Catriona McCuaig is a Welsh-Canadian author who lives in the Canadian bush where she likes to watch wolves and bears passing by. She is well known to British readers through her writing in the *People's Friend* and *My Weekly* Story Collections.

SNARES AND NETS

When Nesta Davies comes to Holyhill from Oxford in 1533, to care for her son's ailing wife, she learns that an old woman has died there in mysterious circumstances. After a young woman is lured to her death, saved only by Nesta's intervention, she vows to uncover the truth. As a midwife who delivers babies and lays out the dead, Nesta has access to every household in the district. Can what she learns there help to solve the increasing lawlessness in the hamlet?

Books by Catriona McCuaig
Published by The House of Ulverscroft:

ICE MAIDEN
MAIL ORDER BRIDE
OUT OF THE SHADOWS
ROMANY ROSE
DOWN LILAC LANE
AT SEAGULL BAY
GHOST WRITER
WHEN THE DAFFODILS BLOOM AGAIN
DARK MOON
TO LOVE AGAIN
IN A WELSH VALLEY
BITTER HARVEST
CHERRY STONES
HEART OF DARKNESS
FOLLOW YOUR HEART

CATRIONA McCUAIG

SNARES
AND NETS

Complete and Unabridged

ULVERSCROFT
Leicester

First published in Great Britain in 2009 by
Robert Hale Limited
London

First Large Print Edition
published 2010
by arrangement with
Robert Hale Limited
London

British Library CIP Data

McCuaig, Catriona.
Snares and nets.
1. Midwives- -Fiction. 2. Great Britain- -History- -
Henry VIII, 1509 – 1547- -Fiction. 3. Detective and
mystery stories. 4. Large type books.
I. Title
813.6–dc22

ISBN 978–1–44480–406–5

Published by
F. A. Thorpe (Publishing)
Anstey, Leicestershire

Set by Words & Graphics Ltd.
Anstey, Leicestershire
Printed and bound in Great Britain by
T. J. International Ltd., Padstow, Cornwall

And I find more bitter than death the woman, whose heart is snares and nets, and her hands as fetters:
whoso pleaseth God shall escape from her, but the sinner shall be taken by her.

Ecclesiastes 7:26

1

Nesta Davies straightened for a moment, clamping her bloodstained hand in the small of her back. Bending over the low-slung bed for such a long time had stiffened her and she longed to stretch out and wait for the ache to subside, but there was no time to waste.

The combined odours of blood, sweat and the tallow candles which relieved the darkness in the tiny room made her want to vomit but she fought against the urge as she bent over the bed again.

'Is she all right, mistress? Is there nothing we can do?' the other woman whispered. 'When I had trouble birthing my first they shook pepper under my nose and that helped. When I sneezed it stirred the babe, and out into the world he popped!'

Nesta shook her head. ''Twould only make matters worse in this case, I fear. The child means to come feet first.'

The girl's mother sucked in her breath. It was well known that such a difficult delivery could cause the death of both mother and child.

'We'll have to turn the child in the womb,

1

Mistress Baxter,' Nesta muttered, her face wrinkled with tension. 'Your hands are small. Can you try?'

'I'll see what I can do, but I'm that frightened. I've done it on the farm with a calf once or twice, but a real baby? I don't know if I dare.'

Unspoken between them was the fear that any intervention might harm the infant, maim it for life, perhaps.

'You must dare, if you want your girl to live.'

Taking a deep breath the woman advanced on the bed, her face set in an expression of grim determination. The young wife let out a scream which made Nesta's ears ring.

'There, I think I've managed it.'

The pair sighed with relief. 'Just as well she fainted while that was going on,' Nesta remarked, holding a feather to the candle flame. 'I'll need to bring her round now, though, for she needs to push.'

The acrid smell of the burning feather filled the room, as young Lizzie regained consciousness with a bewildered shake of her head.

'That's right, my girl! It'll soon be over now! You'll have to push when I tell you.'

'I can't! I can't!' the girl screamed.

'You can, and you must. Now you take

hold of that rope I tied to the bed, and haul on that. Your ma is here to help you.' She nodded at Mistress Baxter, who stepped forward, a wet rag in hand, to mop her daughter's face.

Within minutes the baby had slid into the world, protesting in a reedy little voice. 'No need to slap this one's bottom,' Nesta noted with satisfaction, as she tied off the cord and snipped it with the expertise that came from long practice.

'A boy!' the new grandmother sang, while tears of gladness rolled down her face. 'Your Harold will be that pleased, that I know!'

Lizzie held out her arms to welcome the little stranger who had caused her so much trouble. 'Where is Harold, Ma? Can he come in now?'

'Not just yet,' Nesta interrupted. 'I've got a bit of clearing up to do first. Can't have him seeing you in a welter of blood, can we?' Although it might do the fellow a world of good, she told herself privately. If men knew what we poor women have to go through they might think twice about having large families!

Now she could afford to relax. Blood had been shed, and a battle fought and won. For a while it had been touch and go, but now it was safely over, and young Lizzie and her husband were rejoicing over their newborn

3

son, radiant with happiness and pride.

Nesta Davies and the girl's mother, meanwhile, had retired to the kitchen to relax over a generous measure of home-brewed mead.

'You did well to bring her through her ordeal, and I'm that grateful,' Mistress Baxter said, smacking her lips in enjoyment of the reviving drink. 'I swear I thought we were going to lose my poor girl.'

'Ay, it's always a possibility when the babe tries to come feet first. But we managed to get him turned in the womb, and all's well that ends well,' Nesta agreed. And nobody knows how many prayers I sent up while poor Lizzie was writhing in agony on that bed, and me all of a dither because her mother was seeing all, and trusting me to produce a miracle!

Mistress Baxter had come bursting through the door when labour was well advanced and although Nesta soon had reason to be glad of her presence, she'd been none too pleased at first to be working under the keen eye of her patient's mother.

'I take it you'll be here to help with her lying-in,' she remarked now. 'Two weeks in bed she'll need to get her strength back.'

'Yes indeed. I promised the girl I'd be here when her time came, seeing as it's her first.

Her Harold's a nice enough young fellow, but I couldn't depend on him to take proper care of her. She'd be hopping up and down getting his meals and all the rest, never mind doing all the washing that comes with a new babe.'

'And that's another thing. She'll need plenty of nourishing food broth and so on.'

'I'll see to it, never you fear.'

Now that the drama was over, the mead had loosened the woman's tongue.

'I'm from Hollyhill, as perhaps you know, mistress, and I've brought a message from your son. When he heard I was coming to Oxford he asked me to seek you out. I was that surprised to find you as the midwife at Lizzie's side when I thought I'd have to go traipsing all around the town, searching!'

'And what does my Jack have to say for himself, I wonder?'

'Only that he wants you to come up and lend a hand there, if you can, mistress. His poor wife, it seems, is fading fast and he's in sore need of help in the house. You can be a comfort to them all, if you will come, he says.'

'I'll go to them of course, gladly, although I don't know so much about being needed. Young Kate, my granddaughter, is there,' Nesta remarked. 'Surely she can run the household while Joan is abed?'

'Too ham-fisted to be of much use, so I

hear, and would rather be wandering the countryside than taking a pride in her father's home! A disgrace, that's what it is! Fifteen years old, he tells me, and many a girl is a wife and mother at that age, with her days of freedom long behind her.'

Nesta bridled. The girl had her faults but it wasn't this woman's place to say so! 'Oh, well, she's young yet. She'll mend her ways in time, I don't doubt.'

'Huh! She'd mend them a deal faster after a good whipping, and if she was any child of mine I'd see that she had one before she's very much older!' Noticing the midwife's black expression the woman broke off in confusion.

Nesta took pity on her. 'Ay, well, if I'm to go up to Hollyhill tomorrow I must bespeak the carrier's cart! It's too far to walk, at my age, though there was a time I'd have done it without giving it a thought. Now you listen to me. Your girl has had a hard time of it. As I said, make sure she keeps to her bed for a full two weeks, and feed her plenty of nourishing broth. She has her babe to feed now!'

'I'll stay as long as she needs me, mistress. You get along now; we can manage here. I'll just fetch Harold out to settle up, and then you can be on your way. Rest assured I'll remember you in my prayers for this day's work!'

Nesta was pleased to be given a handful of small coins in payment for her services, something which did not always happen. People were usually grateful, of course, but poor people often paid her in kind, depending on their means. In the past she had received a bag of vegetables, or a loaf of new bread, and on one occasion even a plump rabbit. All very acceptable, of course, but not much use if you needed money.

One of these days she'd like to find some patients among the gentry, who could afford to pay well, but until that day came she was thankful to work among the poor and thus make a modest living for herself.

Meanwhile her visit to Hollyhill would make a change, although she was distressed to hear that her daughter-in-law's condition had worsened. She suffered from the coughing sickness, for which there was no cure.

Nesta had been annoyed to hear that young Kate hadn't been pulling her weight in the house, especially now, when she was needed so badly. Had the Baxter woman exaggerated the situation? Or perhaps Jack asked too much of the girl, expecting her to keep up the standards of his competent wife and, before her, his own mother.

'Tomorrow morning? I can take you as far

as Bicester, missus,' the carter said, when she routed him out of his hovel, mumbling and grumbling. 'More than that I can't promise, but 'tis not so far from there to Hollyhill. I suppose you can go the rest of the way on Shanks's pony?'

Nesta agreed that she should indeed be able to walk the remaining few miles. Having come to a satisfactory arrangement as to payment, there was nothing left to do but to pack her few possessions in readiness for the morning's journey.

And now I must go to bed, she told herself, or I'll never be up at daybreak. And that will never do, or I'll find myself limping the whole way to Hollyhill, and that would be too much of a good thing!

2

Nesta paused with her fingers on the door handle before changing her mind about stepping inside. After dropping her bundle on the step she hobbled to the rear of the house where Jack had his workshop at the end of the vegetable garden.

He looked up as she entered. 'Mumma! You came!'

'Of course I did! You sent for me, didn't you?'

'Well, yes, but I wasn't sure you'd get the message. Mistress Baxter seemed all of a dither when I spoke to her.'

'As it happens I was helping her daughter to birth the child, so the woman didn't have to seek far to find me.' Nesta stroked the fine leather of the half-finished boot on her son's workbench. 'This is fine stuff, Jack! It cost a pretty penny, I'll warrant.'

He grimaced. 'Nothing but the best for the lord of the manor. I can only hope and pray he pays me on time, or I'll be in a fine muddle.'

'Are you afraid Sir William will cheat you?'

'Not that, but he's been known to take his

time about paying his debts. The thing is, I've this leather to pay for, and it don't come cheap!'

'Then next time you just ask him to pay something down before you make a start on the work. Say you need to buy materials.'

'That's not how it works in the trade, Mumma. Don't want the customers going elsewhere, do we? Plenty of other shoemakers about!'

'Pshaw! My feet are killing me, Jack Davies, and I haven't come all this way to argue. Now, before I go indoors, how doth Joan fare? And where are the children?'

Jack began to rub his hands together. Worried, his mother thought. Wringing his hands like that. Seems I was right to come, take some of the burden off his shoulders.

'Joan is weak as a newborn kitten. She puts a brave face on it, but I'd say she's not long for this world, Mumma. Coughing up blood now, and you know what that means.'

Nesta did. Casting about for words of comfort and finding none, she repeated her question about her grandchildren.

'I sent the boy on an errand. He'll be back soon.' Young Jonno was apprenticed to his father, which was fortunate for him because it meant he could live at home and be fed properly, as many apprentices were not. Nor would he suffer frequent beatings, the fate of many a boy with a stern master, although Jack was not averse to dishing out a clout when necessary.

'And Kate? Indoors, I suppose, putting the house to rights?'

Jack scowled. 'Kate, doing housework? I doubt she's doing any such thing. A sore trial to me, that girl is, Mumma. She won't do a hand's turn, and my poor Joan is at her wits' end with her. No, she'll be off wandering the highways and byways without a care in the world.'

Nesta nodded sagely. Some young man would be at the bottom of this, she reckoned. She'd have a word with that young woman when she got herself settled in. She was about to tell Jack this when her grandson arrived.

'Gramma! Dad said you were coming.' The boy flung himself into Nesta's arms, grinning.

'We'll talk later,' she told him, returning his hug. 'I shall look in on your mother now, and after that wash the dust of the road off me. I've walked all the way from Bicester and my feet are as black as your hat!'

'I'll bring in a bucket of water for you, Gramma,' the boy said eagerly, and she nodded her thanks. At least one of her grandchildren knew where his duty lay!

Joan was lying in a rumpled bed beside a

wide-open casement. She struggled to a sitting position when she saw her mother-in-law.

' 'Tis good of you to come, Mumma. The house is all of a muddle, I'm that ashamed I can't tell you. I just can't seem to find the strength to get out of bed these days.'

Nesta shivered. The bedroom felt as damp as a tomb but cold air was the only known treatment for the coughing sickness. Apart from the sheen of sweat on her brow the younger woman looked well enough, with the roses in her cheeks, but Nesta knew from her long experience with the sick that the hectic flush was just another symptom of the disease.

'Never you mind, gal! I'm here now, and I'll soon have the place put to rights. I'll make some pottage and have it all ready to serve when your Jack comes in looking for his dinner. And we'll have to feed you up, as well.'

'I couldn't eat a thing. I don't seem to have no appetite these days.'

'I'm sure you could manage a nice drop of custard, gal. Let's see, shall we?' Nesta pretended not to notice as Joan was seized with a racking cough. She slipped out of the room and went to investigate the kitchen. The place could do with a good scrubbing, she noted, but that would have to wait until she had the meals organized. A lump of stale bread amid the dirty crockery on the table showed that the menfolk had breakfasted none too well.

One of her first tasks would be to set some dough to rise. There was nothing better than a chunk of fresh bread to brighten the spirits, especially when washed down with beer. Meanwhile, she would see what the garden yielded in the way of vegetables for her pottage. The stale bread would at least yield the crumbs necessary for that.

Someone had done a good job of keeping the patch free of weeds, she saw, as she selected peas and onions for the tasty dish. And to judge by the cackling coming from the hen house there would be eggs aplenty for both the pottage and the custard for Joan.

Humming happily to herself she set about preparing the food. Despite the sad reason for her coming to the hamlet, she was looking forward to the change of scene. She loved the noise and bustle of Oxford, yet Hollyhill had a charm of its own. The peaceful place was set in pretty countryside and, although the people were suspicious of strangers she knew she would be made welcome, as Jack's mother.

'Gramma! Dad said you were coming!'

The girl had entered quietly, making Nesta jump. Planting a dutiful kiss on her grandmother's face, she sniffed the air like a rabbit scenting danger.

'Something smells good! We've not had much more than bread and cheese since Mumma fell ill.'

And whose fault is that? Nesta thought, but she bit back the words, muttering something noncommittal instead. It wouldn't do to irritate the child right off. Best to bide her time and wait for the right moment.

What on earth had Kate been up to? The hem of her gown was thick with mud, and wisps of corn-coloured hair had escaped from her cap.

'What news from round about, grand-daughter?'

The girl shrugged. 'Goody Clapton died in the night, or so I heard.'

Nesta frowned. 'Who might she be, then?'

'An old woman who lived in a cottage down the end of Church Lane. A midwife, she was, like you.'

When a bowl of custard had been taken to Joan, and the rest of the family were seated around the table, Kate repeated the news.

'I could've told you that,' Jonno muttered. 'Heard it when I was out carrying errands for Dad.'

14

'Goodwife Clapton, eh?' Jack remarked. 'Poor old duck. Gone at last, has she? Well, she was a good age. Must have been ninety if she was a day. She brought you both into the world, you know. Well, I wonder what they'll do now, then? Nobody to bring people's babes into the world nor to lay them out proper when they come to an end. I thought she'd be with us for ever. What will you do when your time comes to provide me with grandchildren, then, Kate?'

To his surprise the girl jumped up, red in the face. 'I'm never getting married! Not ever!'

'Hey, I haven't said you can leave the table, gal!' Jack called, but the girl had gone, slamming the door behind her. 'What's the matter with her?' he demanded.

His mother shrugged. She thought she knew what that was all about. Kate had been racketing round the country with some young swain, who'd now given her the push. It was to be hoped that matters hadn't gone too far. It was common enough for a boy to be a devoted lover until his ardour bore fruit, and then, aghast by what had happened, he'd be off before the priest could catch up with him and make him wed the unfortunate girl in question.

With his mouth full of barley bread, Jack

spoke up again. 'Here's an idea for you, Mumma! Why don't you move here permanent like? They'll need someone with the old gal gone. Joan and I always said we'd make room for you here when you got too old to manage alone, not that you're ready for the knacker's yard yet! All you'd be doing is moving in a few years early, and delivering babes would put a few groats in your stocking for a rainy day.' He beamed at her, well pleased with his notion.

'It's something to think about,' she admitted.

3

Nesta was sweeping dust out on to the street when a girl appeared in the doorway, coughing and spluttering.

'Pardon me, gal! I didn't know you were passing by.'

The girl appeared to be about the same age as Kate, although not as pretty. Dressed in a plain grey gown, and wearing the usual white apron and cap, she presented a demure appearance which suggested that perhaps she was a servant, home on leave from some large establishment.

'Are you the midwife now?'

Nesta blinked at the abrupt tone. 'Well, if it's a midwife you're looking for you've come to the right place, although I've brought no babes into the world in Hollyhill. I'm here from Oxford, visiting my son and his family. Was it for yourself I'm needed?'

The girl didn't look as if she was *enceinte*, but she might only just have learned of her predicament. Nesta hoped she wasn't being asked to help the girl rid herself of an unwanted encumbrance. Not only was she against any such action for its own sake, but it was a crime, punishable by hanging.

'No, of course I'm not expecting a child! What do you think I am? No, it's a love potion I want. You do make them, I suppose?'

'Well no, I don't, so I'm afraid I can't help you there. Sorry!'

The girl's eyes flashed and for a brief moment Nesta felt chilled. So might an adder look before it struck, she told herself.

'Goody Clapton would have given me one, but she's dead!'

'Perhaps if you speak to someone in her family they could help you?'

'She had no family, mistress. I went to her cottage and searched all about, but I couldn't find what I wanted. She had potions aplenty, but who knows what they were for? I might swallow the wrong thing and be poisoned.'

'You might, indeed,' Nesta assured her. 'Some things are used on the outside of the body. They aren't meant to be swallowed. Salves for wounds, for instance, and cures for warts.'

The girl's eyes narrowed. 'Then you do know about herbs and such!'

'A few simple remedies only. Not the sort of thing you mean. My advice to you, young woman, is to go home and forget about this young man, whoever he is. Plenty more fish in the sea, as they say!'

The girl gave her a black look and flounced off. It occurred to Nesta then that the girl had spoken of taking such a potion herself when surely any such mixture should be used on the object of her affections, not herself. Just as well she'd had enough sense to refrain from tasting any of the nostrums the old woman had left behind.

Nesta shuddered. No doubt Goody Clapton had supplemented her income by making up a few herbal remedies and other items calculated to appeal to foolish young women like this morning's visitor. In doing so she had left herself open to a charge of witchcraft, like other poor souls Nesta had heard about. All it would take would be an accusation by some dissatisfied customer, or some farmer's beasts dying of the murrain, and the blame would be laid on the old woman, for her to be tried as a witch.

First would come trial by water. The woman would be thrown into the river with her wrists and ankles bound. If she sank, she was proved innocent; it was too bad if she drowned as a result. If she floated, that showed her guilt, and she was sentenced to death by burning.

No doubt Goody Clapton was fortunate to have died of old age, in her own bed, if she possessed one. Nesta continued her work, wondering as she wielded her broom whether Kate had visited the old crone, looking for some potion or other. If so, pray heaven it was a case of unrequited love and not something worse! Her father would have the hide off her back if she brought shame on the cordwainer's house!

Unbeknown to Nesta, the constable from Hethe was at that very moment standing in Jack's workshop, asking awkward questions, while Jonno listened with his mouth open.

The hamlet was too small to have a constable of its own and it had to make do with one lone man who served several parishes. This Sam Fowler was a burly man with a curly black beard. Above average height, he was capable of striking terror into any minor villain or drunken man. On this occasion, however, he had come riding in to Hollyhill on more important business.

'Poisoned, you say? Surely not!' Jack said firmly. 'Unless of course she was ailing and, trying to help herself, took one of her own remedies by mistake. Yes, that would be it. She was getting on a bit, you know, and I've heard tell her sight was failing.'

'And I say she was poisoned, Master Davies.'

'But how could anyone know?'

'Because of the state she was in when she

was found. Tom Robinson called there to bespeak the woman for his wife when her time comes; it's their second and he's worried. He came in just as the poor old soul was having fits and she'd been sick all over the floor, too. He bent down to see if there was anything he could do, but she died, right before his eyes. There wasn't even time to fetch the priest to her, not that she'd have thanked him for it because as I've heard it she never darkened the church door from one year to the next.'

'People do have fits. P'raps one came over her natural like.'

'Same thing happened to the dog,' the constable told him. 'Dogs have fits too, we all know that, but cur and mistress, stricken down all in the same moment? Don't sound right to me.'

'Murder, then?'

'Don't know what else you'd call it.'

'Cor, cruel, that is, poisoning a dog!' Jonno interjected, earning a glare from his father.

'Just you get on with your work, boy, and never mind what don't concern you! What is it you want with me, then, Constable? 'Tis years since I've seen the woman, God rest her soul. Jonno here is our youngest, twelve come Michaelmas. We've had no need to summon a midwife since he was born, and even if we had, my mother would have stepped in and done the job.'

'A midwife as well, is she? She knew the old woman, then?'

'No, no. She's from Oxford, Mumma is. Just came yesterday to help us here. It's my wife, Joan, see. In a bad way with the coughing sickness.'

The constable nodded. 'I'll be on my way, then, seeing as you've nothing to tell me. I have to speak to everybody while I'm here, or the sheriff will have something to say.'

★ ★ ★

'Who are you, then?' Nesta opened the door to a tall bearded man. It gave her a crick in the neck, gazing up at him. 'If you want my son, he's in his workshop, around the back.'

'I'm the constable from Hethe, mistress. I've spoken with Master Davies, and now I want a word with you.'

'Oh, yes? What about, then?'

'I'm enquiring into the death of the woman who was murdered.'

'Murdered!' Nesta's voice came out in a squeak She looked back over her shoulder, as if she expected the axeman to be creeping up behind her. 'Who's been murdered, then?'

'Goody Clapton, the midwife. You knew

her, of course, you being in the same trade, like?'

'Er, no, I never met the poor soul. I'm from Oxford, you see, born and bred. I just arrived yesterday. My son sent for me because his poor wife is sick unto death.'

'Funny, that, you living there and him here.'

'Not funny at all! My husband had a cousin living here in years gone by. An old bachelor, he was. When my boy finished his apprenticeship Cousin Micah made a place for him here. Said if Jack came and gave him a hand in the business he'd leave the place to the lad when he died. And that's how Jack came to Hollyhill.'

'And very nice, too! Some fellows gets all the luck. I wish somebody would leave a nice house to me. Then I'd be able to get married one of these days.'

'But what happened to Goody Clapton? Bludgeoned over the head, I suppose, by some vagrant passing by on the road, who wanted to steal whatever she had put by.'

'More like somebody with a grudge against her.'

Nesta listened in horror while the constable recounted the gory details.

'I daresay you'll be taking over now she's gone,' he suggested, watching her closely to judge her reaction. 'Lucky for some!'

'What! If you're trying to say I killed the poor old soul so as to take over her business you're very much mistaken, my man. And unless you want to feel my fist in your chops you'll take that back, constable or no constable!'

'Only doing my job, mistress.'

'Then you can get off and do it somewhere else!' she told him, her bosom heaving. When he had taken himself away she had to sit down. He couldn't possibly have suspected her, could he? No, he was just being awkward, nasty piece of work that he was. However, she didn't relish the idea that someone was going about doing murder.

4

'I don't want you wandering off on your own while there's a murderer on the loose,' Jack Davies warned his daughter.

'Aw, Dad!'

'Don't you 'aw Dad' me, my girl, and you can take that look off your face unless you want to feel the weight of my hand. I don't want you coming to grief. Anyone who'd do harm to a poor old widow woman wouldn't think twice about killing a pretty young gal, or doing summat worse!'

Kate lapsed into a sullen silence.

'Did you hear what I said, gal?'

'Yes, Dad.'

'What I don't understand is why they poisoned the dog,' Nesta said, her brow furrowed.

'To keep it quiet, of course, so it wouldn't bark, Mumma. Perhaps the fellow wanted to look around inside to see what he could find, so he came prepared.'

'But how did he do it?' Jack shrugged. 'How should I know? Put the poison on a bit of meat and threw it to the animal, I expect.'

'It must have been someone we know,

then,' Jonno piped up.

'How d'you make that out, then?'

'Well, it was somebody who knew the old woman kept a dog, and how many people are there around Hollyhill? Stands to reason.'

'You're so simple, Jonno!' Kate's voice dripped with scorn. 'Somebody tramping the roads could have been watching the place. It doesn't take much brain to spot a dog!'

But, as they later learned from the miller, who had come to collect his new boots, the real story was rather different.

'People are saying that whatever finished off poor Hawisa was in the dog's dish, as well. The constable found her trencher half-full of grub, and the same sort of vegetable stuff was given to the animal. Either she was used to sharing her bit of food with old Towser, or she didn't fancy the taste and she passed it on to him.'

'Doesn't mean that's what poisoned them,' Jack told him.

'Oh, no? Constable saw the vomit and he said it looked the same as the other.'

'Ugh! Do we have to listen to talk like that?' Kate rushed out of the room, her hand over her mouth.

'Never mind her. She's only a girl.' Jonno grinned, eager to hear more.

'You know what this means, don't you?' All

26

eyes turned to Nesta. 'It must have been someone she knew.'

'How do you make that out, mistress?'

'Why would she have accepted food from a stranger, already prepared, much less eaten it without a qualm? And, come to that, how would a traveller passing by have the means to cook the dish? As I said, it had to be someone known to her, somebody she trusted.'

'I don't know who it could be,' the miller mused. 'We all know she's no kinfolk hereabouts. You wouldn't know about that, Mistress Davies you not living local, like.'

'It doesn't have to be someone related to her. I'm a midwife, too, you know, and people often pay for my services in kind. Not with food already cooked, I must admit, unless you count a loaf of bread or a jar of honey.'

Jack frowned. 'But, Mumma, why would a grateful customer want to kill the old gal? That don't make sense.'

'Unless whoever cooked it gathered up wild stuff and made a mistake. Used toadstools instead of mushrooms, let's say.'

Needless to say, these ideas had already occurred to the constable. He'd interviewed anyone who had produced a baby in the past three months, but nobody had thought to take a tasty dish to the old midwife.

'Well, they would say that, wouldn't they?' Nesta muttered, exchanging the latest gossip while attending to Joan. 'If it was deliberate, the poisoner would never admit to it, would he? Or she,' she added thoughtfully.

'Why is everyone saying it must be murder?' Joan wanted to know. 'Surely she could have done it herself by mistake? Pulled hemlock, thinking it was wild parsnip?'

'Except that she is supposed to have been knowledgeable about herbs and simples. That kind of thing is passed down from mother to daughter, you know.' Nesta suddenly remembered the girl who had called on her, demanding a love potion.

'Silly girl,' Joan laughed, on hearing this. 'Some people will believe anything.'

In the end the coroner, brought unwillingly from Oxford, gave a verdict of accidental death. He had better things to think about, and he was not about to waste his time on one old crone, who had been nearing the end of her life in any case. Hawisa Clapton's corpse was shovelled into a hastily dug grave at the back of the churchyard, where in time a grassy mound would be the only sign that she ever existed.

'Where did she come from, does anybody know?' Nesta wondered, but the old dame had been by far the oldest person in the hamlet and nobody could remember a time when she hadn't been part of the scenery.

'Thing is, what do we do for a midwife now?' the baker wondered, when Nesta called in for a quartern loaf. 'Some of the womenfolk will take charge at a birth, I daresay, but what if things go wrong, eh? You need someone who knows what she's doing at a time like that.'

'I'm a midwife, myself. I suppose I could lend a hand if necessary, just while I'm staying here. Mebbe you've heard; I'm looking after my daughter-in-law at present.'

'Ay. Mebbe you should stay on, permanent like.'

'I'll give it some thought. Good day to you!'

Jack had made the same suggestion. Perhaps it was a good idea. After Joan had gone — don't dwell on that now — he would need his mother to keep the house in good order. She could be useful there, and when the time came that she was old and feeble and no longer able to work for a living, she would still have a roof over her head.

On the other hand, wouldn't it be wise to keep her independence? Jack might remarry in time — men did — and the new wife mightn't want to share her kitchen with an older woman.

Nesta knew she would miss Oxford if she never returned there. She loved the busy streets, the market place, the bustle around the numerous inns and taverns. There were ancient churches and a number of university colleges, some of them several hundred years old.

By contrast, Hollyhill was a quiet place. Long ago it had been known as Holy Hill; people said that a hermit had dwelt nearby and that was how the place had come by its name. Time had corrupted that title and Hollyhill it had become, even though there were no hollies growing in the nearby woods.

Nesta decided that she could probably settle here and live in contentment. Nothing was carved in stone, she reminded herself, and there was nothing to prevent her from returning to Oxford if things didn't work out. For the moment, though, she was needed here. Poor Joan had more bad days than good now, and her husband could not look after her and run his business at the same time.

Then there was young Kate. Something had to be done about her. If she was determined not to marry she could not expect to spend the rest of her life under her father's roof, enjoying life while contributing nothing to the household. What if she was trained up to become a midwife? Would that suit her? It might be worth sounding out Jack on the subject.

Nesta nodded to herself, pleased with the notion. If he agreed to the idea she would take the girl with her if she was called to attend a local woman in childbed. Not that the girl would be of much use, but at least they could see if she was suited to the task. Either she would be awestruck by the miracle of birth as a new babe slid into the world, or she would be appalled by what she saw and that would be the end of that!

'He might let her try it,' Joan whispered, when she heard what Nesta had in mind. 'She's got to be taken in hand, Mumma. I worry about her and I wish I could see her settled before I go to my last rest. It's not so much that she's cack-handed in the house; she'd learn all that in time if put to the test. It's this running about the countryside like a young deer that worries me. What is she up to, Mumma? That's what I'd like to know!'

'Have you questioned her?'

'I've asked till I'm blue in the face, and much good it does me. 'Walking by the river,' she'll say, 'or sitting in the woods, listening to the birds.' Does she think I'm simple? She must be doing more than that. One of these days she'll come to grief, especially now, after what's happened to poor old Goody Clapton.

Oh, I know what the coroner had to say, but nobody truly believes that, do they?'

Nesta shook her head helplessly. 'With a girl of that age there are other things to worry about, Joan. All this talk of never wanting to wed could be just a smokescreen to hide the fact that she has a lover.'

'Then why can't she bring him home and let us have a look at him?' Joan cried, and her agitation brought on a fit of coughing which effectively ended the conversation.

5

The watcher in the wood drew back as the girl approached the concealing bushes. It was her again, the shoemaker's girl, still mooning over that worthless youth. Anybody with half a brain in their head could have told her that that little affair would come to nothing, but she'd flown into it headlong.

Oh, yes, the fool had met him here every day for weeks, flattered no doubt by the attentions of the eldest son of the lord of the manor. Easy to see that on his part it was just a fleeting dalliance, a pleasant encounter to help him wile away the summer days before he took up his place at Court. No doubt the girl had been dazzled by his fine clothing and by the fact of who he was. Most of all, she seemed impressed by the fine gret palfrey which came stepping proudly through the wood. Ah, thought the watcher, she seemed to love that animal almost as much as she did the boy himself! How daintily the creature accepted the apple from her outstretched hand, and how willingly the girl sprang up behind the young man when he offered her a ride into the nearby countryside.

The watcher had been there on the black day when young Will had come to tell the girl he was leaving. All decked out in a new red doublet, he was, with dark-green hose beneath, and there was a great feather in his hat. The faithless youth hadn't even dismounted, but had stayed in the saddle while he gave the girl the news she had never thought to hear.

'But you said you love me,' she pleaded. 'Don't leave me, Will!'

'It can't be helped.' He shrugged. 'My father has made all the arrangements and is highly pleased with them, and I must obey. Surely you can understand that?'

'Then take me with you, Will. Please? I won't go home; I'll come with you now.'

'And what would you do at Court, sweeting? 'Tis no place for . . . ' he broke off, not wanting to hurt her any more than was necessary. The watcher, more experienced than the girl, had understood what must be going through the lad's mind. Even in some relatively minor capacity he would fit in with the others there, all of them gently or nobly born. What was Kate Davies? Only a shoemaker's daughter.

'We could be wed,' she said timidly. 'Then it would be all right.' Perhaps it might have been, had the boy insisted on it, for wives took their status according to their husband's rank. But Will knew what was expected of him. He must take a bride who brought a substantial dowry with her. He didn't need his father to point that out to him.

'I must get on,' he muttered. 'I only came to let you know so you wouldn't wonder.'

And that was more than some men would do, at that, the watcher thought, grim-faced.

'Will, no! Don't go!' The girl stumbled after the horse, taking hold of the stirrup. The boy shrugged her off and spurred his horse into a canter. Within minutes he had disappeared from view.

Now the girl came here every day, crying, and peering into the distance. More fool she, the watcher grunted. It was obvious that the boy was never coming back. This Kate was young and pretty; she should find herself another sweetheart. Or, she could take her destiny into her hands and do what the watcher had done, except that she'd never have the gumption.

The watcher stiffened, and drew further back into the sheltering foliage. A man was approaching, a man the watcher recognized. Tom Robinson, by all that was holy! Don't say he was after that little hussy now, and his wife about to give birth at any moment!

He had come up to the girl now, and they

were speaking, but they were too far away for the words to reach the watcher's ears.

'Ah, Kate Davies, isn't it?'

'What if I am?'

'Your granddam; is she still staying at your house?'

Kate nodded. 'Yes, she is. She's come because my mother is ailing. Why do you want to know?'

'I need her to help my wife when she's brought to bed. Old Goody Clapton attended her last time, but no doubt you've heard what happened to her, God rest her soul.' He looked at Kate with his head on one side and she smiled up at him.

'I'm going home for my dinner now, Master Robinson. You can walk with me if you wish; my grandmother will be in the house.'

The watcher's eyes narrowed. What were they up to now? The pair strolled off, side by side. The girl was smiling and chattering now, faithless wench!

★ ★ ★

'This is Master Robinson, Gramma.' Having made the introduction Kate wandered off to see how her mother fared.

Nesta looked at him with interest. 'Ah!

'Twas you who found poor old Goody Clapton, I hear. 'Tis the talk of the neighbourhood.'

'Ay. I've seen a few sights in my time, but that fair turned my stomach over. I thought I'd heave my innards up, the way the poor woman looked, lying there. But never mind that; 'tis over and done with now, and she's at peace.'

'So now you've come to me. I'll call on your wife in a day or two, to make sure that all is well with her and the babe.'

'Ay, you do that. We can't have anything going wrong this time.'

'Why, was there something amiss with her first?'

'You could say that, mistress. It was a girl! If she knows what's good for her she'd better produce a boy this time or I'll know the reason why!'

He went on his way, leaving Nesta standing in the doorway with her mouth open.

'What's wrong with girls, I'd like to know?' she demanded as she carried a bowl of broth up to her daughter-in-law. 'The world would be a sorry place without them. And why blame his poor wife if she doesn't have a son this time? It's God who decides that. And you should have seen the way he glared at me, the fool! As if I could somehow manage to deliver a boy for him. I don't have magic powers!'

'It all has to do with the King,' Joan sighed. 'He put his poor wife aside because she was barren, and took up with this Nan Bullen instead. It gives ordinary men the wrong idea about how to treat a woman.'

'Barren, my foot! Poor Queen Katherine had a quiverful of children. She did her duty. If it pleased God to take them to himself again, that is hardly her fault. Although I must say I wonder why the Lord would let a woman go through nine months of misery followed by an agonizing birth if he didn't mean the children to stay. By all accounts there's nothing wrong with the Princess Mary, but no, Great Harry wants sons!'

'Every man hopes for a son to follow him in his own trade,' Joan countered, quoting her husband.

'And you've done well to provide Jack with one,' Nesta remarked, nodding her approval. 'I suppose it's different in the King's case. We need a man on the throne to rule the country, especially in time of war. If Harry Tudor died tomorrow, how should we manage with a little girl left in charge? What galls me is the notion that the man could divorce his wife and take up with this young hussy instead, even defying the Pope to get his own way. What if it came about that every man in the kingdom could do likewise, eh? Let him fancy a pretty wench and take her into his house in place of the wife who'd served him faithfully all her days. What would the wife do then, cast out to wander the countryside, with no roof over her head? It don't bear thinking about, and I'm sure that every woman feels the same!'

'It will never happen,' Joan said, smiling. 'No need to get so worked up, Mumma! We don't want you falling with an apoplexy! I expect the king is in love with the Bullen girl, but doubtless he's sincere about the need to get sons.'

'Ah, but will he get them?' Nesta looked sceptical. 'She seems fertile enough but she's just given birth to a girl, hasn't she! Never mind that all the astrologers promised a boy. The poor Queen must be rejoicing over this outcome, that's all I can say.'

Two days later Nesta paid the promised visit to Sally Robinson. She found the young wife dandling her baby daughter on her knee.

'And who is this, then?'

'This is our little Catherine, Mistress Davies.'

'Named in honour of the Queen, I suppose, like my own granddaughter. Have you chosen names yet for this new babe?' With the rate of child mortality being so high the priests insisted on baptism taking place as soon after birth as possible in case the infant did not survive. Thus it was essential not to linger over the choice of names. 'Perhaps you'll call this one Harry, after the king, if it's a boy?'

'Oh, no. He'll be Adam, after my father.'

'And if it's a girl; what then?'

Nesta was surprised to see the girl's face turn white.

'Oh, it must be a boy, mistress! Please, oh please, you must make sure it's a boy!'

'I'm sorry, my dear, that's not something I can do. I'm just the midwife, not God.'

'Goody Clapton could have. She promised!'

And more fool she, Nesta thought. If she was murdered, perhaps it was a dissatisfied customer who finished her off. She little suspected how close she was to the truth.

6

Nesta glanced up at the sky and frowned. It looked threatening, with enormous black clouds which provided a marked contrast to the bright foliage on the trees, which was just beginning to change colour.

She had just pegged out a line of washing, which she knew was probably a useless exercise, except that Jack didn't like it if the house was festooned with dripping linen. Poor Joan had night sweats which necessitated changing her nightwear and bedding on a regular basis. Not wishing to make work she had assured her mother-in-law that she could manage, but Nesta had ignored her protests.

'Lying in bed in a clammy night rail will do you no good at all, gal! Besides, I like doing laundry, so I won't hear another word about it!'

It was true; it was in her nature to find things that needed fixing and put them right. It gave her a sense of satisfaction to take garments that were grubby and give them a good pounding. Then she would spread them out over the lavender bushes to bleach in the sun and later, when they were dry, bring them indoors again, inhaling their delicate scent as she came.

Not much chance of that today, she told herself glumly. Perhaps if a good wind blew up the clothes might dry after all. Or pigs might fly, if they had wings.

Sure enough the first drops fell before she had covered the few yards between the drying-green and the back door. Of young Kate there was no sign. Nesta had coaxed the girl into helping her squeeze the excess water out of the bedding; it was easier if two people did the task between them, turning the cloth over and over and wringing it out firmly. A well-brought-up girl would have carried the basket out to the clothes line without a second thought, saving steps for her grandmother, but not Kate Davies! Not for the first time Nesta wondered how the child had reached the age of fifteen without being trained up sensibly. This of course was Joan's job, but somehow she had failed. Was it because she had been too ill of late to keep her household in order? Or did her daughter have an uncommonly stubborn streak?

Nesta was itching to fetch the girl a good clip round the ear, but she knew she must keep her temper in check. Joan had enough to worry about without having to witness a set-to between her daughter and her mother-in-law. And what about Jack? It was a funny thing: people could moan about their relations until the cows came home, but just let an outsider say the same, and that would not go down well at all.

There was a saying that you could catch more flies with honey than with vinegar. All right, so she would appeal to Kate's better nature. 'Why don't you lay the table while I scrub these carrots?' or 'Be a good girl and collect the eggs for me, won't you?'

Kate would usually do as she was asked, but not before heaving a heavy sigh and flouncing out of the room. Obviously stronger measures were called for. Nesta noticed that the floor needed a good scrub, and she vowed to put the girl to work on it. Unfortunately she was nowhere to be seen, so Nesta stepped outside to see if she was anywhere in the vicinity.

Her hand flew to her mouth when she noticed the clothes'-line. It had come adrift at one end and the garments were languishing in the mud, apart from a few which were still aloft, supported by the forked prop. Why had the line collapsed? It was made of good new rope, recently purchased from the chandler. Moments later, holding the broken line in her hand, she understood what had happened.

The rope had been neatly severed by a knife. This had been no accident.

'Kate!' she bawled, trying to contain her fury. 'Whatever you're doing, get out here at once! I want a word with you!'

'What is it, Gramma?' Kate came around the corner of the house, clutching a spray of rose hips in her hand. 'Look, I've been collecting hips. I thought some syrup might help Mum. Partial to a sip of syrup, she is.'

'Never mind all that! Just look at my clean washing, all over mud!'

'The rope is broken. Perhaps a rat chewed through it and the weight of the clothes made it snap. You know what they're like, trying to gather bits and pieces for their nests.'

'A two-legged rat, my girl! This rope has been cut deliberately. Are you sure you don't know anything about it?'

'I haven't seen anyone about, Gramma.'

'That's as may be. Meanwhile, you can gather this lot up and give it a good rinse through, while I try to repair this clothes'-line.'

'But, Gramma — '

'But me no buts, Kate Davies. This rope isn't the only thing that needs to be made to bear its weight. You do as you're bid, and when you've finished, you and I are going to sit down and have a quiet talk.' She raised a hand to stop the flow of words which seemed about to erupt and, sullenly, the girl began to gather up the sodden garments.

Nesta was sure that Kate wasn't responsible for the cut line, but then who could have done it, and why? Jonno was a sensible boy and in any case he'd been hard at work all morning under his father's watchful eye. No, it could not have been Jonno. Therefore it had to have been someone from outside the family. Some child, probably, playing a malicious prank. If she ever found out who had done it, she would make sure the culprit received a good thrashing.

Later, grandmother and granddaughter faced each other across the table. Kate sat with her arms folded tightly across her chest, her lips pressed into a thin line.

Annoyance welled up in Nesta's breast. 'And you can take that unket look off your face!' she snapped, not for the first time since coming to Hollyhill. She received a glare in return, although she managed to stare Kate down.

'Listen here, my gal, and listen well,' she began, striving to keep her voice even. 'There's too much work in this house for one woman and I'm relying on you to help. You're big and strong and it wouldn't hurt you to step forward and do a hand's turn, without waiting to be asked.'

'You're not my mother!'

'No, but your poor mother is much too ill to do anything in the house, or to keep you up to the mark, come to that. That's why I'm here, at your father's request. It's up to us to work together, to save your mother worry she doesn't need. Even if she wasn't ailing, you should have learned to take charge of a household by now. You're of marriageable age, Kate. No man will tolerate a wife who can't cook and clean and bake, and bring up his children in the proper manner.'

'Huh! I'll never marry, Gramma!'

'You want to enter a nunnery, then, is that it?'

'What? No, of course I don't!'

Nesta was silent for a moment. Poor Joan wasn't long for this world, and when she died Jack would naturally expect his daughter to keep house for himself and his son, at least until he remarried, which he probably would, in due time. This wasn't something that she should bring up now. Nor should she probe any further. She suspected that Kate was going through the throes of young love, and that something had gone awry. Perhaps the young man she fancied was betrothed to someone else. Parents often arranged marriages for their children in their infancy and such engagements were as binding as a marriage.

'Marriage isn't for everybody, child, although you may well change your mind in the future. But if you mean to become an old maid, then you must learn some way of making a living, should the need ever arise. And don't say that won't happen,' she said firmly, to forestall an interruption, 'because no one can foretell what the Lord has in mind for us. I thought that I'd grow old along of my Mark, but he died before his time, and I had to turn to and try to make money to support myself.'

'So you chose to become a midwife?' Nesta was quick to note the spark of interest in Kate's lovely brown eyes.

'I did that. I worked alongside an old gal who'd brought hundreds of babes into the world, and seen off a good many folks at their end. I learned my trade well, and I'm good at it, though I says it as shouldn't. I can teach you, Kate dearie. What do you say to that, then?'

Kate bit her lip. 'Maybe. I don't know if I could stomach all that screaming and gore.'

'You'll get used to that. Mind you, I don't know if I'll get much call for my services here. People in country places are slow to try something new and them hereabouts might not want me, even though I'm the cordwainer's mother.'

'Where else would they go, with Goody Clapton gone?'

'As to that, we shall have to wait and see. Tell you what, I'll take you along with me on a couple of cases and you can see if mebbe you'll take to it. I can't say fairer than that, now can I?'

Ignoring Kate's hesitant look, Nesta got up and went outside. She vowed to make sure that the girl would go with her next time, and if she hated every minute of the experience, why, that might make housekeeping seem pleasant by comparison.

7

'Come as fast as you can! My Sal said to tell you the baby's on its way!'

Nesta grinned at the panting man. 'Steady on, Master Robinson! If things have only just started we'll have plenty of time to spare.'

'I want you there right from the start!' he blurted. 'Nothing must go wrong with this child, Mistress Davies. Nothing, I tell you!'

'And I'm sure that nothing will. Is anyone with your wife now? Then go back and sit with her. I'll be there shortly. I must just gather up my things.'

The man left at a trot. Nesta nodded approvingly. It was good to find a man who was concerned about the health of his wife and new baby. So many men were glad enough to play their part in making a child, but when it came to actually bringing it into the world, they were no help at all. She knew of some whose little ones had been stillborn or lost through miscarriage, and what did those husbands tell their wives? 'Never mind, sweeting, we can have more.' Just like the king, no doubt. His poor Queen went through a dozen pregnancies and miscarriages, only to be punished for her failure to produce a living heir. As if it could be her fault!

Nesta put on her sacking apron in place of the white one she normally wore.

'Kate? Where are you?' she bawled. 'Mistress Robinson's time has come. Quickly, now! No time to waste!'

Kate appeared in the inner doorway. 'I don't think I'll come, Gramma. Perhaps the next time. I have a headache and I need a bit of a lie down.'

'Headache, is it! That's nothing to what that poor woman will be going through shortly. You promised me you'd give this a try, so stop fiddling about and get that apron on!'

Sullenly the girl moved forward and tied the apron around her slender waist.

Tom Robinson sprang to his feet when the women arrived. 'Thank the Lord you've come! She's in a terrible state. Just look at her!'

Nesta approached the bed, pushing aside a frightened maidservant who was hovering nearby. Poor Sally was tossing and turning, moaning dreadfully.

'Now, now, Sally, stop this nonsense. What on earth is the matter? You surely can't be in this much pain yet. You must save your strength for what lies ahead. You've already gone through this once, you know what to expect.'

Sally continued to thrash and moan. Kate's eyes opened wide.

'What's wrong with her, Gramma?'

'I'll know better if you let me near the bed and take a look at her. Stand aside, do!'

Moments later, she nodded her head in satisfaction. 'All's well. You just calm down, Sally. Do you want to mark the child?'

The young mother shook her head and lay still, holding herself rigidly, only to writhe in agony a few second later.

'Can't you do something, Gramma?' Kate whispered, her face puckered in dismay.

'Have no fear, Kate! This is quite normal, you know. Her pains are coming close together now, so it won't be long.'

Nesta spoke truly, yet she wondered what had provoked the young mother's dreadful distress. After all, this wasn't the first time she'd given birth, so she must know that everything was as it should be, painful though it was.

Within half an hour it was all over, and both mother and child had come safely through their ordeal. 'A lovely little girl!' Nesta announced, wrapping the child in the blanket proffered by Kate. She was surprised by the young mother's reaction.

'I don't want to see her!' she wailed. 'Take her away!'

'Come now, dearie, you don't mean that. You've a beautiful little daughter, sweet as can be. Come, I'll let you hold her for a minute before we swaddle her.'

Sally turned her face to the wall. When the baby had been washed and dressed, Nesta carried her outside to meet her father.

'A boy?' he asked eagerly.

'Another little girl. Strong and healthy, with all her fingers and toes!'

His shoulders sagged and he did not return her smile.

'So she's failed again!' he muttered. 'Better she had died, methinks.'

Utterly shocked, Nesta watched him leave. What on earth was the matter with the man? He was just an ordinary labouring chap, not Harry Tudor! Sons might bring home a wage, in time, perhaps even follow their fathers into their chosen trade, but it was daughters who supported parents in their old age.

It suddenly occurred to her that she hadn't been paid. That wouldn't do at all! It was too bad if the man was disappointed in the sex of his child, but that was hardly her fault.

'God's teeth!' she muttered, furious with herself for not having asked him to stump up. Now she would have to come back on the morrow to get what was due to her. On second thoughts, that might not be a bad idea. If Sally was determined to reject the child, something would have to be done. The poor babe couldn't be left to die for want of nourishment. People were such kittle kattle. You never knew how they were going to react, and by and large folks such as Nesta Davies were left to pick up the pieces.

Later, when they were trudging home, Nesta waited for her granddaughter to say something about the birth, perhaps to ask questions about what she had witnessed. Then she could give a little talk about the whole business of labour and delivery as part of the girl's training in the art of midwifery. Surely Kate would have been impressed by the miracle of birth? Nesta had attended dozens of women in childbed but she had never ceased to marvel each time a new little person came into the world in front of her eyes.

However, there was something else on the girl's mind. 'Why was Master Robinson so cross, Gramma?'

'Don't ask me, gal! Miserable sinner that he is, he was expecting a son and a daughter just won't do, it seems.'

'Why are men so cruel, Gramma?'

'It's a mystery to me,' Nesta told her.

'Mind you, not all men are like that, as you'll find out for yourself as life goes on. Your own father is a good man, and there was no nonsense about wanting sons when you were born. Happy as the day is long, he was, when you came into the world, and that I know for a fact.'

Kate smiled briefly. 'Ay, I think he loves me well enough. When he's not scolding, that is.' She fell silent then, and Nesta had the sense that the girl wasn't thinking so much about Tom Robinson as of something closer to home.

As they walked on she heard footsteps behind them, and the heavy breathing of someone who was moving too fast for comfort. Swinging round she recognized the pasty-faced girl who had come to her, asking for a love potion.

'Have you come from Sal Robinson's house?' the girl panted.

'We have indeed, and all is well. Mother and babe came through it safely.'

'The babe, mistress. Boy or girl?'

'A beautiful little girl.'

A queer expression passed over the girl's face, gone in a flash.

'That's good then. That's very good.' Then she threw back her head and laughed, before racing back the way she had come.

'What an odd sort of girl that is,' Nesta remarked. 'Do you know her, Kate?'

'Oh, that's Frances Cropwell. Fanny, they call her. I've known her all my life, but we've never been friends.'

'She seemed quite concerned about Sally, though, which was kind. Are they related to each other, perhaps?'

Kate shrugged. 'They could be, for all I know. Everybody in these villages seems connected in one way or another. Most likely Fanny and Sal are cousins of some sort.'

Nesta did not sleep well that night. She was sure that the new mother would have got over her feelings about the new babe, all in good time. In fact, having seen Tom Robinson's reaction to the news of his daughter's birth, she thought that the young woman probably feared her man's wrath and her dismay was due to the expectation of that, rather than any negative feelings towards the babe itself. But somebody had to make sure that the man calmed down, or the stress would stop Sally's milk coming in, and the babe would suffer.

Morning came at last. The Davies family had broken their fast, and the men had repaired to the workshop. Joan had been made comfortable, and Kate had been given certain tasks to do while Nesta was out.

'I shan't be long,' she told the girl. 'As soon

as I've made sure that all is well at the Robinsons I'll be back to see how you've got on.'

She hurried off, pleased to be out in the crisp morning air. When she reached the bridge she was surprised to see a little knot of people, nudging each other and whispering. A body had just been dragged from the water and dumped on the riverbank. Two sturdy men, with dirty water dripping from their clothing, stood about helplessly, looking down on the corpse that they had apparently just recovered.

With a sinking feeling Nesta drew closer and, to her horror, she recognized the sodden figure as that of Sally Robinson.

8

'Out of my way!' Nesta pushed through the little knot of onlookers without regard for their grumbles. 'Don't just stand there like a heron on a rock! Help me turn her over, somebody, do!'

'It's no use, mistress. Deader than a doornail, far as I can see!' The speaker was the local blacksmith, identifiable from the leather apron he wore.

Nesta struggled to turn the girl onto her face and was relieved when one of the dripping rescuers came forward to help her.

'I've seen this trick work before,' she panted, pushing down on Sally's back with both hands.

'Can't you see she's gone, mistress? There's nothing you can do now so you may as well save your strength.' It was the same doomsayer as before. She ignored him and worked on. Moments later she was rewarded when a stream of water gushed out of the girl's mouth.

'That's right, gal! Better out than in!' She sat back on her heels as Sally coughed and choked. A frightened murmur rippled through the crowd as Nesta helped the girl into a sitting position, wiping away a strand of pond-weed.

'Someone better go for the priest,' she heard a voice say.

'No need for that, you fool! Can't you see she's come round now, and no harm done?'

'She's tried to do away with herself, ain't she? Mortal sin is that! She'd have gone straight to hell, unshriven, 'cept you come by and done a miracle.'

'We don't know what she did or didn't do. She could have slipped. Did any of you see what happened?' People exchanged frightened glances but nobody replied.

'There you are, then! You don't know what you're talking about. Don't go spreading gossip or you'll be the one in trouble with the priest. You know what the commandment says about not bearing false witness. You'll get a clout round the ear from Tom Robinson if he gets to hear that sort of talk, and mebbe a thump from the priest to back it up!' She looked down at Sally, who was still looking pale and dazed, as well she might.

'Now then, we're closer to my son's place than Robinson's, so we'll take her there before she catches her death of cold. Two of you chaps make a chair with your hands and hoist her up, and we'll get going.'

'Gotta wait for the priest,' the bossy fellow insisted. He quailed under Nesta's glate.

'That's your job, man! You wait here and let Feyther know where we've taken the poor gal. And mind you do, or you'll have me to reckon with!'

So the damp little procession set off, with Sally perched precariously on the men's linked hands, with Nesta supporting her from behind.

They had not gone far when they came upon a young woman loitering beside the road. She seemed to be gathering a nosegay, but she stopped when she saw the little procession and stepped into their path.

'What's happened? Has there been an accident?'

'Yes, that's right. And you can help by running ahead of us and passing on the news. You know where the cordwainer dwells? My son, Master Jack Davies? If my granddaughter is there, tell her to boil water in readiness, and heat stones as well.'

The girl nodded and sped off. Of course, Nesta thought, that was the girl who wanted a love potion. Well, let her do something useful for once, instead of mooning over some chap who doesn't know she's alive!

However foolish the girl might be, she had obviously delivered her message sensibly enough, for when Nesta arrived home everything was in readiness. She nodded approvingly when Kate appeared in the doorway with a blanket in her arms.

'That's right. Now then, lay her down gently, you men, and we'll soon have her put to rights.'

This done, they stood watching in bovine fashion until Nesta shooed them away.

'You've done well to help, but this is women's work now. We must get her out of this wet gown and into something warm and dry. No doubt Master Robinson will want to thank you properly when he hears about this.'

They nodded and moved away, although the smaller of the two men looked longingly at the hot drink which Kate had prepared. Nesta hoped that Robinson would indeed offer the pair some reward, not to mention those who had pulled Sally from the river in the first place. Not that he struck her as being a particularly kind or generous fellow, but there was nothing she could do about that.

She conducted a quick inspection to make sure that all was well with her patient whom, after all, she had delivered of a child not long before. Then, helped by Kate, she quickly stripped off Sally's soaking garments, substituting a voluminous bedrail of her own. When at last the girl stopped shaking Nesta handed her the hot posset, which she held in both hands while she sipped.

'What's happening down there? Is everything all right?' Joan's anxious voice floated down from above.

'Up you go, Kate, and let your mother know all's well. I can manage here.'

'Yes, Gramma.' Kate climbed the stairs slowly, looking back at Sally, eager not to miss anything, Nesta supposed. Well, it was just as well if the two of them were alone. Sally might not want to say much in front of an audience.

'Now then, gal, are you going to tell me what all this is about?'

'I don't know what you mean, Mistress Davies.'

'You must know how you ended up in the water, gal! If those two chaps hadn't happened on the scene in time you wouldn't be here now to tell the tale. And I might as well tell you that Feyther Wagstaffe will be here at any moment, and you'd better get your story straight before he comes, for I hear he's good at tripping sinners up when they don't make a good confession!'

'Confession?' Sally's eyes opened wide. 'What do I have to confess? I've hardly been out of bed since the babe arrived. I haven't even been churched yet! I've no sins on my conscience, Mistress Davies. At least, only a little one,' she whispered, so that Nesta had to strain to hear.

During her years as a midwife, Nesta had known of several women who had suffered melancholy after giving birth, although fortunately none had tried to do away with herself. Could Sally have proved the exception to the rule? She had certainly seemed downcast in the beginning, refusing to hold her babe.

A knock at the door heralded the arrival of the priest. Completely expressionless, he looked down at the pale girl on the bed.

'Should I leave, Feyther?' Nesta spoke meekly, hoping he wouldn't say yes. How was she to know what was going on if she was banished from the room? Fortunately he shook his head impatiently as he pulled a chair closer to the pallet where Sally lay.

'Not unless Mistress Robinson has something to say to me in confession.'

'I was just asking her how she came to fall into the river,' Nesta explained, stretching a point. 'As far as I know, there were no witnesses when it happened.'

'So I understand. The current is strong there and the men who pulled her to the bank say she was washed up on a rock in the middle of the river, otherwise she might have drowned before they came on the scene. Now then, my child, let me hear your story, if you please.'

'Yes, I'd like to know what you were doing so far from home, and you only just out of childbed,' Nesta interrupted. 'I'm the midwife who attended Mistress Robinson's confinement,' she explained, unabashed by the priest's frown. Sally drew her hand across her forehead, suddenly becoming agitated.

'Tom! Where is he? What's happened to him?'

'I'm sure he'll be along as soon as he hears of this,' Father Wagstaffe soothed.

'No, no! You don't understand! A boy brought a message this morning, to say that Tom had been set upon by brigands and left for dead near the bridge! He wanted to see me before he died! Of course I came as soon as I could, but when I got near there was no sign of him. I was looking all about and that's when someone came up behind me and gave me a hard push in the back. That's all I can remember.' She started to shake again and Nesta drew the blanket up and went to the fire to fetch another hot stone to place at the girl's feet.

'It was foolish of you to come alone,' the priest said reprovingly.

'I didn't stop to think. I only knew I had to

get to Tom before it was too late. And there was nobody else in the house, save for Polly and the children.'

'Who was the boy who came with the message?'

'I never saw him. 'Twas Polly who went to the door and he was gone by the time I came downstairs.'

'Attempted murder!' the priest announced. 'The constable must be sent for, and meantime you must stay here, where you'll be safe with Master Davies. I insist that you make no attempt to return home for the present.'

'But the children!' Sally wailed. 'I must go to them!'

'Polly will care for them,' the priest said, as he got up to leave.

9

'I must get home!' Sally insisted again. 'Polly can't manage the two babies by herself, and little Mary needs to be fed. And it's kind of you to say they can come here, Mistress Davies, but I can't impose. Not with Joan ailing upstairs. Think of the noise, for one thing! Every time Mary cries, it sets Catherine off, too. She's jealous of the new baby, Catherine is. She tried to push her off my lap this morning. You'd hardly believe the strength she has, and her only ten months old!'

'Mary, is it!' Nesta said. 'A name that will wear well. After the princess, I suppose, or the Lady Mary, as we're supposed to call her now!'

Sally looked away, her face sad. Nesta wondered whether by giving her baby that name, the girl was making a statement. After all, the husband, God rot him, had made as much fuss about his beautiful new child as if he were the King himself. She was pleased to see that Sally had apparently bonded with the babe after her first rejection.

'Yes, you must go home, child,' she said

now. 'Never mind what the priest said about you staying put. Men don't understand these things. If the sheriff wants to talk to you, he can see you at home, just as well as here.'

So Jonno was sent to fetch a neighbour who came with his cart, willingly enough, being eager to hear the tale of the day's doings. Sally answered his questions meekly enough, hoping, no doubt, to quash any rumours which were flying around concerning her attempted suicide. Nesta was thankful when they arrived at the Robinsons's cottage and the man had gone away.

When she had seen Sally tucked up in bed, with little Mary in her arms, Nesta went downstairs and looked about her. Having sent the neighbour on his way she would now have to walk home, but she wanted to have a quiet word with the young maidservant, Polly.

The house, solidly constructed of wattle and daub, was large for a labourer's cottage, and well appointed, with decent furniture and well-polished pewter pieces. Much better, in fact, than she had expected. She said as much to the sandy-haired girl in the grubby apron, who came to ask if she needed aught.

'A tankard of beer would ease my throat before I start on the road home. I'm told that you answered the door and took the message up to your mistress. Who was the boy who brought it, do you know?'

The girl's hand shook as she put the tankard down at Nesta's elbow.

'I never saw him before. I'm not from these parts, see. I come from over Banbury way.'

'How did you come into service here, then?'

'Oh, old Mistress Critchley — Sally's mother, that's dead, you know — she was a sort of cousin to my mother. When this new baby was expected, Master Critchley sent for me to come and help in the house. Part of the time I go over the fields to his place, to tackle the rough work. His other married daughter keeps house for him; she lives there with her husband, Peter Dilley the glover.'

'And your mother didn't mind you leaving home?'

'Bless you, no! I'm the middle one of fifteen, and I've never known a time when there was enough food to go round the lot of us. Not that they all live at home now, o' course. There's some married and off her hands. I send her what they pay me, not that it's much, and everybody's happy.'

Except you, poor little mite, Nesta thought, looking at the girl's red hands and anxious expression. 'And I suppose this house belongs to Master Critchley?' she hazarded, and was proved right when the girl nodded.

'But the boy. What did he look like? How old would you say he was?'

Polly wrinkled her nose. 'Like all little chaps. Dirty and ragged. About eight or nine, mebbe. My brother Wat's about that size.'

'And what did he say, exactly?'

'Come quick, come quick! Yer husband's been set on by robbers and he's lying down by the bridge, bleeding like a stuck pig. Come at once, he says, cos he ain't got long to go and he wants to say goodbye.'

'So you went up and repeated the message to Mistress Robinson?'

The girl looked at Nesta as if regarding a simpleton. 'Of course I did. 'Tweren't my husband, was it? I had to go and say.'

'So he didn't actually call Master Robinson by name,' Nesta mused.

'I told you, didn't I. Yer husband, that's what he says, plain as day.'

'Then for all you know the child might have come to the wrong house by mistake, and the message wasn't about Sally's man at all.'

Polly's jaw dropped. 'Oh, lawks a mussy! If I done the wrong thing I'll be for it when the master gets home. Of course, when the woman up the street stopped in and told me how Sally tried to top herself, I knew I'd get it in the neck anyway, for not watching over her better.' She hid her face in her hands and

68

began to rock back and forth.

'She did not try to top herself, Polly. She fell in the river by accident and luckily two chaps fished her out. And you can't be blamed, because for all you knew the tale was true and it was your duty to pass it on. Sally would never have forgiven you if her husband truly had been mortally wounded and she hadn't been there to say goodbye.'

'You mean that, missus?'

'I do, but you'd better prepare yourself for some awkward questions when the constable gets here. You must repeat what you've said to me, and all will be well.'

Polly sighed. 'I was thinking mebbe it was some sort of prank.'

'Funny sort of prank, if you ask me! Somebody lured poor Sally out of the house and all the way down to the river, and her still weak from giving birth. What would be the point?'

But of course the point had been to push Sally to her death. Not that she wanted to explain that little detail to Polly. She'd learn about it soon enough, but it was better not to put ideas into her head until the constable had spoken to her.

'Like me to pour you some more?' Polly asked now, peering into Nesta's empty tankard.

'No, no. That was very nice, but any more and I'll be tipsy. The next thing we know, I'll be in the river myself, and we don't want that, do we?'

Walking home, Nesta tried to sort things out in her mind. It could be someone with a grudge against Tom Robinson. She dwelt on that for a while. But if that was the case, why take it out on his poor wife? Let's say it was a warning gone wrong. Was he a gambler, or had he borrowed money and failed to pay it back? One did not necessarily cancel out the other. It was possible to imagine someone threatening the man. Pay what you owe, or your wife will suffer, and see how you like that!

She would have to make a few enquiries, starting with Jack. What was known about Tom Robinson? Or could someone be trying to get back at Adam Critchley, Sally's father? Apparently he was quite well to do, which might well arouse envy in the breast of someone less fortunate. Had he perhaps dismissed an employee, who was now seeking revenge? Or thrown someone off his land, say a poacher, and turned him over to the law? There were endless possibilities and Nesta couldn't follow them up without knowing more.

Then there was the murder of poor old

70

Goody whatever her name was. Could the two crimes have been connected? Surely it was unusual to have two suspicious deaths in such a short time in a law-abiding place like Hollyhill? Although actually, one murder and one attempted murder, she corrected herself.

All these ruminations got her nowhere, and it wasn't until the next morning that she heard the sequel to that day's events. She answered the door to a bright little woman who explained that she was a friend of Joan.

'My boy and her Jonno were born the same week, see. That's how we got together in the first place. You know how it is, you like to talk about babes getting a first tooth, and what to do about colic, that sort of thing.'

'Yes, yes,' Nesta said, feeling impatient and wanting to get on. 'Did you come to see Joan? She had a bad night, I'm afraid, and she's only just dropped off to sleep. I'd let you go up, only she really needs to rest.'

'No, no, I'll come back another time. Just give her this honey cake, if you'll be so kind. Fresh baked this morning. I thought she'd like a little treat.'

'That's good of you. Is there any message?'

'No, unless she wants to hear the latest gossip. I suppose you heard what happened to poor Sally Critchley yesterday? Ah, but of course, you was the one as brought her round. I remember that now. Well, the news is, they've arrested her husband, Tom Robinson, for trying to do away with her.'

'No!'

'Uh huh! The constable came for him at cock-crow and hauled him off to the lock up. Desperate she'll be, poor dear. Not only because her man's bound for the gallows, but on account of him wanting her dead. I mean, husbands are more trouble than they're worth at the best of times, as every woman knows, but finding out they mean you real harm, that's another story altogether!'

'Yes, indeed,' Nesta murmured thoughtfully.

10

'I must say I'd never have believed it of Tom Robinson,' Jack muttered, chewing hard on the end of a loaf of barley bread. 'Trying to do away with his poor wife like that. Now, I could understand it if she was a nagging sort of woman, but she's always seemed like the meek sort to me.'

'I wonder if he done for old Goody Clapton as well?' Jonno piped up.

'I don't see why he'd want to do that, son. What was the poor old gal to him?'

'She brought his daughter into the world,' Kate observed. 'The old baby, not this new one.'

'What's that got to do with the price of eggs, then?'

'Everybody knows he was expecting a boy this time, Dad. Mebbe he blamed Mistress Clapton when it turned out to be a girl.'

'Stuff and nonsense. You should know better than to go round saying such things.' Jack reached for another chunk of bread. 'Good stuff this, Mumma! You should teach our Kate how to make it.' Kate glared at him, but he reached for the honeypot and didn't notice.

Nesta rubbed her nose. 'None of this makes sense. If Tom wanted to kill his wife, why go to all that folderol about luring her away from home? I could understand it if he'd lost his temper for some reason and throttled her in the heat of the moment, but this other business?'

'Constable will get to the bottom of it,' Jack told her, wetting a finger and mopping up the crumbs he'd let fall on the table. 'Come on, Jonno. Time we was getting to work. If you're a good lad I'll let you go out later, make some deliveries for me.'

Jonno's eyes lit up. A few hours spent away from the workshop was a rare treat.

'I'm going over to see how young Sally's getting on,' Nesta remarked, to no one in particular. 'She's bound to be all of a dither, with her man locked up.'

'Can I come too, Gramma?' Kate seemed unusually eager, Nesta thought, but then it wasn't often that the dull routine of daily life was interrupted by anything so interesting as attempted murder.

'I suppose so, gal, but stay in the background, you hear? Poor Sal won't want everybody and his cur making remarks. Come to think of it, you might be able to help. You take that Polly aside and see if she's remembered anything else about that boy, the child who brought the message. Seems to me the whole mystery will be solved when we know who he is.'

'Won't the constable seek him out?'

'Of course he will, but we want to know as well, eh?' The two of them exchanged knowing grins.

Sally Robinson was surprisingly well composed for one whose husband was held in gaol and in danger of hanging. Nesta said as much to the girl.

'They can't do much to him, can they, Mistress Davies? I wasn't killed, and I don't know who tried to push me in the river. They can't make me say it was my Tom; not that I believe he had anything to do with it. Why should he?'

A thought occurred to Nesta. 'You say you were pushed into the water. How did that happen? I mean, was it a hand on your back, or a blow behind the knees, let's say?'

'Two hands on my back.'

'But where exactly? Above or below the waist, let's say.'

Sally hesitated for a second or two. 'One hand quite hight up on my back, and another on my left shoulder, I think. Yes, that's how it was.'

'Not a nine-year-old boy, then. He wouldn't have been tall enough.'

75

'Who said it might have been a nine-year-old, then?' Sally seemed genuinely puzzled.

'Oh, nobody. There were no witnesses, you see. It's just that Polly thinks that the boy who brought the message that lured you away was about the age of one of her young brothers.'

'I wish I'd got a look at him. I might have known who he was, seeing as I've lived here all my life. Come to that, I wish I'd taken the message myself, or I might not have gone haring off the way I did. That was such a stupid thing to do.'

'No, no,' Nesta said soothingly. 'Any woman would have done the same if her husband was thought to be dying. It does strike me as strange, though, that you didn't see anyone nearby when you reached the bridge.'

'They must have been crouched down behind all those willows. Whoever it was couldn't have been far off if they were able to spring on me as soon as my back was turned.' She shivered, remembering. 'Why are they holding on to my Tom, Mistress Davies? When are they going to let him come home?'

Nesta had no answer to that. 'They have to make sure of their facts, I suppose. Don't take this the wrong way, gal, but men have been known to murder their wives. They have to work out that he's not one of them.'

'Oh, Tom would never get rid of me,' Sally said, her tone bitter. 'He's too much to lose. If I can only produce a son for him by this time next year he'll be sweet as pie, just you wait and see.'

'I'm fed up hearing about men and their sons!' Nesta burst out. 'They're all the same, it seems, from Old Harry on down. You and Tom have two beautiful daughters. What more could anyone ask for? Tell me that!'

'You don't understand, mistress. There's more to this than meets the eye. I wish I could tell you, but I can't.' Loud wails floated down from upstairs, and Sally heaved herself to her feet, saying that she had to see to the baby.

'I must be on my way,' Nesta told her. 'Where has that granddaughter of mine got to, I wonder?'

Kate had been chatting to Polly, and when she and her grandmother were on the road again, she had a morsel of news to relate.

'Polly went to market this morning, Gramma. She likes that, it's about the only time she gets a minute to herself these days. Mistress Robinson doesn't mind if she takes her time about it. She likes to look at the gewgaws and the sweetmeats on some of the stalls, even if she doesn't have the money to buy anything for herself.'

'What of it?'

'Well, everybody was talking about Tom Robinson being in the lock-up, and naturally she stopped here and there to have a listen.'

'Naturally!'

'They say he goes out to the Bird in Hand of an evening, and when he's in his cups he says things.'

'What sort of things?'

'How he's married to a useless women who can't bear sons. How he'd like to get rid of her and take up with somebody better. That's what he's supposed to have said, Gramma, on my oath!'

'Don't listen to such talk, my gal! To start with, that young Sally has borne two children in less than a year. If God wills it, she'll live to bear many more, including a clutch of boys. And when a man talks of getting rid of his wife he doesn't mean murder. It's like that King of ours throwing poor Catherine of Aragon on one side to take up with that Boleyn hussy, 'cept he's royalty and can get away with it. There will never come a time when ordinary chaps can do likewise. The women of England would never stand for it. Tom Robinson must know all that. Talk's cheap. You mark my words, there's nothing in it.'

'But somebody tried to drown Sally,' Kate argued.

'True enough, but who was it? That's the question. Let's say it was Tom. Why go to all that trouble, sending messages and that. He'd be found out, sure as eggs is eggs. Much easier to take her out for a walk some evening, like husbands do, then give her a push when nobody was about. Then he'd come bleating to the priest, about how she slipped on wet grass and went over, and nothing he could do to save her.'

'You sound like you've made plans to get rid of someone yourself, Gramma,' Kate teased, but Nesta was perfectly serious.

'I know people, child, that's all.'

'If he did do it, Gramma, it must have been somebody different who poisoned Goody Clapton, mustn't it?'

'Yes, indeed. I've yet to meet the man who would stoop to cooking up a nice dish of food, and that includes your father!'

Kate looked startled. 'So you're saying it was a woman who poisoned old Goody?'

Nesta realized what she'd said. 'Oh, I don't know about that! Some men work as professional cooks, I think. I've heard tell that the King has such fellows. Pastrycooks, who make puddings and pastries. And as far as I know, the great nobles and mebbe even the gentry might have them too. Stands to reason, doesn't it? You don't get duchesses and grand ladies doing their own cooking.'

'But there's none of them in these parts, unless you count those folk over at the hall.'

'Oh yes? Who are they, then?' Nesta was surprised when Kate's expression became suddenly grim, and the girl ran on ahead, as if the seven devils were at her heels.

11

In due time Tom Robinson was released from gaol. 'From lack of evidence' the constable said, but his wife insisted that he was innocent.

'No denying he can be a bit awkward at times, but he'd never do me harm,' she told Nesta, who had called on her yet again, to check on the health of mother and child.

'Poking her nose in,' Tom said sourly, but when his wife pulled him up short he admitted that they had cause to be grateful, 'seeing as how she brung you back to life when everybody thought you was gone.'

The days grew shorter, and the morning air was crisper. Gradually everyone forgot about the strange happenings at Hollyhill, although the priest kept a watchful eye on his flock. Greatly daring, for she was afraid that she'd be told to mind her own business, Nesta asked him if he had any idea who the mysterious boy might be. For hadn't he baptized every child born within a ten-mile radius?

'I cannot think who it might be,' he told her, scratching the tip of his nose. 'The blacksmith's boy fits the description but although I've questioned him closely with threats of hellfire, he swears he's done nothing wrong. I did hear about a vagabond family camping on the common at the time; they've moved on now. I believe it might have been one of them.'

The inhabitants of Hollyhill accepted his pronouncement with some relief. Hadn't they always said that it must have been a stranger? Some child — or even a midget — with the devil in him. None of them would have tried to dispose of poor Sally, and that was plain as day.

That autumn confinements were few and far between. So much for teaching young Kate a useful trade, Nesta mourned. Just as well they had Jack to provide for them, or it would be slim pickings indeed. Back in Oxford it would be a different story; the place was teeming with people and it wasn't unusual for the midwife to attend to two or three women in one week.

In November, though, they were called to the wife of a shepherd, who lived on the outskirts of the hamlet. It being her first child, the labour was a long one, and Kate fell asleep on the settle while they watched and waited. Eventually the time came, and the screams of the poor woman as she writhed in the second stage of her travail brought the girl to her feet.

'A lovely boy!' Nesta beamed as she placed the child in the arms of the new mother, whose smile of relief soon turned to agony as she clenched her fists again.

'Gramma, what's wrong?' Kate cried. 'What's happening?'

'Unless I'm very much mistaken there's another little man in there,' Nesta told her, pulling back the covers. Sure enough, another baby, smaller than the first, slid into the world, giving an indignant cry.

'Two sons! Your husband will be pleased,' Kate cried, remembering Tom Robinson and his callous rejection of his little girls. The shepherd, when he was eventually readmitted to the house, looked at his sons with awe.

'You done well, gal! Mind you, you had no call to summon Mistress Davies like you did. I could have brung them two along meself. I've brought twins into the world afore now!'

'Them's lambs, not humans,' his wife retorted. 'And right ham-fisted you'd have been, too! A woman needs other women around her at a time like this.'

'Ay, well, I hope you told her we can't pay! I've no money until quarter day rolls round, and that's all there is to it!'

'You can owe it to me till Christmas,' Nesta

sighed. This was beginning to be an old familiar story. But her patient had other ideas.

'Just you reach up there on that shelf and hand me down that shawl,' she told Kate. 'Here, mistress, you take this. Brand new, it is. I made it meself. Gave me something to do to wile away the long months of waiting for this pair.'

'Mary, this is lovely,' Nesta told her, as she unfolded a beautiful shawl. 'I could do with something like this, with winter coming on. Are you sure you want to part with it?'

'Didn't cost me nothing. Spun and wove the wool meself, I did. One of the perks of being a shepherd's wife, that is.'

When Nesta and Kate stepped out into the cold dawn, it was to see a cart approaching.

'That's Peter Dilley, Gramma,' Kate told her.

'Oh, yes? Who might he be, then?'

'Sal Robinson's brother-in-law. He's married to her sister, Anne.'

Nesta regarded the man with interest. 'What's he doing out here at this time of the morning, then? His wife's not expecting, is she? He can't have come looking for me.'

But the man had come for them, as he explained when he came level with them.

'Heard you was here. The old man wants a

word with you, so he sent me to pick you up. Save you a walk, he said.'

The two women clambered up on the cart. It smelled strongly of cow manure but they were grateful for all that.

'I'm glad of a ride after the night we've had,' Nesta told him as the horse began to amble along.

'All's well there, I hope?'

'Yes, indeed. Twins. Two boys. Mother and babes hale and hearty.'

'Two boys!' he marvelled. 'Some folks have all the luck!'

Not another one! Nesta thought. Pasting a smile on her face she asked: 'Perhaps your wife is *enceinte*?'

'What? No, she is not, more's the pity! Why do you ask?'

'I thought mebbe that's why you've come for me, so I can take a look at her. See that all's well. Her father would wish her to be well looked after at such a time, especially when he came so close to losing Sally.'

'No, mistress; it's for himself he wants you. He thinks you can cure his gout. In agony with it, he is, and cross as a bagful of weasels. Goody Clapton always gave him a salve to put on his foot, which seemed to do the trick.'

'Oh, dear! I don't have anything of that

kind about me. I will come and look at him, though,' she amended hastily, in case he asked them to get out at the crossroads. Adam Critchley's house was some miles out of their way, but it still brought them closer to home and her feet were throbbing. The older man wasn't the only one with problems.

'Can you do anything for gout, Gramma?' Kate was regarding her anxiously. Nesta had told her often enough that she wasn't skilled in the use of herbal remedies as Goody Clapton was said to have been. Nor did she wish to get that sort of reputation. There was a fine line between being an honest healer and one who dealt in mysterious potions. Best to leave that sort of thing to apothecaries, who were trained in the art; otherwise, sooner or later, one ran the risk of a charge of witchcraft.

'Oh, yes. The juice of marigold leaves, mixed with vinegar, gives relief to any hot swelling, child. And late in the year though it is, there are still marigolds growing well in the shelter of the garden wall. Methinks we should gather them all, to keep by us in case of need.'

Kate gave a sigh of relief. It was well known that the plant was named in honour of the mother of Our Lord, so there was no possibility of any spiteful person accusing her grandmother of any wrongful use of it.

Adam Critchley groaned when he heard that Nesta was unable to help, and would have to return the next day with the marigold decoction.

'I can't stand another day of this, mistress! 'Tis worse than hellfire!' He pointed to his inflamed toe joints, stabbing a finger in fury.

However, his daughter, who had been hovering nearby, spoke up boldly. 'We have marigolds here, Dad! I can gather some right away, if Mistress Davies will tell me what to do.'

'It's the leaves you want,' Nesta explained. 'And you can save yourself all this misery if you change your ways, Master Critchley.'

'What do you mean, woman?'

'Gout is caused by too much rich food and drink. Eat moderately and drink less and you should see some improvement.'

'Lot of nonsense,' he growled. 'Do you mean to stand there all day, daughter? Get me that marigold juice, or whatever it is, so I can get relief. Marigolds, indeed! Hawisa Clapton charged me a pretty penny for what is freely available from my own garden. I might have known she was a cheat. Still, she got what was coming to her in the end, so there is some justice in the world.'

Since Nesta had been brought here all the

way for nothing, as Critchley described it, Dilley wasn't asked to bring the cart out again to take them the rest of the way home. Kate thought this very unfair, and said so. 'Gramma told Mrs Dilley what to do for you, Master Critchley. She wouldn't have known otherwise, would she?'

'You keep a guard on your tongue, gal, or I'll teach you a lesson you won't forget!'

Nasty old curmudgeon! Nesta thought. Kate spoke truly. No need to threaten her like that. But before they left, she gleaned some very interesting information.

12

Nesta was plodding down the lane leading away from the house, when she heard her name called.

'Don't mind Dad,' Anne Dilley panted. 'He can be a bit awkward at times. He's only out of sorts now because of this miserable gout.'

'I'm sure it's very painful.'

'Oh, it isn't just that. No, he's thinking of getting married again, and he's afraid she won't take him if he looks like being laid up half the time.'

'My goodness, who is the lucky bride? Anyone we know?'

'Her name is Jane Pettapiece, from over Cottisford way. She's been married and widowed twice already, never mind she's not thirty yet.'

'Poor girl! What happened to the husbands, then? Met with accidents, did they?'

'They both died of natural causes, as far as I know.' Anne spoke primly, no doubt well aware of the scandal that had affected her family ever since her sister had almost been drowned. 'They were both old men; marriages arranged by her parents, no doubt. She happens to be a cousin of Margery. Dad's been lonely since my mother died, so he had a chat with Margery and this is the result.'

'Margery? I don't think I've heard of her, have I?'

'Margery Dawes, Dad's half sister. She lives over at Hardwick-cum-Tusmore so you wouldn't have met her.'

'I see. Well, I hope it all works out as your father would wish. I'm a widow myself, so I know a bit about loneliness. Come along, Kate. Time we were off.'

Anne took Nesta by the arm as she turned to leave. 'Do you know of any cure for barrenness, Mistress Davies? Some herb or simple that would help me bear a child?'

Nesta had to think. 'There's catmint, of course, that's said to be a help, but whether you are supposed to take it internally or use it on the outside, I can't say. How long have you been married, then?'

'Nigh on three years,' the girl said, biting her lip. 'I did think I might be *enceinte* once, but I lost the babe early on, and never a sign of one since.'

'And I suppose you long to have a child of your own in your arms, now you've seen your sister with two babes on her knee. Never fear, dearie, your turn will come. I've seen many like you, slow to get started, then once the

90

first one arrives at last, they can't get stopped! Bringing up children is hard work. You take my advice, and enjoy your free time while you can.'

'You don't understand!' the younger woman wailed. 'If Dad weds Jane Pettapiece she could give him half a dozen children in half no time!' Clamping her hand over her mouth as though she was about to vomit, she ran back the way she had come.

Nesta looked at Kate and shrugged. 'What on earth is the matter with that family? They all seem obsessed with the idea of reproducing themselves. Never mind; if they do, all the more work for us, eh?'

'I suppose so.' Her granddaughter sounded gloomy. 'Can we get home now, Gramma? I'm so hungry I could eat Will Rouse's wooden leg!'

Nesta was too exhausted to ask who Will Rouse might be, or how he'd come by his wooden leg. It occurred to her that it was almost twenty-four hours since she'd eaten, and she was almost as desperate for a meal as Kate seemed to be.

Later in the day, however, she had cause to recall this little scene. Jack had come to the house for a drink, bringing news with him.

'The miller just came by, and what do you think he had to say? They've taken young

Philip Dawes in for questioning now. This just gets worse, doesn't it?'

'Dawes? Now where have I heard that name before?'

'You know, Gramma!' Kate reminded her. 'Adam Critchley's sister is a Mistress Dawes. Anne Dilley mentioned her this morning.'

Nesta clapped a hand to her forehead. 'Of course! Dear me, I must be getting on a bit. I'm a real forgettery Fan. Is this Philip a nephew of old Critchley, then?'

Jack nodded. 'Seems he was loitering near the mill when the constable caught up with him. Not that there's any harm in taking it easy when you're out from under your master's eye!'

He caught sight of Jonno grinning and hastened to put right what he had said.

'Don't you go getting any ideas, my lad. I was talking in general, like. What I meant was, the Dawes boy didn't seem to be doing owt wrong, only Sam Fowler's on the lookout for anyone looking suspicious and so he took him for questioning.'

'And did that come to anything?'

'As far as I know the boy is still locked up, but what that means I can't say.'

When Jack and Jonno had returned to work, Nesta smiled at Kate.

'I do believe you should go down to the

lock-up and see what you can find out from the Dawes boy, gal.'

'Me? They won't let me in, Gramma!'

'You don't want to get inside, you silly girl. It's got a window, ain't it? Talk to him through that, and make sure the constable don't catch you.'

'But what shall I say? I can't go up to him and ask if he tried to murder his cousin, can I? Why don't you come with me, Gramma? You're better at this sort of thing.'

'He won't fancy talking to me, gal. Seeing a pretty young thing in front of his nose would please him. Make up some tale that'll loosen his tongue. And while you're at it, take him one of my honey cakes, to get things started.'

'Hullo! Anyone in there?' Kate hovered nervously in front of the lock-up, praying that the constable wasn't inside. Then she realized that the great plank was in place across the door, and the man could hardly have locked himself in.

'Hullo!' she called again, this time raising her voice. A face appeared at the window.

'Who is it? What do you want?'

'I've brought you a honey cake. I thought you might be hungry.'

A thin hand reached through the bars and snatched it from her.

'Manners!' she muttered, as the boy began

to tear at the food.

'Got any more?' he begged, with a last swallow.

'No, I have not, and that's the last you'll get from me if you can't even say thank you. What are you doing in there, anyway?'

'I wasn't doing nothing wrong,' he whined. 'I was on the way to see my uncle with a message from my mother. I stopped by the river for a bit, to see if the fish were biting. Thought I might try my luck on the way home if Uncle Adam didn't keep me long. Then along comes the constable and grabs me by the scruff of the neck and says he wants to talk to me. Seems somebody tried to drown my cousin Sal the other day, and he thinks it might be me.'

'But why suspect you? You don't even live in Hollyhill.'

'That's the trouble. According to him, a boy took a message to Sal, saying her husband was hurt, but the child wasn't from these parts. Now the fellow's off to Hardwick, to see if any boy there fits the description Polly gave. That's Sal's maid,' he explained.

'I know Polly. And I suppose he thinks that you came to Hollyhill, meaning to kill poor Sally, and you brought the boy with you, a child who nobody from round here knows,' Kate remarked. 'I shouldn't worry too much.

If the constable finds any suitable boys, all he has to do is parade them in front of Polly, and that will be that. And I happen to know that there weren't any witnesses when Sally fell in the water, and she has no idea who pushed her, so that will be that. They'll have to let you go.'

The boy's gloomy expression didn't change. 'Trouble is, Peter Dilley spoke out against me, the dirty gallus.'

'Peter Dilley? What does he know about it? And he's your cousin, isn't he? Why would he do that? Blood's thicker than water, I've always heard.'

'He's only married to my cousin. He's got no time for me. Besides, he'd be glad to get rid of me, same as someone poisoned that poor old gal as lived in the wood.'

'Now you're being fanciful. Surely you don't really think the man would try to do you harm?'

'All I know is, I'd never take a bite or sup in that house, not when he's around.'

'Your wits are addled, boy.'

'Think what you like. He'd like to see me swinging from a gibbet at the crossroads, and that's no word of a lie.'

'I must be on my way,' Kate remarked, since there seemed to be nothing more she could glean from this sullen youth. 'I'm always in trouble for wandering off instead of working in the house like a dutiful daughter. If my dad finds out I've been here I'll get a proper whipping!' This, of course, was a thumping great lie, but one that was justified, she felt, if she was to establish a rapport between them.

'Come again!' he called after her. 'And bring one or two of them honey cakes with you and a sup of ale!'

She walked away briskly, just in time to avoid the constable, who was striding towards the lock-up, coming from the direction of the church.

13

Nesta, hobbling upstairs with a bowl of broth for Joan, wondered how her granddaughter was getting on with Philip Dawes. She had flattered Kate into going alone because she herself was suffering badly after all the walking she'd done in the past few days. She'd been walking great distances all her life, of course, but now her hip was giving her trouble.

It occurred to her that she should gather some herbs, before winter killed off the plants. There was nowhere in Hollyhill where spikenard and ginger could be had, but when she next went to Oxford she could procure some from the apothecary. These items, mixed with the juice and seeds of the sage, were a known cure for rheumatic humours. In the meantime the juice, taken with honey, could sometimes stop the spitting of blood in those with the coughing sickness, such as Joan had.

She also had a dim recollection of being told, by the old woman with whom she learned the midwifery trade, that salted sage juice often helped barren women to conceive.

It might be worth mentioning that to Anne Dilley. It could do her no harm and it might do some good.

There was silence in Joan's room, but as Nesta paused at the door she saw that her son had his head down on Joan's bed. His shoulders were heaving, and his wife laid a loving hand on his head, running her thin fingers through his curls to comfort him. Nesta tiptoed away. The broth could wait.

There were some who would have counselled Jack to stay away from his wife, for it was well known that the disease could spread all through a family in some mysterious way. But that would be too cruel. Joan must know that her days were numbered, just as Jack knew that the woman he'd loved since he was a lad would soon be gone beyond his reach. They needed all the comfort they could give each other.

The children, too, must be aware that their mother wasn't long for this world. Was this why Kate stayed out of doors so much? Out of sight, out of mind, as the saying went. If she was away from the house she could pretend that all was well at home. As for Jonno, he was a happy-go-lucky boy who seemed to live for the day. Don't cross a bridge before you come to it might well have been his motto.

Kate came home, yawning. 'I don't know when I've felt so tired,' she complained. 'I think I'll go and lie down.'

'When you get to my age you'll know what tired is, gal!' Nesta snapped. 'You'll wake up when you get busy sweeping this floor. It hasn't been touched for days, and it looks like it. First, though, tell me what you found out from young Dawes.'

'Nothing much.' Kate sighed, sinking down on a bench and reaching for a half-eaten crust of bread, left behind by Jonno. 'He swears he hasn't done anything to get himself locked up.'

'Of course, he would say that, wouldn't he? What I want to know is why the constable picked on him. He doesn't even live in this parish.'

'He says that Peter Dilley ratted on him to the constable.'

'What? That don't make sense, gal. Anne Dilley and this lad are sort of cousins, as far as we know.'

'That's what I said, but according to him Dilley has something against him, and he reckons it all fits in. What I mean is, nobody can work out who the boy was, the one who gave the message to Polly, so it stands to reason that the child is probably a stranger, brought here by Philip.'

'That tale is about as likely as babies being found in the cabbage patch! What I'd like to know is what brought the lad to Hollyhill in the first place, if he's so innocent.'

'He says he was carrying a message from his mother, to Master Critchley.'

'Well, then, if that be true, his mother will speak up for him and all will be well.'

'I don't suppose she'll be believed, Gramma. She is his mother after all, and in any case she wasn't anywhere near Hollyhill when the attack on Sally happened. What do you think will happen to him now?'

'I suppose they'll have to let him go in the end. I'm beginning to think that Sally wasn't pushed at all. She was bound to be weak and dizzy after giving birth not long before, and she must have got too close to the edge and tumbled in. No mystery there.'

'But the boy, and the message, Gramma. Was that just a prank, then?'

'A very nasty prank, if it was! I suppose we may never know. This will be a nine days' wonder, and then everything will settle down the way it was, you'll see.'

'Poor old Goody Clapton, though. That was no accident, was it!'

'There's some as believe it was. She was getting on a bit and her eyesight was poor by all accounts. She probably picked the wrong stuff by mistake and cooked it up with other bits and pieces she found in her patch of garden. Then she shared it with her dog, and that's how the pair of them died. That had nothing to do with Sally's accident. How could it have been possible?'

'I suppose you're right,' Kate mused, 'but I wish we could find out what really happened. I don't like not knowing, do you?'

'And I don't like knowing that that floor ain't been swept for days,' Nesta reminded her. 'Are you going to get on with it, or do you mean to sit there all day, like you've taken root?'

'Aw, Gramma!'

'Don't you 'aw Gramma' me! I've got to make an apple pie, and I don't want the dust swirling about while I'm doing it. Now do let me get on!'

The watcher in the wood had noticed Kate going to the lock-up, and followed at a discreet distance. Luckily the building was in an isolated spot beyond the church, with plenty of shrubbery to act as concealment.

'Young slut!' the watcher mumbled. 'Just look at the hussy, flirting with every man above the age of ten! First Tom Robinson, now Philip Dawes, and heaven knows who else! If her father was any kind of a man he'd put a stop to her wandering before she gets herself in a peck of trouble. And that grandmother of hers is no better, letting the girl go with her every time some woman gives birth. Goody Clapton, now; there was none of that with her. She kept herself to herself, and her secrets died with her!' The watcher gave an unpleasant chuckle at the thought.

The boy seemed to be pleading with the cordwainer's girl. No doubt he was telling her of his innocence, but there was only one person who could verify that, and the watcher did not intend to confess to what had been done!

Perhaps the lad was begging the girl to let him out of his prison. Over the hills and far away he'd be, if that happened, which would not be a bad idea. If he became an outlaw, with a price on his head, that would serve the watcher's purpose well enough, unless another killing became necessary. Then the constable might begin to wonder if the boy was guilty after all.

No, it was best if the lad remained in custody. Perhaps he would hang, and thereby two birds would be killed with one stone. The watcher shivered with excitement, waiting to see what would happen.

The girl, it seemed, had a certain amount of sense, for now she was walking away. What did she have in mind, though? Did she intend to return after dark, to release young Dawes? Kate disappeared round the corner.

Now the constable was approaching. The girl must have noticed him and decided it was best not to be caught loitering. Fowler pulled the iron bar free of its moorings, uttering an oath as the boy appeared in the doorway. When the door closed behind him, the watcher sidled up to the building and crouched down beneath the aperture which let air and light inside. Angry voices were easily heard.

'How long are you going to keep me here? I've done nothing wrong! I've told you why I came to Hollyhill. Hasn't my mother explained?'

'Your mother can explain till the cows come home, boy! Why should I believe her? She's not going to see you hanged, is she?'

'So she did agree with what I said?'

'As it happens, she did, but that's not good enough for me.'

'Then what happens now?'

'I don't have to tell you anything, boy, but if you must know, I'm taking young Polly back with me today. We'll get all the Hardwick boys lined up for her to take a look at. According to her, if the little messenger is there, she'll know him at once.'

'She won't find him there, and that I can swear to.'

'Oh? And why would that be? Hidden him

somewhere, have you?'

'You won't find him because he doesn't exist.'

'Oh, he exists, all right. Let there be no doubt about that. Mebbe he's not a Hardwick boy after all, though; is that what you mean? Never you mind. I'm ready to search the whole of the shire, and mebbe beyond until I find the little varmint. I'm off now, to fetch Polly. You just sit there, my lad, and think about your sins.'

'You can't leave me here, with no food or water!'

'Can't I! We'll see about that, my lad!'

'But I'm starving! I've had nowt to eat since you brung me here!'

Liar! the watcher thought. *I saw the girl handing you that cake!*

14

A loud noise from outside startled Nesta so much that she dropped an iron pot on the floor, narrowly missing her foot. A weak voice wafted down the stairs.

'What happened? Is anything wrong?'

'All's well, Joan!' Nesta bawled back. 'There's something going on outside, though. I'll just go and see what it is.'

Chaos reigned out in the road. A small coach, the sort that had curtained windows, behind which ladies travelled safe from the public eye, was lying half in the ditch and the driver was in the act of taking the agitated horse out of the traces. A wheel had come loose and was lying on the ground some distance away. Two women, visibly shaken, stood watching.

Jack Davies came around the corner of the house alerted by the noise, with an excited Jonno hard on his heels. Nesta stepped forward to offer assistance.

'That wheel's done for,' she remarked.

'And there's no wheelwright in Hollyhill,' Jack observed, as the coachman came up to their little group, muttering calming words to the frightened animal. 'Jonno, you run and fetch the smith. Mebbe he can do something about this, at least do a botch job until these ladies can get where they're going.' Jonno sped off, highly pleased with his errand. Not only was he freed from a very dull piece of work, but he also had a fine tale to impart to anyone he might meet on the way. This was high drama!

'Where are you ladies bound for?' Jack asked now, addressing the elder of the two, whom he judged to be a married woman in her late twenties.

'We hoped to make for Adam Critchley's today, and then on to the manor,' she replied, in a honey-sweet voice. 'Should we try to walk on, think you?'

Nesta's ears pricked up at that. 'It's much too far for you to walk to Master Critchley's, let alone to the manor,' she murmured. 'You must come inside and rest awhile. There is nothing you can do here. It will be some time before my grandson gets back with the smith, even if the man is at home. I thought I heard someone say that he might be going to Oxford today.'

Her son gave her an odd look. 'First I've heard of it,' he muttered. What was Nesta up to now? But whatever it was, she had one thing straight, and that was that Jonno would be gone for a while. The ladies would be better off inside the house, with his mother plying them with refreshments, than they would be wandering about here.

As Nesta had guessed, this was Jane Pettapiece, who was meant to be marrying Adam Critchley. With any luck she'd be able to find out a bit more about this mysterious family.

'As a matter of fact I happened to be visiting Master Critchley yesterday,' Nesta murmured, when her guests were seated at the table with food and drink in front of them. 'I'm the midwife who delivered his new granddaughter, you know.'

'Oh, yes?'

'He has gout, I'm afraid. He sent for me to see if I could provide him with a remedy.'

The woman raised her eyebrows. 'I don't believe in old wives' remedies. Prevention is better than cure, they say. A proper diet is what he needs, and I'll make sure he takes better care of himself once we're married.'

'Very right and proper,' Nesta agreed, wondering as she spoke what the woman's last two husbands had died of. She turned to the young girl, who so far had not spoken a word. 'And is this pretty young maiden your daughter?'

'Hardly! Blanche is full fourteen! This is

my niece. I've brought her with me so that her betrothal can take place.'

'Oh, she's to marry a brother or son of Master Critchley, then?'

Kate gave a ghost of a smile. Trust Nesta to squeeze out information in a round-about way!

With an exasperated cluck of her teeth, Mistress Pettapiece set her straight. 'Of course not! Master Critchley has no sons, and his brother is three times her age!'

'It wouldn't be the first time that such a marriage has been arranged, mistress. I've heard of many such unions. If her intended husband isn't one of the Critchleys, then who is it?'

'Young Will, son of Sir William Mowbray at the manor. It's an excellent match.'

'Not one that I care about!' the girl stammered. 'I've never met the boy. He might be cross-eyed with warts for all I know!'

Neither Nesta nor Jane Pettapiece noticed that Kate had turned white. She fled from the room, clutching her stomach. A moment later Blanche Bellefleur followed. Her aunt made no move to stop her.

'Foolish child! She should be thankful we've arranged such a great match for her. The boy is at Court even now, and if he plays his cards right he may do great things there.

He might even find himself in the king's favour. I've told Blanche that she may even rise to become a lady in waiting to the Queen, but will she listen? No, she acts as though we're sending her to become a scullery-maid.'

'Which queen?'

'Why, Anne, of course. Whom did you think I meant? Not old Catherine; she's out of favour. The Princess Dowager is what we're supposed to call her these days.'

'Ah, well, the girl is young yet. Happen she'll change her mind when she meets the young man and falls in love. He may not be as ill-favoured as she makes out.'

'Is that your granddaughter, then, the girl who was here until a moment ago?' Mistress Pettapiece, well-bred as she seemed to be, obviously thought she should keep the conversation flowing. Or perhaps it was just that she wanted to change the subject when it came to the Critchley family, Nesta thought. Surely she must have heard of the strange things that had happened of late.

'Yes, that's Kate, baptized Catherine, of course, after the old Queen, as so many girls were. Mebbe all the new girl babies will be called Anne now. You don't have children of your own, I gather?'

'I haven't been blessed with any as yet.'

'Ah, well, you're still young, and about to remarry. You'll produce a quiverful in time.'

'I hope so.' The woman sounded doubtful. 'Master Critchley has no sons, as perhaps you know. In fact, I expect that's the main reason he wishes to marry again. As for me, I'm content as I am, but you know what they say. Third time lucky!'

It was impossible to know whether she yearned for the babes which had so far been denied her, or perhaps her previous marriages had been less than satisfactory and she hoped for better this time around.

'You haven't ever thought of marrying again, Mistress Davies?' she asked.

'Chance would be a fine thing!' Nesta replied, laughing. 'Now, where on earth has that Jonno got to? He should have been back ere now. Come to that, where are those two girls? They've made friends, mebbe, and Kate is showing your Blanche about the place. There are few young things of her age nearby and I think she longs for companionship.'

In fact, Kate was lying face down on the drying-green, her shoulders heaving. The other girl approached, timidly.

'Are you all right?' There was no reply and she tried again, raising her voice.

'I said, is there anything I can do?'

Kate rolled over, squinting up at the other

girl. 'I heard what you said, and no, I'm not all right!'

Blanche came to sit beside her, gingerly feeling the grass first to test for damp.

'I don't know what the matter is, but whatever you're feeling, it can't be as bad as what's going to happen to me! They're forcing me to marry a man — a boy, really — whom I don't even know. My aunt tells me the same thing happened to her, and she grew used to it in time, even though in her case the man was much older. I don't want to get used to the idea, I don't!' Her voice was shrill and her fists were clenching and unclenching, almost as if she was wringing the neck of a chicken, Kate thought.

'You love someone else, then?' Kate's expression was sad as she spoke these words.

'What? No, there's nobody else.'

'You're lucky, then. It would be much worse if you loved someone who was taken away from you.'

'Is that what's happened to you?'

'Oh, yes. I could have sworn he loved me true, but now he's to wed someone else. I don't know how I can bear it, Blanche. That is your name, is it not?'

Blanche nodded. 'Can't you talk to him, beg him to wed you instead of this other one?'

'All the talking in the world would not alter this. He was betrothed once, when he was a baby, but the girl died. Now it seems his father has made new plans for him, and he durst not go against them.'

'What is his name? Mebbe 'twill help if you talk about him.'

'His name is Will,' Kate muttered, her tone bitter. 'Will Mowbray.'

15

'Oh.' The other girl was silent for a moment, digesting this. 'You mean he's the same Will they're forcing me to wed! Well, then, as far as I'm concerned you can have him, and gladly.'

'If only it were that simple,' Kate said, her eyes filled with tears.

'Does he love you, then?'

'I thought he did, but it was only dalliance on his part. I'm only poor Kate Davies, the cordwainer's girl. What do I have to recommend me? I have no wealth and no high-born relatives. Of course he could not wed me!'

'If he truly loved you he would dare all,' a voice announced. Startled, the two girls looked up, to find Frances Cropwell looming over them.

'What do you know about it?' Kate spoke crossly. 'You should not be listening to what does not concern you!'

'I could not help it,' the older girl remarked. 'You were speaking loud enough for the whole hamlet to hear. I was just passing by, and stopped to see what the commotion was. There is a fine conveyance standing in the forecourt, and a man holding a horse which he has taken from the traces. Fine visitors for such as you, Kate Davies! Someone wanting boots made for them, perchance?'

'The carriage belongs to my cousin,' Blanche said, looking down her nose at the intruder.

'Ah, I see! And where are you bound, mistress?'

'To the house of Master Critchley, as it happens. My cousin is to marry him this winter.'

Frances threw back her head and laughed. 'Oh, that is very good! Very good indeed. And is she young and fair, this cousin of yours?'

'I don't see what business that is of yours!' Blanche spoke stiffly.

'Ah, but 'tis everyone's business when such a fine, upstanding man weds for the second time, you know. So little of interest happens in a place like this that all must share his joy, don't you see? And think how joyful he will be if the lady provides him with a covey of fine sons! His first wife failed him badly, you see. The poor man has nothing but daughters now.' She laughed again, a tinkling little sound which had something malicious in it.

'And you, mistress. You're going there to be a companion to the lady; is that it? She will need someone like you. His daughters are little likely to welcome her into their hearts. That I do know!'

'I do not see how you can know anything of the sort,' Kate said, as she scrambled to her feet to face Frances. She held out her hand to Blanche, who came to stand beside her. 'This is Blanche Bellefleur, who is to be betrothed to Will Mowbray.'

'So I heard, but it seems the lady has little liking for the idea.'

'No need to speak of me as if I wasn't here,' Blanche said with spirit. 'And why should I like the notion of being married off to someone I've never even met? Why, he might be cross-eyed with a wart on his nose, for all I know!'

'I believe the lad is more comely than that,' Frances said softly. 'Just ask Kate here, if you do not believe me! The fortunate wench who weds the only son of Sir William Mowbray will have a good life, no matter what the lad looks like. The man has more money than a king's ransom, I've heard, and young Will is set to inherit all when the old man goes. Give the fellow a bevy of grandsons and he'll provide you with anything you ask. A different gown for every day of the week, and food and drink that such as we can only dream of. No need for tears, Mistress

Blanche! Heaven has smiled on you, no doubt about it.'

'Heaven did not smile upon my sister,' Blanche responded, her eyes full of fear. 'She was wed, two years ago, and happy enough at the beginning. But she came to grief, nonetheless.'

'Was her husband unkind, then?' Kate asked.

'Oh, Richard was pleasant enough, I believe, but she died in childbirth, and the babe with her. Wed in December, she was, and gone to her grave by September. Richard offered for me then, but I refused. We were all in such grief then that my father bowed to my wishes, but this time there is no avoiding the marriage. It saddens me greatly to think that I may have but a year to live. To die at the age of fifteen is a terrible thing.'

'Plenty of people die from other causes,' Frances said. 'And come to that, who is to say you would die in childbirth? My grandmother had fifteen children, and eight of them survived.'

Looking at Frances's sturdy frame, Kate thought that the grandmother had most likely been a strong peasant woman, built for childbirth, and very different from the fragile Blanche, with her delicate bones. She sought for words to comfort the girl, who seemed to be on the verge of tears.

'My gramma is a midwife, and I am learning the trade with her,' she said proudly. 'I am sure she will attend you when you are confined, and we shan't let anything bad happen to you.'

'Fine for you to say!' Frances snorted, but she quailed under Kate's angry look, and muttered something about being expected at home.

'What an odd girl!' Blanche burst out, when they were alone once more. 'Is she a friend of yours?'

'Oh, no. I hardly know her. She lives on the edge of the wood, I believe, with an ancient uncle. Pay no heed to what she says. I never do!'

A little cloud of dust on the road drew their attention to the fact that a vehicle was approaching. As the cart drew near Kate recognized the blacksmith in the driver's seat, with a grinning Jonno lolling in the back with his legs protruding over the edge.

'You hold the horse steady, lad, while I go and speak to the women,' the smith ordered, as the boy sprang to the ground.

'What's going on?' Kate demanded. 'Is he going to fix the carriage?'

'Can't. Spokes are busted. 'Tis a job for the wheelwright, and he's not at home.'

'Then perhaps we cannot go on,' Blanche told him, looking hopeful.

'Oh, yes, the smith will take you. He's not busy today, so he won't mind the journey, he says, 'specially if the lady greases his palm with silver.'

Blanche wrinkled her nose. 'Aunt Jane won't want to travel in that! It's nothing but a farm cart!'

'It's that or Shanks's pony!' Jonno retorted. 'Anyway, here she comes now.'

Sure enough, Jane Pettapiece was tottering out to the cart in her fashionable shoes, with Nesta close behind. The blacksmith held a travelling-bag in each hand and the visitors were helped into the wagon in short order.

'Well! That was interesting!' Nesta said, as the cart disappeared in a cloud of dust. 'It lent a bit of excitement to the day, even if we didn't get our work done. I'm all behind like the old cow's tail now!'

Kate said nothing. Nesta looked at her closely. 'And where did you get to, gal, rushing off like that?'

'I came over light-headed and wanted some air.'

'Light-headed, is it! Nothing wrong with you, is there?'

Kate flushed. 'Of course not, Gramma!' She knew what the old lady was thinking, although her grandmother could not have guessed anything about her dalliance with Will.

'That's all right, then! But there was something as made you run out of there like a hare that sees a dog coming!'

Suddenly Kate could bear it no longer, and it all came rushing out.

'Life is so unfair, Gramma!'

'Are you only now finding that out, gal? What's brought this on, then? Let me guess. It's young Blanche, isn't it!'

Kate nodded.

'I see it all now. Here she is, a child younger than you, all set to be married, petted and made much of. Are you jealous, then?'

Kate hung her head. Nesta peered at her more closely. 'But why? Ever since I got here you've been insisting that you never mean to wed. That's why I'm training you in the midwife's skill along of me, so you'll have something to fall back on in the future. Now this girl comes here on the way to her betrothal, and you're pouring like a babe!'

'Blanche doesn't want to be married, Gramma. Her sister died in childbirth when she wasn't married a year, and Blanche is afraid it will happen to her, too.'

Nesta sighed. 'That's a chance we all must

119

take, gal. Every midwife loses a patient now and then, even if she has all the skills in the world, and that is a great sorrow. But we must not question the will of God, Kate. He alone knows what is best for us all.'

Kate refused to look Nesta in the eye. God's will, indeed! Was it his will that she should be left yearning for the man she loved, while Blanche, who had no desire to be married at all, should be yoked to Will Mowbray? Or did God concern himself with matters of the heart at all? She had prayed and begged that Will would defy his father and turn to her, and this was his response!

16

Joan was all agog to hear about the visitors. 'I wish I could have met them,' she said wistfully. Of course, it would have been asking for trouble to bring strangers within touching distance of someone suffering from consumption. People with the deadly disease were to be avoided at all costs. It hardly ranked with leprosy, or the plague, but even so nobody who contracted it ever recovered, and it meant a lingering death.

'It was Mistress Jane Pettapiece,' Nesta told her.

'Pettapiece. That sounds familiar, somehow.'

'Yes, I've mentioned the name, I believe. She's the widow who means to wed Adam Critchley. Do you know him?'

'Well, not to say know him, exactly, although he has given Jack one or two orders and he does pay up promptly. I think I saw him once at the livestock market; a rather overweight man, with a high colour?'

'That sounds like him, all right. Florid isn't the word for it! Eats and drinks far too much, I'm sure. No wonder he suffers from gout.

The new wife will have to take him in hand, if she doesn't wish to be widowed for a third time!'

'What did she have to say for herself, then?'

'Not a lot. Thinks herself a bit above us, I daresay. She was forced to be pleasant, of course, seeing as she was here in the house, being given refreshments.'

'I thought I heard another voice. A young girl. Her daughter, perhaps?'

'No, no; she's childless. I think she hopes to get with child once she's married to old Critchley, though. He's already got daughters, so anything's possible. With any luck she'll send for me when she becomes *enceinte*.'

'But the girl?'

'Oh, that was Blanche. A niece, I gather; one with a nice little dowry. Apparently she's to be betrothed to young Mowbray; not that she's happy about it, mind you. Just fourteen and young in her ways. Probably led a sheltered life and fears to come out into the wide world. I'll tell you one thing for nothing, Joan, the child is terrified of childbirth. According to Kate, she had a sister who died that way. Less than a year married she was, poor girl.'

'It doesn't run in families, does it? Dying in childbed, I mean.'

'Not necessarily, although this Blanche is pale-skinned with sandy hair, so one never knows. Some redheads tend to bleed, you see. For all it's an old wives' tale I've known it to happen more than once.'

'Queen Catherine's a redhead, they say, and she's had a dozen babes and lived to tell the tale, even though they did not.'

'Ay, there is that.' Nesta fell to thinking about their two visitors. Perhaps Blanche, too, would need her services before long. She was beginning to feel restless because since coming to Hollyhill there had been little call on her services. Not like Oxford, where she had been known to attend two or three confinements in the same day! A thought struck her.

'Isn't young Mowbray at Court, Joan?'

'So I've heard.'

'Then I suppose he'll take his wife there after they're married, and they won't be calling on me when she gives birth.'

'Unless she retires to the manor. I wonder whether the weddings will taken place here, or wherever it is those two are from?'

'Marriages usually take place in the bride's parish,' Nesta reminded her.

'Yes, but when they're marrying important men?'

Nesta shrugged. She hoped that the

weddings would take place here. A bit of jollification would do them all good. At the very least the women and children would line up outside the church to see the newly married couple coming out. The apparel of the bride and her attendants would be something to talk about during the long winter months to come, and the old women would keep a close eye on the bride, to see whether she seemed happy or sad.

Then, too, Sir William would probably provide a feast for all his tenants and neighbours, to celebrate the marriage of his son and heir. This would probably take place in the tithe barn, if it was cleared out in time. About Adam Critchley she wasn't so sure. He had a reputation for being tight-fisted, and any feasting might be confined to his close family and other kinfolk.

Either way, poor Joan would not be present among the observers. Still, the family would come home to regale her with tales of all that had happened, and Nesta herself would attempt to secrete a delicacy or two in her apron pocket to bring home to tempt the invalid's appetite.

'Did she say anything else, Mother?'

'Who?'

'That Mistress Pettapiece.'

Nesta had to think. 'She did say that the

Critchley girls seemed cool towards her, the one time she happened to meet them. I think she feels a bit awkward, coming into the house now, but as I told her, it's not as if they are children now, to take a dislike to a stepmother. They'll soon shake down together.'

'I wonder how Jonno and Kate will get on when my Jack takes another wife,' Joan remarked.

'Here! that's enough of that, gal!'

'It's true, though, isn't it? We both know I'm not long for this world, no getting away from it.' She broke off in a spate of coughing. Nesta helped her to sit upright, banging the pillows into shape with unnecessary force.

'We've all got to go sometime, sweeting, but I don't think your time has come yet.'

'It's in God's hands.' Joan sighed. 'Whether I'm taken early or late, Jack will be a widower eventually. We've been happy together, mebbe better than most, and I hope he'll miss me for a little while, at least. After that, it's only to be expected that he'll marry again. Men have needs, after all.'

'No need to think that way now, gal. If anything happens to you, I'll be here to look after Jack and the children, don't you fret.'

'That's not what I meant.'

'I know, gal, I know.' They clung together for a moment, while Nesta tried in vain to blink the tears away from her eyes. It was as well for them both that just then a loud crash came from down below.

'What the devil?' Nesta hopped up and went to the door. 'Who's down there? What's going on?'

'Only me, Gramma!' Jonno called. 'Dad sent me in to fetch him a drink and the barrel fell off the shelf. That's all it was.'

'That better be all!' Nesta said grimly. 'If that barrel has burst it'll be a waste of good cider, not to mention the mess all over my clean floor! It'll be sticky for a week, no matter how hard I scrub!' She hobbled downstairs, but on arrival in the kitchen she was pleased to see that the barrel was intact, lying on its side against the table.

'I told you all was well,' Jonno insisted. 'When the barrel rolled against the table some pans fell off, and that's what made the noise, you see?'

'I'll give you noise, my lad!' she told him, raising a hand to box his ears, but he side-stepped neatly and darted out of the door, leaving her to right the offending barrel. She couldn't lift it by herself, so there it would have to stay until Jack came in.

Standing alone in the kitchen she was suddenly overcome with a wave of great grief for poor Joan, who seemed to have given up on life. It was one thing to accept the idea of one's own death, but quite another to give up all hope of survival. That, as everyone knew, was a sin. Nesta wasn't sure why that should be so, but she had heard many a sermon preached on the subject. She supposed it must have something to do with failing to believe in God's omnipotence.

Joan needed to be taken out of herself. She might not be able to leave her bed — or at least, not very often — but something could be done to keep her spirits up. And who in this household could do that, if not Nesta Davies? Jack tended to treat his ailing wife like a fragile piece of pottery, likely to break into shards if he wasn't careful. As for the children, they didn't know how to treat their mother now, and who could blame them?

Joan had shown an interest in the forthcoming marriages, so why not learn more details with which to regale her? Nesta would go to the Robinson house, on the pretext of enquiring after Sally's health, and that of the new baby. It would be easy to bring up the subject, since Mistress Pettapiece had actually called at the Davies home, and from there it was a short step to finding out how the Critchley girls felt about their father's forthcoming nuptials.

Then, too, there was the mystery of who

had tried to drown Sally! The heated gossip concerning that event had all but died down, but possibly the Robinsons had found out something which they were keeping to themselves.

Yes, Nesta would set forth in the morning, and this time young Kate should be left at home. This investigation would call for a certain amount of cunning, and she didn't want the girl blurting out something which might interfere with Nesta's plans.

17

Sally Robinson received Nesta with a show of surprise, which called for an explanation. Apparently old Goody Clapton had not been in the habit of making follow-up calls to check on the progress of mother and child. Once the babe had been brought safely into the world she was inclined to take her money and depart, never to be seen again until her services were needed once more.

Yes, the new babe was thriving, and Sally was making a good recovery, although something else was bothering her. It concerned her husband, she whispered. He was pestering her to resume her marital duties and she needed more time, especially since her recent ducking had brought on an attack of the rheumatics.

'Can't you give me something to put in his food?' she asked, looking so serious that Nesta was hard put not to laugh.

'A sort of love potion in reverse?'

'I reckon so. You must have something, Mistress Davies! Goody Clapton had herbs for all purposes.'

'Well, I don't. Just the ordinary things,

meant to heal stomach upsets and the like.'

'You gave my dad summat for his gout, and that worked a treat.'

'That's true. How is he, anyway? I hear he means to marry again.'

Sally pulled a face. 'So he says, the old fool! Why he can't settle back comfortably into old age, I can't think! It isn't as if he's on his own, with nobody to care for him! My sister is there, and I'm near by, as you know. And as for that woman he's betrothed to, she's been wed and widowed twice already. What sort of wife will she make him? I ask you!'

'Mistress Pettapiece? She seems capable enough to me. Surely she'll be able to take some of the responsibility off your shoulders?'

Sally's eyes opened wide. 'You know Jane Pettapiece, do you? How can that be? I thought you'd lived in Oxford until recently.'

'She stopped at my son's house when her conveyance broke down,' Nesta explained. 'It fell to me to entertain her, since my daughter-in-law is unwell and has taken to her bed. Mistress Pettapiece seems a pleasant body. Childless, of course, but she can't help that. Mebbe she'll fare better this time around.'

A curious expression flitted across Sally's face, so quickly gone that Nesta wondered if she'd imagined it. 'I'm sure she's looking forward to her wedding day,' she went on. 'Is it to take place in our church here?'

'No, no. Dad will have to go to Cottisford for it. Jane means to be wed in her own parish, as is right and proper.'

'That's too bad. I do like to see a new bride coming out of church, decked out in all her finery, don't you?'

Sally was saved from having to answer by the sudden appearance of her husband.

'What's she doing here?' he growled, by way of greeting. 'Come to collect your money, I suppose!'

'Well, yes, now you come to mention it,' Nesta remarked. 'I would like to have my pay, if you don't mind. Actually I came to see if Mistress Robinson and the new babe are quite well. All part of the service.'

'Goody Clapton never did that.'

'I don't suppose she did. She seems to have been a little lax in her care for her patients. Now myself, I like to make sure that my mothers are quite well before they breed again.' She turned to Sally, giving her a brisk nod.

'Now remember what I told you. You must not consider becoming *enceinte* again until this new babe is weaned.'

'Here, none of that! 'Tis no business of yours, what goes on betwixt man and wife.

131

You keep a civil tongue in your head or we'll look elsewhere for a midwife in future!'

Nesta's mind whirled for a few seconds, as she desperately tried to think how she might respond, and then she hit on a likely answer.

'You want a son, don't you?'

He stared at her, as if she was mad. ''Course I do. Doesn't every man? And me more than most! What's that got to do with the price of eggs?'

'If another babe comes too soon, it will be another girl, that's what.' She was spouting nonsense, and she knew it. She crossed her fingers inside her apron pocket.

'Thass an old wives' tale,' he spluttered.

'Is it? What about your two childer, then? Born so close together as to be almost twins, and look at them! Both girls!'

There was nothing he could say to that, so when Nesta held out her hand he fumbled in his money pouch and pulled out the necessary coins, slapping them into her outstretched palm with ill grace. She took her leave, well pleased with herself.

It was only when she was well down the road on her way home that she remembered why she had come. Other than learning that the Critchley wedding was to be held at Cottisford, which meant no feast for either the eyes or the stomach, she had gleaned very little information. Ah, well, at least she had been able to winkle her money out of that uncouth Tom Robinson, which was something. She resolved that in future she would demand her money from any new father while he was still caught up in the euphoria of the birth.

Joan greeted Nesta expectantly. 'Did you find out anything? Are the weddings to be held in Hollyhill?'

'Mistress Pettapiece will marry in her own church, as we expected. I heard nothing about the girl, Blanche. I did manage to put one over on that oaf Tom Robinson, though!'

Joan listened to the story with sparkling eyes. 'You cunning thing! That's not true, though, is it, what you said?'

'Of course not. I made that up. Mind you, there's something to be said for having the childer spaced out a bit. If a woman doesn't have the strength to bear one after another it doesn't help her. Babes can be born dead then, and oftentimes the mother, too. It won't do that Robinson any harm to do without for a bit, unless he wants to lose his wife, poor girl. She came close to drowning, after all. I can't think that that did her any good.'

It wasn't until Sunday that they learned more about Blanche Bellefleur and her intended nuptials. The priest called the first banns, which caused a ripple of anticipation to pass through the congregation. This of course meant plenty to look forward to, not least the feast which was sure to be provided by Sir William.

Nesta was taken aback to hear a loud gasp from Kate, who was seated beside her on the bench. Before she could say a word the girl had sprung up and run down the aisle to the door.

'What's up with her?' Jack whispered, looking annoyed at the disruption.

'Not feeling well,' Nesta hissed. 'Women's problems. I'll see if she's all right.' That would shut him up, she decided. Men shied away from any hint of things like that. She got up and quietly made her way out of the church.

Kate was nowhere to be seen. She could not have gone far, Nesta reasoned, so she must be somewhere near by. She began a tour of the churchyard, and eventually found her granddaughter sprawled on the ground, hidden behind a tombstone dedicated to the memory of Anne Russell, virtuous wife and mother.

'Get up off that damp grass! Do you want your gown all over green stains? I've better things to do than scrub your clothes for you, miss!'

Kate got up reluctantly.

'Now, do you want to tell me what all this is about, or shall I leave it to your father to worm it out of you?'

'It's nothing, Gramma!'

'Nothing, is it! You disgrace your family by rushing out in the middle of Mass, and you say it's nothing! I'll tell you what it is, my gal. You were quite all right until Father read out the banns of marriage, and then you got upset. And why should that be, eh?'

'I felt faint, that's all.'

'Stuff and nonsense! You're healthy as a pig in clover! This can't have anything to do with Blanche, I trow. You hardly know the child. It's that Will Mowbray, eh? How can you possibly know him, anyhow?'

Kate took a deep breath, suddenly glad to be able to tell all. 'We love each other, Gramma! 'Tis only his father who stands between us. And then Will was sent away to Court, and now they're marrying him off to that mewling Blanche. Oh, I'm so unhappy I could die!'

Nesta raised her eyes to heaven. 'Has he made you any promises, sweeting?' Her voice was gentle. She must tread softly if she was to have any hope of getting to the bottom of this.

'He said we'd wed some day, Gramma. That counts as a betrothal, doesn't it?'

'Were there witnesses, Kate? Was anything written down? Well, then, it meant nothing, I'm sorry to say.' Alarmed by Kate's wail, she took the girl into her arms. Pray Heaven their relationship had gone no further than that. She had no wish to serve as midwife to her own great-grandchildren, or at least, not yet!

18

'There's a man on a horse!' Jonno panted.

Nesta stared at her grandson who had poked his head around the door and was now watching her, bright-eyed.

'So what? Did you have to rush in here just to tell me that, scaring the wits out of me? You almost made me drop this pot!'

'But he's come all the way from the manor house, Gramma, and he says 'tis you he wants!'

'There must be some mistake. I can't think what he wants with me, not unless Sir William has gout like old Critchley. Far as I know, there's no woman there having need of my services.'

'You've got to come, Gramma!' the boy insisted.

Nesta heaved a sigh. 'Then you go and tell him I can't leave my cooking and he'll have to get in here, if it's truly me he wants. You can hold the horse's head and talk to the beast. You'll like that.'

'I'll get a clip round the ear from Dad if I don't get back to work right this minute!'

'And you'll get a clip round the ear from

me, my lad, if you don't do what I tell you. Now get off with you!'

The man who sidled into the room, nervously holding his cap in front of him, was obviously an outdoor servant, judging by his shabby garments.

'Well, what is it? Speak up, man! I haven't got all day!' Nesta was annoyed at the interruption and made no attempt to offer any refreshment, even though new-made bread was cooling on the window sill, filling the room with its tantalizing aroma.

'You be the midwife, ain't yer?'

'What if I am? Your wife in labour, is she?'

'What wife? I ain't married.'

Nesta raised her eyes to heaven. 'Then who needs a midwife?'

'Nobody as I knows of, missus.'

Drumming her fingers on the table, she spoke slowly and distinctly, as if to a simpleton. 'My grandson tells me you've come from Sir William. If nobody needs a midwife, then what does he want of me? Can we settle this now, and let me get on with my work? There's a sick woman upstairs, waiting to break her fast.'

'He wants you to come and see to a deader, missus. Old Goody Clapton, she used to lay them out, only she's gone, and there's nobody else to do it.'

'There's been another murder?' Nesta squeaked.

'Nobody said nothing about murder, missus.'

Lord give me patience! Nesta thought. 'Then who died, man? Can you at least tell me that?'

'Ol' Jem, the steward. Clapped a hand to his head like he was thinking, and then fell down, pollaxed, like. He never got up again.'

'He took an apoplexy, mebbe. Are they sure he's gone? I've seen people struck down like that, only the life is still in them.'

'Give up the ghost, right enough,' the man replied, with gloomy relish. 'Master said so, and he seen plenty of deaders in his day. So are you coming, or not?'

'I'll have to speak to my son first.'

'Ay, you do that, missus. Best not wander off without his permission, eh?'

Fuming, Nesta went in search of Jack. Not that she needed his permission, not by a long chalk. She simply needed time to think.

'You'd best go, Mumma,' he decided.

'Oh, yes?'

'My best customer, is Sir William. We don't want to fall afoul of him. Next thing we know, he'd be telling all his friends I'm not obliging, and then where would we be? Anyhow, he'll probably pay you for the laying-out, and that would be a bit more in your stocking, eh?'

'I daresay, but I'd lose the whole day, come time I go there and back. Surely there must be someone up there who could lay the old chap out? Maids, and that!'

'I dunno, but if Sir William's sent this chap and his horse to fetch you, stands to reason it's you he wants. You go, Mumma. See what you can find out about young Will's wedding. You know how Joan does love a bit of gossip.'

That decided the issue, and in due course Nesta set off, riding pillion behind the messenger; the groom, or whatever he was. The weather was crisp and clear, and she decided that she might as well enjoy the outing, although she knew she'd pay for it the following day, with sore bones and stiff muscles.

The manor house was an imposing building, half-timbered and possessing several leaded windows. A pretty penny that must have cost, she thought. The horse, which had plodded along wearily for the last few miles, now picked up speed, obviously knowing the way to its stable. The man slipped out of the saddle and reached up to help Nesta down, almost falling backwards with the effort.

'Get your hands off me, man! I can manage!' she insisted, not wanting his grimy hands on her clean white apron. If she was to meet the lord of the manor she wanted to appear clean and tidy.

'Suit yourself,' he grumbled. 'Only trying to help!' He marched off with the horse, leaving her standing alone.

'Where do I go?' she bawled after him.

'Kitchen door. Over there,' he shouted, pointing. Nesta picked up her skirts and hurried in.

She found herself in a huge room, where several maids were busy with various tasks: slicing, chopping and stirring. They stopped and stared as if they'd seen a ghost. Nesta stared back. A tall woman detached herself from the rest, looking her up and down.

'I'm Mistress Davies. I'm told that Sir William has sent for me.'

'Ah, the midwife, I suppose, come to see to poor Jem. You'd best get on with it, then. Bessie will take you to his room, and see you have everything you need. And don't you be all day about it, Bessie Hawkins, or I'll box your ears for you!'

Bessie, the frightened little scullery-maid, scurried down dark hallways at such speed that Nesta had to trot to keep up.

'Where is everybody?' she wondered, but the child only shook her head and kept on.

'In there,' she whispered at last, pointing to a heavy oaken door behind which, no doubt, the steward was sleeping his last sleep.

'Don't you run off now, gal. I want you to wait while I see if everything is in order here.'

'I ain't going in no room with no deader,' the child bleated, her eyes wide and frightened.

'Nobody's asking you to. Just stand here. I'll be back in two shakes of a baa-lamb's wagger.' A quick look around reassured Nesta that somebody had indeed made the right preparations, although why they couldn't have carried on with the job instead of sending for her was anybody's guess. 'Off you go, then, gal. I'll be all right now!'

Nesta performed the last offices with the respect due to the dead and with a skill born of long practice, although she could have wished for a second person to assist her. It was hard to turn the corpse without help. As she worked she noted that the man did indeed seem to have died of natural causes. There were no marks of violence on the body, and the face was in repose. At last she managed to wrap him in his shroud, and commenced to sew him into it with small, neat stitches. He was ready for his coffin now, if indeed he would be accorded such a privilege. The poor often made do with a rough wooden box, or went into the ground with no protection at all, but presumably some better provision would have been made for this man, who had served the nobility in his day.

Right, then! She would return to the kitchen. She hoped to be fed there, having left home without breaking her fast. Then, too, she was determined not to leave without her pay, and there was also the question of how she was to get back home. Not on foot, she very much hoped.

Luck was with her. The servants were about to sit down to their midday meal, having served their betters and brought back the dishes, all good pewter, Nesta saw.

'You can sit there.' the cook said, as she pointed to a space on the bench, an announcement which led to giggles on the part of the other servants. 'It was Jem's place, but he won't be needing it now.'

Nesta sat down thankfully, licking her lips in anticipation when a trencher was set down in front of her. Good quality bread, by the look of it, not that miserable barley stuff. A second maid ladled a generous helping of rabbit stew onto it. Nesta was hungry and the aroma was delicious. They seldom had meat in the Davies household, and this was a rare treat. She said as much and the cook replied that the gamekeepers trapped the rabbits to prevent them from demolishing the crops. And why waste good food, when there were plenty of folks here to eat them? Chewing happily, Nesta agreed.

19

The meal being over, the male servants went about their business, while the maids were directed by the cook to get on with their various tasks. She herself remained sitting at the table, obviously enjoying a well-earned rest before beginning to prepare the next meal.

'I suppose you'll want to be on your way now,' the cook observed, when she could think of no further orders to give.

'I shall, when I've been paid,' Nesta said firmly. 'And I hope that someone has given thought to how I'm to get home. It's much too far to walk!'

'The steward usually sees to all that.'

Nesta pulled a face. 'Dead men have no pockets! Is Sir William about, I wonder?'

'He's given orders not to be disturbed. Can't you come back another day?'

Nesta was furious. 'No, I cannot! He sent that foolish groom to fetch me, interrupting my day's work, and here I am. The least he can do is pay me my due!'

The cook knew when she was beaten. 'Nan! Run after Samuel and tell him to get back here. He's wanted!'

Nothing loath the girl scurried off, to return within minutes with a handsome young man who was some sort of house servant.

'Mistress Davies here come to lay out Jem. Now she wants her money, and who's to give it her? You'll have to beard the master in his den and see that she gets it!'

While she was waiting, Nesta decided to flatter the cook into giving her the information she wanted.

'I suppose you do a lot of special cooking for the gentry,' she began. 'Sir William entertains a lot, does he?'

'Now and then. Not so much since his wife died, o' course. Mostly his men friends.'

'That's a shame. I'm sure you'd like to see all the grand ladies coming here with their gowns and jewels.'

'Not much of that round Hollyhill, mistress.'

'No, but isn't young Master Will at Court these days? I'd've thought he'd be bringing his friends home once in a while. Some special young lady, perhaps?'

'Oh, no. He's betrothed, you see, and he's to wed soon enough, we hear.'

'How lovely! It's too bad that you won't be able to cook the wedding feast, though.'

'What do you mean by that?' The cook frowned. 'I can bake and cook with the best of them, and I've served Sir William well for many a year. Why shouldn't I make the feast for his only son's wedding?'

'I meant nothing by it, mistress, only that the wedding will take place in the bride's parish when the time comes. Isn't that the usual way of it?'

'Mebbe so, but it'll be in our church here. Where the girl comes from, they have only a chapel of ease, too small to take in all the guests. The wedding feast will be in this very house, except that the common folk will be served out in the barn, if there's room now the harvest is in. They'll be coming here from miles around. I expect we'll be seeing you here then.'

'That will be something to look forward to. Who is the bride? Have you met her?'

'A young girl, barely fourteen. Blanche Bellefleur, her name is. She was here for the betrothal, and a poor creature I thought her. Hanging her head and not saying a word. She'll have to do better than that if she's to hold young Will. He's got an eye for the girls, that one has. I have to watch him with my maids, that I do.'

'Afraid of marriage, is she?'

'Hmph! I only wish I'd had such a chance,

146

when I was her age. Girl like that doesn't know she's born! She's to be married to a handsome young chap, and live on the fat of the land. She'll even go to Court, if she plays her cards right! Not like my girls here in the kitchen, sent out to work from the age of eight, working from dawn till dark. Do you know, Mistress Davies, I started out by scaring the birds off the fields at planting time, lest they gobble up the seeds, and I was all of five years old.'

'Hm,' Nesta responded. It was a familiar story. 'Does young Master Will want to marry this Blanche, or whatever her name is?'

The cook shrugged. 'Not up to him, is it? He has to do what his father wants, and the girl is well dowered. He knows what's expected of him. Wed the girl, get heirs on her, and then he'll be free to take up with whoever he prefers. That's life, isn't it?'

Nesta repressed a shudder. Kate had had a fortunate escape. She might be hurting now, but in time she'd come to see it. For people like the Mowbrays, a girl of her class was there to be used and cast aside. She hoped that when the boy returned from Court he'd be taken up with his young bride for a time and have no need to be chasing after poor Kate.

The servant returned, carrying a small

purse, which he held out to Nesta. 'Here's your money, then.'

'Did he say anything? Send me any message?' Nesta demanded.

'Sir William? Nay. Just gave me this and went back to what he was doing.'

No word of thanks, then. Well, maybe it wasn't to be expected. She had done the job and now received pay. Sir William would think no more of it.

'Then how am I to get home, you tell me that!'

He shook his head. 'Didn't say nothing about that.'

'Then you'd better find me a bed for the night! 'Tis a good ten miles from here. Even if my legs would carry me I'd never get home afore dark, and tisn't safe for a lone woman to be on the roads then.'

He sniggered, and she felt fury welling up inside her. Did he think that it was only young and beautiful women who were attacked by wandering footpads?

'You get about your work, my lad, or you'll feel the back of my hand!' the cook cried, obviously in sympathy with Nesta. He swaggered off in a show of dumb insolence.

'Don't mind him. He's not been with us long, and he's not trained proper. One of these days he'll get what's coming to him,

148

and no mistake. Now listen; the carter is due here at any minute and I daresay he'll be travelling on in your direction. Mebbe you can get a lift with him.'

'I'd be glad indeed,' Nesta said. 'Now you were telling me about young Master Will?'

'Well, he's always been a favourite of mine, or mebbe 'tis the other way round! Used to come down here when he was a little boy, begging me for treats. Marchpane and that. Oh, he loved his marchpane! I remember once, when it was his birthday, I fashioned a little pig from marchpane and coloured it pink, and he loved that. He didn't want to spoil it so he just ate the tail, and kept the rest till it got too hard to bother with. Now what do you think of that?'

Not much, Nesta wanted to say. 'You'll be making a lot of special dishes for the wedding guests, then, I expect?'

'That I am, and don't ask me where I'm going to find the time! Master said something about hiring extra women to help with the work, but I've heard no more about it, and time is running out.'

'I think I could spare the time,' Nesta murmured. 'I'm a good hand in the kitchen. That's if I'd be paid for it. I've got to think of my old age, you know.'

'So have we all,' the cook sighed, 'although

where I'm concerned it'll be a case of keep working till I drop in my tracks. Happen to know of anyone else who'd be willing to come, do you?'

'My granddaughter, Kate,' Nesta said at once. 'Mind, if you need us for more than one day, they'd have to find us a place to stay. 'Tis too far to be going backwards and forwards from home.'

'Oh, we'll find you both a bed, never fear!'

Of course, Kate was neither a good cook nor an enthusiastic worker, but surely she'd make an effort in this case, with the cook to chivvy her along! She'd be thrilled with the notion of seeing inside the manor house, the very place where Will had grown up, and no doubt she'd like to see Blanche again.

Nesta was so wrapped up in thoughts of what was to come that she hardly noticed when the carter came in, clamouring for a glass of ale. 'The lad is watering the 'oss, and I'm dry as a bone, same as 'im,' he told the cook, winking at her cheekily.

'You can have it if you say you'll take Mistress Davies to Hollyhill with you. She come here to lay out poor old Jem, and now she's stuck without a ride back.'

'I can take you as far as the crossroads, then I'm bound for Cottisford. Can't say better than that!'

'That will do very nicely, thank you,' Nesta told him, thinking she could just about manage the two miles from there to home. And just wait until Kate heard about the plan she had up her sleeve!

20

The sun had gone down and the twilight hour was upon them by the time the carter drew his horse to a halt at the crossroads.

'Here we are, then, mistress! You'll be all right now, eh? Not far from home!'

She scrambled down, murmuring her thanks. She felt bruised and weary after the ride over the rutted track and the thought of the two-mile walk ahead of her was almost too much to bear. She hoped that young Kate would have a meal waiting, or at least a hot drink. Well, it was either get on with it, or sit here until morning, she told herself, so she squared her shoulders and marched on.

She must have gone about half a mile when she heard a horse approaching. By the sound of things it was moving too fast for safety. Who would be foolish enough to gallop along in the gathering dusk? Prudently she stepped aside, waiting with one foot in the ditch until the rider went by.

When the animal reached her it bucked nervously before charging on. Even in the gloom she could see that it was riderless, the reins flapping uselessly on its neck. Well, there was nothing she could do about it. It would be folly indeed to step into the path of a terrified animal and she didn't possess the strength to stop it, even if she could somehow managed to grasp the bridle.

No doubt she would come upon the rider further down the road, cursing mightily and giving her some tale about a bird which flew out of the hedgerow, causing the horse to shy and rear.

Having trudged not more than a furlong, Nesta heard a groan coming from the ditch. She hesitated. She had heard stories of footpads who pretended to be injured so that they might accost some good Samaritan who stopped to help them. A lone woman like herself had better be careful. Then she chided herself for her cowardice and began to look about her for the source of the sound. No footpad would chase his horse away in such a manner, and in any case what would be the point of loitering here on the off-chance that somebody would come by, all ready to be robbed? No, there had been an accident, of course, and as there was nobody else about it was up to her to do something about it.

The sound came again, louder now. She peered into the ditch and after some moments saw a man lying there, moaning. She slid down and leaned over him.

'Are you all right, master?' Silly question! Of course he wasn't all right! Why else would he be sprawled there, and in such a state?

'Set upon!' he muttered. 'They stole my horse!'

'No, no,' she soothed him. 'The beast passed me on the road. Somebody will catch him ere long and keep him safe until you can claim him.' She squinted in the half-light, thinking that she knew him. Of course! It was Sam Fowler, the constable!

'I'll go and fetch help. The blacksmith lives just around the corner. He'll know what to do. You stay there till we get back.'

Another silly thing to say! The man swore, but she ignored him and scrambled back into the lane. It was getting darker now, and she only hoped she could find the blacksmith's cottage without doing herself a mischief. It stood some way off the road and she had never been there on foot. A dog began to bark hysterically and she followed the sound, shuffling along in case something lay in her path.

'Hold on! Hold on! I'm coming!' The blacksmith stared at her in surprise. 'Why, it's Mistress Davies, ain't it? Jack's mum. What be you doing here after dark, all by your lonesome?'

'There's been an accident. Sam Fowler's lying in the ditch up yonder and I've come to get help. He may need carrying.'

'What's he doing that for, then? Broke something, has he?' The blacksmith scratched his head, looking doubtful.

'How should I know? His horse threw him, most likely. The beast passed me on the road going like the seven devils was after him.'

'I'll fetch my 'prentice, and we'll take torches. You can get off home now, mistress. You've done your bit.'

Nesta bridled. 'I'll do no such thing! First off, I can show you where the chap is. Then I can take a look at him, see if anything's broken, for I have a certain skill. It was too dark to see anything before.'

'Suit yourself, but don't blame me if it makes you late home, and the road black as pitch! There'll be no moon tonight.'

'Then you can lend me a torch, man! Now let's be on our way. The sooner we get Fowler indoors and out of the damp, the better!'

By the time they reached the constable, he was sitting up with his head in his hands. The young apprentice looked at him, all agog.

'I'm surprised your 'oss threw you,' he laughed. 'A gentle beast, that, as I knows from getting him shod.'

'You mind your tongue, my lad,' the constable said. 'And for your information I didn't come off. I got down to help someone in trouble and the next thing I knew I got a crack on the head and it all went dark.'

'Footpads!' the boy remarked, not one whit abashed. The blacksmith fetched him a cuff on the side of the head and he subsided.

'Yes, you've quite a bump here,' Nesta announced, running her fingers over the constable's scalp, as he shrank back from her touch.

'Here, steady on! That hurts!'

'Nothing that can't be cured,' she said cheerfully. 'Now, then, you two, haul him up and we'll get him to the forge. Give me that torch, boy! You can't carry that and the constable too. He won't want his hair set alight, to add to his troubles!'

Soon the injured man was lying on a pallet in front of the fire in the blacksmith's house. Having seen him into the tender care of the blacksmith's wife, Nesta went on her way. Surprisingly she was no longer tired, and she covered the last mile at speed.

'Mumma! Where on earth have you been? I was just about to come looking for you, thinking you were lying hurt somewhere in the lane!'

'It wasn't me as was lying hurt out there,' Nesta retorted. 'No, I'll tell you no more till I get settled, with a bit of something inside me. And my feet is all wet with dew, so you can fetch me a hot stone wrapped in a bit of sacking, Kate.'

'Is that Mumma? Is she home safe?' Joan's anxious voice floated down from above.

'All's well!' Nesta bawled in return. 'I'll come up and see you later, and tell all!'

Later, the whole family crowded into the upper chamber, 'to save me telling it twice,' as Nesta remarked, when they were all settled.

'Do get on with it, gal!' Jack ordered. 'You said someone was lying in the lane. Not another deader, was it?'

'No, but it could have ended up that way, if I hadn't happened by. Lying out of doors all night would have done the chap no good. No good at all.'

'What chap, Gramma?'

'The constable, Jonno. Sam Fowler.'

'Whatever was he doing that for?'

'The way he tells it, he heard a cry for help, got down to see what he could do, and got a wallop over the head.'

'Footpads!' Jonno declared, unconsciously echoing the apprentice's words.

'Oh, no, Jonno, I don't believe so. Whoever it was let the horse go loose. It passed me on the road afore I found the constable. It's my belief that someone meant to do for the constable, only it didn't quite come off.'

'I doubt that, Mumma!' Jack looked

157

sceptical, as well he might. 'Who would want to harm an officer of the law? They'd be in big trouble for that. Could even be a hanging offence.'

'It certainly would be if they'd managed to commit murder, son.'

'Who said anything about murder? The boy is right, I expect. Some stranger set on the man, not knowing he was the constable, and in the scuffle the horse got away. Then the villain heard you coming, and ran off, before he could be caught.'

'Oh, Mumma!' Joan said, wide-eyed. 'Something could have happened to you, out there all alone.'

'Well, it didn't, so there's no point dwelling on it. And I said murder, because I'm sure that's what it was meant to be. They've never found the person who killed poor old Goody Clapton, or tried to drown Sally Robinson. The constable is still making enquiries, and mebbe he was getting too close to the truth, or at least the murderer thought he was, and didn't want to take any chances.'

'What about that man you went to lay out, Mumma? Do you suppose the same person killed him as well?'

'No, Joan. It's my believe the steward died of natural causes, probably an apoplexy. There were no signs of violence on the body,

158

and who should know that better than me? By the way, I've found out a bit more about the plans for young Will's wedding.'

'I'm going down to lock up!' Jack decided. 'Come on, young Jonno. Weddings is women's talk. Nothing of interest to the likes of us!'

21

'First of all,' Nesta began, 'the wedding is to be held in our church here.'

'Mistress Pettapiece, you mean?' Joan frowned. 'I thought she was getting wed closer to home.'

'No, no. I'm talking about the young couple. Blanche Bellefleur and Master Will.'

Kate looked down at her lap, twisting her skirts into a ridge on the right side.

'The good news is that everyone is invited to the wedding breakfast afterwards, so that's something to look forward to, isn't it? Mind you, I hear there's to be two feasts; one for the honoured guests and another for the peasants — tenants and servants and the like. I daresay there'll be some difference between the two, but with any luck there'll be meat on both tables, and mebbe scraps to take home afterwards.'

Joan smiled. 'I'll have to make sure that Jack fetches me something nice, then.'

'Of course he will, and I'll tell you something for nothing! I'll be able to bring you something dainty from the squire's table, that's if all the lords and ladies don't scoff the lot before I get a look-in.'

'How will you manage that?'

'Because they're taking on extra cooks, and I'll be one of them, gal!'

'Never! How on earth did you manage that?'

Nesta looked smug. 'I was in the kitchen, wasn't I, having a bite and sup before I started back, although I could have starved for all Sir William cared! Fetched me up there fast enough, didn't he, to see to old Jem, but never a moment's thought as to how I was supposed to come home. Anyway, I was sitting with the cook having a bit of a natter, and she told me all about it. Took me on like a shot, she did, when I told her as I could cook. Be a bit of money in my pocket, I said, and that was that!'

'Well, I never did. That'll make a bit of a change for you, eh? If I didn't have this wretched sickness I'd be up there with you, taking it all in.'

'We'll tell you everything, gal, never fear.'

'We?' Kate's head came up and she ceased to pluck at her dress.

'Well, yes, child. There's a job going for you, too, if you want it. I spoke for you, and the cook approves. The more the merrier, I think, or the poor soul will be going round in circles, come the day.'

'You know I can't cook, Gramma.'

Joan reached out to pat her daughter's arm. 'You're coming along nicely, dear. That gruel you made for me this morning was quite tasty.'

'Gruel! I'm sure Sir William wants that served at his son's wedding! They may want you to cook, Gramma, but I'd be down with the scullions, and that I won't have.'

With a sudden flash of insight Nesta understood what was on the girl's mind. Young Will was her true love, but he'd merely dallied with her and moved on. Now he was to wed a girl with a fat dowry while poor Kate was made to scour pots and pans, used in the preparation of his wedding feast.

'Listen to me, my girl! We want to get to the bottom of what's been going on with that Critchley lot, don't we? Where better to hear the gossip than up at the manor house? Jane Pettapiece will be there, undoubtedly, and if the servants don't have plenty to say about her, I'll eat my cap. You'll be sleeping in the servants' *dortoir*, where you can hear every word spoken.'

'I told you. I'm not going.'

'Wouldn't you like to have a bit of money you can use to buy yourself something nice, sweeting?' Joan spoke softly. 'Have a look at the caps and gowns the guests are wearing, and see what you fancy. Then we'll see about getting it copied for you.'

Kate shook her head mutely.

'We won't even ask you to give any of the money to us,' Joan pleaded. This was a handsome offer, for when children went out to work it was expected that they would hand over a goodly portion, if not all, of the money they earned to their parents, to help support the family.

'If I'd behaved like this when I was your age I'd have got a thick ear!' Nesta sniffed. 'Whatever happened to honour thy father and thy mother?'

'Mumma, please! Kate is my daughter and I'll deal with her as I think fit,' Joan protested, in a rare show of spirit.

Nesta was stung into a retort she regretted as soon as it was out of her mouth, but she wasn't prepared to back down now. 'Your way of dealing with her has produced an idle, good-for-nothing lump of a girl! Fifteen years old, and not yet capable of running a household as any respectable woman should!'

Tears welled up in Joan's eyes. 'And so you've had to give up your good life in Oxford to come here and look after things!'

'Now, now! I said nothing of the sort, gal. I was glad to come and help in your hour of need. That doesn't mean I have to stand by and watch Kate shirking her duty. I've done my best to take part of the load off her shoulders, and I'm giving her the chance to learn a useful trade, in case she doesn't marry. And what does she give me in exchange? I ask for one small thing, and she turns me down!'

'Don't talk about me as if I wasn't here,' Kate said, in a small voice.

'Then are you coming with me to work at the manor house?'

'I don't want to, Gramma.'

'That's that, then! Somebody will have to go there and tell them you're not coming, so they can hire somebody else. And just you give some thought as to how this will affect your father!'

'Dad! What's it got to do with him?'

'Don't be stupid, gal! Sir William is one of his best customers. When he hears that Jack Davies's daughter won't come and serve at his only son's wedding feast, he won't be best pleased. He might go elsewhere for his boots, and warn his friends to go elsewhere as well.'

Nesta said this tongue-in-cheek. It was hardly likely that Sir William would come to hear of the desertion of one small scullery maid, but Kate wasn't to know that. If by chance he did so, he was more likely to deliver a sermon on how his tenants should

164

bring up their children to be honest citizens. A good whipping and a week on nothing but bread and water would make Kate Davies change her tune, and Nesta was inclined to agree with the prescription. That should curb her tantrums.

But the stubborn girl still said nothing. Nesta flew into a temper. 'All right, then, have it your own way! But I won't be the one to tell them. I accepted the job for you in good faith and I won't be made to look foolish. No, you can get over there in the morning and ask to speak to the cook. A nice long walk will do you the world of good.'

'She can stay here and look after me, while the rest of you are at the wedding,' Joan murmured, when she could get a word in. 'Then you can go, Mumma, without worrying about me. I know you must find it dull here in Hollyhill, after all the excitement of Oxford. You'll enjoy the hustle and bustle at the manor house.'

Nesta gave up then, suddenly feeling very tired. She needed her bed, and said so. Once on her pallet she lay there for a long time, utterly exhausted but somehow unable to drop off to sleep. What a day it had been! One dead man, decently laid out and ready for his grave. Another man, attacked and left for dead, but fortunately found in time. Had his assailant meant to kill him, or had it simply been a robbery that went wrong?

Joan seemed to think that Hollyhill was a dull place. Well, no doubt it did seem dull to a sick woman, lying in her bed from one week to the next, but as far as Nesta was concerned something was very wrong here. Old Goody Clapton had been murdered. There was no doubt about that, and so far the crime had not been solved.

Someone had tried to drown Sally Robinson, an inoffensive young woman who had harmed nobody. Perhaps that was just a prank? If so, it was fortunate that passers-by had found her in time to save her. And why would anyone want to do such a thing? Someone with a grudge against her, or her husband?

Now there was the attack on the constable. It could have been highway robbery, with only a random target in mind. He had simply been in the wrong place at the wrong time. A few minutes later it could have been Nesta herself who was attacked. She shuddered at the thought. When there were evil-doers about a lone woman stood to lose more than the few coins she might have in her purse.

But what if, she reasoned — what if the three attacks were connected in some way? All thoughts of sleep had now vanished.

166

Presumably the constable was still busy investigating the earlier crimes. Had he come upon something which would lead him to a solution? Had Goody Clapton's killer learned of this, and decided to eliminate him?

The only problem with that notion was the place where the attack had happened. The killer would have had to know that Fowler would be on the road at that time of evening. He could not wait in the trees for days on end, on the off-chance that the man would happen by.

So, Nesta thought, let's look at Hawisa Clapton and Sally Robinson. What could their connection have been? The old midwife had delivered Sally of her first child, of course, but so what? There had to be more to it than that. Still trying to work things out, Nesta rolled over painfully on the lumpy mattress, but sleep still eluded her.

22

'Dad said to tell you the constable's come. He wants to see you.' Jonno's face was screwed up in an idiotic grin and he was shooting his eyebrows up and down frantically as if he was a puppet on a string.

Nesta wiped her wet hands on her apron. 'What's the matter with you, boy? Got toothache or something?'

'No, Gramma.'

'Then stop making that unket face, do. What does Fowler want with me; did he say?'

'He just asked where you were, but I think mebbe he's come to give you a reward, for helping him last night.'

'Fat chance! Well, I might as well hear what he has to say. Go back out and tell him to come in.'

But there was no need for that, for the man appeared in the doorway, not bothering to knock. Jonno scuttled off.

'Good day to you, Constable,' Nesta said. Fowler grunted.

Oaf! Nesta thought. I shouldn't think he's a married man. What woman would have him?

'I've come to arrest you, on a charge of

attempted murder, Mistress Davies. You come along quietly, and you won't get hurt.'

'What?' Nesta reached for the rolling pin, taking a step backwards as she did so. 'Are you mad? That thump on the head has got you mazed, man! I'm going nowhere with you, Sam Fowler, and that's a fact!'

Nesta was well aware that she was shouting. She hoped that Jack would hear and come running to her aid, but Joan was the only one who heard.

'Is everything all right down there?'

'It will be in a minute, Joan, never you fear,' Nesta called back. She turned to face the constable.

'So this is the thanks I get for saving your worthless skin, is it? I should have left you lying there to rot! I don't know what you think you're playing at, you fool, but if it wasn't for me you'd be sick as a donkey with rheumaticks by now, if not worse, instead of running round the countryside accusing honest women of who knows what.'

' 'Twas you come up behind me and give me a wallop that pollaxed me,' he insisted. 'No cause to do that, missus, when all I done was get down off my horse to see why you was crying out like that.'

'You heard someone crying, did you?'

'I did that. A weak little voice, it was. Help!

Help! That's all I remember till I come to and found you poking me about.'

Nesta sat down carefully, still holding her rolling pin. 'Now look here, my man. The shoe is on the other foot now. I was coming home when I heard moaning and groaning coming from the ditch. I was in two minds about taking a closer look, thinking it might be a trick to rob me, but I hope I'm a good Christian woman so down into the ditch I scrambled, and found you there. It wasn't me who walloped you, man!'

'So you say!'

'Do have some sense. That's if it hasn't all been knocked out of you. If I wanted you dead, would I have gone all the way to the blacksmith's in the dark, and then back again to show where you were lying?'

Fowler chewed on his thumbnail without speaking. She fancied she could almost see the wheels turning in his brain. Slow, she thought. Why would they appoint such a man to be constable? Her Jack would make two of him, any day.

'What did they hit you with?' she asked.

'How should I know? Summat heavy, that's all.'

'Then you'd best speak to the carter. He'll tell you I had nothing like that with me when he set me down at the crossroads.'

'Could have picked up an old branch, or

summat.' Dogged to the last, Fowler stared her down.

'Now you listen to me, Sam Fowler! I was up at the manor, laying out that steward who died of an apoplexy in the night. You go and ask Sir William if you don't believe me. I was nowhere near here all day long. I tell you, I was on my way home when I came across you. And supposing I did want to do for you, which I certainly did not, how was I to know you'd be on the road at the very time I was coming along? It had to be someone lying in wait, that's all.'

'But how would that person know I'd be passing by? It's not as if I come this way every day.'

'Mebbe you were just unlucky. If it was some outlaw with robbery in mind, anyone would have done. Why, it could have been me!' Nesta shuddered at the thought.

He scratched his head, wincing when his fingers encountered the wound. 'Mebbe I'll leave it for now,' he muttered.

'If I were you I'd get out there and see what you can find. Whatever he walloped you with may still be there. And shouldn't you be out looking for your poor horse, not standing around here, bothering me?'

'How can I find him? He'll be in the next parish by now.'

The man looked so much like a bewildered child that Nesta suddenly felt sorry for him. Probably he wasn't always this useless. Perhaps his stupidity was the result of his injury. She didn't envy him the prospect of reporting this attack to the sheriff. It would make him appear inefficient, to say the least.

'The animal has to stop, sooner or later,' she reasoned. 'Then they'll get him back to you.'

'Unless it's gypsies,' he said gloomily. 'I know them rogues. They'll dye his coat black so he can't be recognized, and sell him at the next fair. I'll never see him again.'

'Nonsense! If I know horses, he'll make for his own stable. I'd get off home if I were you, and you'll find him waiting for you, sure as eggs are eggs.'

'I dunno. And what am I s'posed to do in the meantime?'

'Go home and rest until you're fit to take up your duties again.'

'Not without I take you to the gaol first, mistress. You come along with me now, and no fancy tricks, mind.'

Nesta picked up the rolling pin again. 'I've told you, man. I'm not guilty, and I'm certainly not letting you lock me up in that damp cell. And I won't come quietly. You lay a finger on me and you're asking for trouble.

The condition you're in, you look like a good push would flatten you, anyhow.'

Fowler's eyes narrowed. 'Are you threatening me, woman?'

'I most certainly am! Now get along with you, and let me do my work. I'm not having my son coming in at noon to find no dinner on the table.'

She waved her rolling pin menacingly, and he took a step backwards. 'Don't think you've heard the last of this!' he growled.

When he had stumbled away Nesta sank down on the bench, surprised to find that she was trembling like an old gaffer with an ague. Surely the carter should be able to provide her with an alibi. He had left her at the crossroads shortly before she came upon the constable, lying in the ditch. Fowler must have been attacked before she had even scrambled down from the cart.

Kate came into the kitchen then, looking shamefaced. Nesta stared her up and down crossly. 'Are you not away yet? It's a goodly walk to the manor and the day will be far gone by the time you go there and back.'

'I'm not going, Gramma.'

'Is that so? I've told you, I'm not the one with explaining to do. It's only right that you make your excuses to the cook up there. She won't much care if you turn the job down now, 'specially if you say your mother needs you at home. It's if you leave her in the lurch she'll be upset, and who's she going to take it out on then? Me, that's what, for I'll be working in that kitchen alongside her.'

'I didn't mean that, Gramma. I don't need to tell her anything, cos I've decided to take the job.'

'Well, praise be! Come to your senses, have you? Or is it just that you can't face the walk?'

Kate shrugged. 'Mebbe working will take my mind off things, is what I thought.'

Nesta understood at once. 'Getting down to work is always a remedy for sorrow, gal. And if setting your eyes on young Will is what you're afeared of, he's hardly likely to appear in the kitchen while you're there. As far as I know he's not even home from Court yet.'

Kate's jaw dropped. 'How did you know, Gramma?'

'Because I was young once, and I know the signs, child.'

'But you don't know how much it hurts, Gramma.'

'First love is painful, but you'll forget about Will when the right man comes along.'

'I never will,' Kate cried. 'I'll love him until doomsday, that I know.'

23

Kate ran blindly out of the house, bumping into the doorframe as she went, giving herself a painful jab which was sure to produce a colourful bruise later. Having no set destination in mind she stumbled on until she reached the riverbank, where she sank to her knees, heedless of the dust on her gown.

She did not know how long she remained there, with the tears streaming down her cheeks, but what did it matter, now that Will was lost to her for ever? Her mind was so far removed from the scene that she did not hear the other girl coming up behind her.

'What's the matter with you, then?'

Kate swung round, clutching her heaving chest. 'Oh, you scared the wits out of me! What do you mean by creeping up on me in that way?'

Frances Cropwell glared at her. 'I don't creep, as you put it! Is it my fault you're in a dream? And what are you doing, out here all alone? Thinking of throwing yourself in, were you? Because of some boy, I suppose! Believe me, no man on earth is worth killing yourself over!'

'I'm not planning to kill myself!' Kate said indignantly. She realized that she was sitting in the very spot from which Sally Robinson had gone into the river, either of her own volition, or because she was pushed. ''Tis mortal sin, as you know very well.'

'But you are howling over some chap, I'll be bound!'

'What if I am? It's not a crime!'

'Ah, there's crimes and crimes, gal! In trouble, are you? If he tells you he loves you, and then leaves you in the lurch, that be a sin *and* a shame.'

'I'm not in trouble!'

'More by luck than judgement, by the sound of things. Who is it, then, this man?'

Kate had never liked Fanny Cropwell very much. Always poking her nose in where it wasn't wanted, and with never a good word to say about anybody. Yet they were much of an age, and it sounded as if the girl had had an unhappy experience of her own. The need to confide in someone was overwhelming, and suddenly the words, pent up for such a long time, came tumbling out.

'If you must know, it's Will Mowbray.'

Fanny's eyes glistened. 'Ah, now I see! He's dallied with you, promised you the moon and the stars, and now he's about to wed another. What did I tell you? No man is to be trusted!'

'It's not like that, Fanny!'

'No? What, then? Tell me!'

'It's his father. First he sent him to Court, and now he's forcing him into marriage with this Blanche Bellefleur!'

'And of course you hate her for it?'

Kate frowned. 'Hate her? I don't think so. She has no taste for this marriage to a man she doesn't even know. How could I blame her for my loss?'

'But you'll come to hate her in time, Kate, when she's wed to Will, and there's no undoing it. Short of death that is,' she muttered, under her breath. 'And it's not just Will she's stealing from you. Think of the life she'll have; the fine house, the clothes, the jewels. And look at you, a simple little country girl from an ordinary family, poor as a church mouse. Why should she have all that, while you have nothing?'

Her voice was shrill, and her figure rigid with anger. Kate scrambled to her feet.

'I have to go home. My grandmother will be looking for me. I can't leave her to do all the work by herself.'

'That's right! Run away!' Fanny called after her. Her voice was lost on the breeze as Kate flew down the path, trembling. There was something about Fanny Cropwell which upset her. How dare she insinuate that the

Davies family was poor and of no account? Jack Davies was a hard-working man, with an honourable trade. They had never gone hungry, and Kate and her mother had always been given new gowns on New Year's Day.

Fanny Cropwell, now; perhaps she did have cause for complaint. As far as Kate knew, she was an orphan, who lived with her aged uncle in a hovel on the edge of the wood. She had no idea what they lived on, for the old man was past working, yet Fanny was obviously not in service anywhere. She seemed free to roam the countryside, much as Kate had done before Nesta had arrived to keep her in order.

Nesta said little when Kate crept into the house, feeling guilty. She had a shrewd idea of what ailed the girl, and decided that it was a case of least said, soonest mended. Once the marriage had taken place, and the girl could see no possibility of any romantic liaison with young Will, she would have to face reality. First love was painful, but it seldom lasted.

When Nesta went out to the community pump, carrying a pail in each hand, she was agreeably surprised to find several other women already there. They greeted her pleasantly, for by now everyone knew who she was, and the reserve due to a stranger in their midst did not apply to her. Polite enquiries as to Joan's health were met with sighs and sad looks, for everyone knew that consumption usually meant a death sentence.

'All this talk of weddings has cheered her up a bit,' Nesta murmured. 'Takes her mind off her troubles, like.'

'Does she mean to go to the feast, then?'

'I'm afraid she's not well enough for that, but we can tell her all about it, and perhaps bring some sweetmeats home, to tempt her appetite.'

'There'll be only one feast, when we was expecting two,' another woman grumbled.

'Oh? How's that, then?'

'Haven't you heard? Master Critchley sneaked off to Cottisford and married the widow Pettapiece there. Any food that was going must have been eaten up there. Nothing left over for the likes of us!'

'Silly old fool,' her neighbour said. 'Getting married again at his time of life. All he wants is looking after, I 'spect.'

'More fool her!' the first woman said. 'Married three times to old men, and no chance of having a family with any one of them.'

'We don't know that Adam Critchley ain't capable,' cackled a third speaker. 'There may be the need for your services yet, Mistress

Davies. And won't that be one in the eye for his sons by law if there is!'

'How do you mean?' Nesta was puzzled. 'The Robinsons have two children, as I should know, having brought the second one into the world. Sally is far from being barren.'

'Oh, I'll grant you that, Mistress Davies, but so far all she's been able to give the old man is granddaughters, and her sister has no children at all.'

Nesta felt it was time to assert her superior knowledge. 'Stuff and nonsense! I do not know what all the fuss is about, this wanting to get sons! Both women are young and healthy and can expect to have many more babes in due course. And what if they are all girls? Master Critchley is an ordinary enough man, even if he does own a bit of land. He's hardly King Harry, who needs male heirs to come after him.'

The women looked about them uneasily. The tallest one licked her lips, hesitated, and then, at a nod from her companion, decided to speak.

'Master Critchley wants to leave his land to a son, or failing that, a grandson.'

'So much I've gathered. Go on.'

'When his wife died, leaving only daughters, he declared he would leave all to the first son born to one of his daughters.'

Nesta began to see. This, then, was why Tom Robinson was so disappointed with his baby daughters. Had they been sons, he would have been in the favoured position of inheriting the Critchley land, or at least holding it in trust. He would be a person of consequence in the community, someone to be reckoned with. If, on the other hand, the Dilleys beat him to it, he would be left with nothing. Peter Dilley would own the very house the Robinsons lived in.

'But what if neither of them has sons?'

'If old Adam dies before that happens, everything goes to his nephew.'

'His nephew! I didn't know he had one.'

'Philip Dawes, his sister's son.'

'What? You mean that lad they kept in the lock-up?'

'That's him.' There were nods all round.

'Of course, if the Pettapiece woman gives him sons, everything changes. A few noses will be out of joint then, I can tell you!'

'How do you know all this?' Nesta demanded. 'Mightn't it be all hearsay?'

The woman stared at her with a triumphant look in her eye. 'Oh, no, it's right enough. My daughter is first housemaid in the Critchley house, and she hears things. Not that she listens at doors, mind you, but when there's words spoken and shouting going on, a person can't help but hear. Now, Mistress Davies, you're not to say a word of this to a soul, do you understand? I don't want it getting back to the Critchleys and my poor girl losing her place.'

24

Nesta had promised not to bruit her new knowledge about, but she did tell Joan. That didn't count. Her daughter-in-law knew how to keep a still tongue in her head, and in any case, who was there to tell? She never had visitors other than the family; people were too afraid of catching the dreaded consumption so they never ventured near.

'You'll never guess what I found out when I went to the pump!'

Joan listened, bright-eyed. 'So that's what it's all about, then! It's a race betwixt Tom Robinson and Peter Dilley, eh? Whoever gets a son first inherits all, while the other gets nothing. You can't blame Tom for being disappointed with the daughters Sally has given him, and as for Dilley, why, his wife is barren as far as anyone can tell. Still, there's time yet, for both of them.'

'Ah, but that's the point, Joan! They could have ten sons for all Adam Critchley cares, now he's wed again. All he needs is for the Pettapiece woman to give him one boy of his own, and that will be that. His daughters' husbands can whistle for the land then.'

'I suppose so. That won't stop them trying, though. Even if he does get sons there's no guarantee they'll live to grow up.'

Nesta bit her lip. 'I pray nothing happens to Jane Pettapiece: Mistress Critchley, as we must call her now.'

'Dying in childbed, you mean? Are you thinking that if she did, and it was you who attended her confinement, you might be blamed? By what you say, it seems that so much hangs on whether she produces a son.'

'I was not thinking that far ahead,' Nesta admitted. 'But look at what has happened already. Goody Clapton murdered, Sally Robinson drowned, but for the grace of God. Now Sam Fowler's had a wallop on the head and left for dead. Things are not right in these parts. Who can tell what's to come next? And before you say it, don't tell me that the constable was attacked by footpads. That doesn't ring true.'

'I doubt they're all connected. Mebbe Sam was getting too close to finding out who did for the poor old gal, and they wanted to put him off the scent.'

'Could be, but what about Sally, then? After what I heard this morning I wonder if it was that Philip Dawes. Kill her off, and he'd be one step closer to inheriting all. I shouldn't be surprised if Sam Fowler thought

184

of that, and that's why he kept the lad in gaol for so long.'

'I thought you said it was supposed to be a secret, all that about who gets Critchley's land?'

'So I was given to understand, but what if Tom Robinson let it slip to Fowler? Swore him to secrecy but said, 'Look, somebody was trying to do away with my wife.' Could be young Dawes. Could be my brother-in-law. You take a look at where they was that day, and you'll see I'm right.'

'It don't sound like much of a secret to me. Before long, everybody and his dog will know what's going on. And why keep it a secret anyway? What's so wrong about the old man wanting a boy to inherit the land and keep it going? Land should be kept in the family, with menfolk to see to things, else you have to squander your money on hiring more labourers.'

'From what I hear, Adam Critchley's not one to squander money. He married over at Cottisford, as we supposed he might, and there's no feast for the likes of us. Not even a drink for the men to drink to the health of the bride and groom.'

Joan sighed. 'Ah, well, I wouldn't have been there if he had invited us all to his table. Never mind, we've got the young folks' wedding to look forward to, and that will make up for being done out of the other celebration.'

'Ay, although I may not see much of it, being busy in the kitchens.'

'That's a shame,' Joan murmured. Nesta, however, was thinking furiously. What did it matter if she missed seeing the bride emerging from the church, on the arm of her handsome young husband? She had seen many a bride come and go; frightened ones, happy ones, even some who looked to be requiring her services at any moment. What was one more? She would hear all about it later, without a doubt.

Meanwhile, she was much better placed to learn something more about the wave of violence which had afflicted Hollyhill. After her latest encounter with that arrogant constable, she was determined to get to the bottom of it all, and not just because she wanted to prove her own innocence. Her curiosity was aroused to fever pitch and why not? After her busy life in Oxford there was precious little of interest to absorb her interest in Hollyhill.

The Critchleys were bound to be at the feast, being local landowners, well known to Sir William. Perhaps she could persuade the cook to let her wait at table, where she could keep her eyes and ears open for anything untoward. Failing that, she could surely pick up a few scraps of gossip while working in the kitchens.

Joan seemed to have fallen asleep, so Nesta tiptoed out of the room. Never mind the wedding feast; there was work to be done in their own kitchen! She found Jack there, with Jonno hovering near the door.

'Felt thirsty,' her son said. 'Came in for a mug of cider. 'Tis warm out there for the time of year. I came looking for you earlier. Where did you get to, then?'

'Had to go to the well. The water butt is near empty. If we don't get rain soon I don't know what we'll do.'

'Ah! Meet anyone interesting on the way, did you?'

'Some local goodwives at the well.'

'What did they have to say for themselves? I s'pose they all wanted to know how you came to rescue Sam Fowler?'

Nesta tapped the side of her nose. 'Little pitchers,' she murmured.

Jonno pricked up his ears at once. 'What, Gramma? What did you hear?'

'Never you mind, my lad. There's some things it's best not to know, not if you want to stay safe.'

'Aw, Gramma! I'm not a baby! And if you

think I'll go blabbing, why, I'm the most trustworthy man in Oxfordshire!'

Nesta grinned. 'Fine words butter no parsnips, Jonno Davies! Now get along with you, do, unless you want to go without your dinner today. I haven't even given a thought to what we're going to eat, and that's a fact.'

But when they had gone she sat down at the table and put her head in her hands. She was suddenly afraid for Jane Pettapiece. Should the woman be warned to watch out for danger? But that would mean having to explain that Adam Critchley's will was common knowledge, and from what she knew of the man, he would not be best pleased. Who knew what he might do out of spite? If he cared to trace the rumour back to its source he might punish the young maid who had passed on the gossip to her aunt, and then the fat would be in the fire. Nesta did not want to be responsible for the child losing her job. They were hard enough to come by in country places.

The main problem was that there was no telling where the danger lay. Say it was one of the stepdaughters' husbands. They would have easy access to Jane at all times, especially Peter Dilley, who lived in the same house. An accident could be contrived — perhaps a fall downstairs — and there would be no way to prove who was responsible.

Or was it Philip Dawes? All he had to do was to lie in wait when the new Mistress Critchley went riding, and leap out of hiding, causing the horse to bolt and, with any luck, to throw its rider, with disastrous results.

A new thought occurred to Nesta. Philip Dawes! Could it have been he who accosted the constable? He must have a grudge against the man, having been kept in that dank gaol for so long. Fowler had probably given the lad a cuff or to, if not worse, to get him to talk. Now Dawes was getting his own back.

The other possibility was that Fowler was on the point of discovering some proof of Dawes's guilt in the Sally Robinson crime, and had to be silenced. Yes, young Dawes warranted a closer look. She must ask the cook what she knew about him. He certainly had a motive for wanting his cousins out of the way.

Of course, there was one flaw in this argument. What about Critchley's other daughter, married to Peter Dilley? As far as Nesta knew, no attempt had been made on her life, and why not? Using her fingers, Nesta counted off the possibilities.

As long as she appeared to be barren, she was in no danger. Naturally that could change in the future; Nesta had known other women, married for years, who produced their first child when they had given up all hope of motherhood. The killer, whoever he was, had no need to act in the meantime. Drawing attention to himself unnecessarily would be a mistake.

What about her husband? Had he tried to get rid of his sister-in-law, leaving the field clear for himself? He would not harm his own wife, of course, for if she died Dilley would have no claim at all to the Critchley estate. But now Adam's bride posed a new threat. Which one was guilty? Dilley or Dawes? As Nesta tried to work it out, a cold feeling settled in her stomach. It didn't have to be either one. Somebody else could have been paid to harm Sally, and that meant that a stranger might be responsible, a man who would be far away by now. How could they ever learn who it had been?

25

When Nesta arrived at the manor house with her granddaughter in tow she found that the whole atmosphere of the place had changed since she was last there. The courtyard was abustle with people coming and going on various errands. Several labourers were struggling to erect an awning, cursing as the wind tore it from their grasp. Other men stood idly by, leaning on trestles which were obviously meant to support tables underneath this shelter.

Nesta smiled grimly. Why didn't they hop to it and help to hold the awning down? That way, it could be erected in half the time. But no; it was easier to stand back and criticize.

'Come on, Kate! Don't stand there gawping! We'd best get inside and see where they want us to go. They'll dock our wages if we don't start on time.' She had no way of knowing if this was so, but she wasn't willing to take the chance. Besides, the girl had to be brought into the proper frame of mind for the work ahead. The cook would be harrassed enough as it was, without having to deal with okkard gals.

The cook greeted Nesta with some relief. 'There you be, then! I was hoping you'd turn up. And this is your son's girl, then?'

'Yes, this is Kate.'

Kate dipped her knee in an awkward curtsy. She wasn't sure if the cook merited such a display, but the woman's pleased expression told her she'd done the right thing.

'See them girls back there? Off you go, and they'll set you right.' The cook turned back to Nesta, sniffing. 'I've never seen such a lot of useless females in all my born days. Some of them can't even handle a knife proper. Young people today! What the world's coming to I just don't know.'

'So they're not all on the staff here, then?'

'Bless you, no. They're extras, taken on special, same as yourself. They've been hired from all around. Some are servants in other places, on loan for the wedding. What about your Kate, then? Already out in her petty place, is she?'

This was a reference to a girl's first job, where she learned the ropes before going on to something better.

'No, she's not in service,' Nesta murmured, loyalty to the family preventing her from bringing up the subject of Kate's failure to conform. 'Her mother isn't well. In fact, she's bedridden now.'

'That's too bad,' the other woman remarked, offhandedly. Chronic illness and early death was so common as to provoke little interest. 'No doubt the girl will be glad of this break, and the chance to earn something for her stocking. Courting, yet, is she?'

'Not at the moment. It seems she has no taste for marriage.'

'Ah, well, it's a good thing we're not all the same, isn't it? I expect her feyther will be glad to have her at home when his wife passes on. Now, if you're ready to get started, I'll put you to work on the pies. Mutton pies we're serving to the common folk.'

'Nothing like a nice mutton pie. I'm partial to one myself, although it's many a long day since I had a taste of one.'

'I have a feeling that most folks will say the same, mistress. There'll be many at this feast who never see good meat from one year to the next. Rook or crow, yes, and mebbe a rabbit, but not much else. Now, I have a rough idea of how many people we're expecting, and I want you to make double the number of pies. What doesn't get eaten at table will get taken away for another day. And mind you keep back your share! May as well make the most of your chances, eh?'

'And I suppose there'll be bread to go with it?'

'Bless you, yes! We've been baking all week, and not just carter's bread, either, but decent raveled bread! It'll be a bit hard and stale by the time it comes to table, but all that free ale will help to wash it down. And there'll be honey cakes and sweetmeats galore, which will please them as has a sweet tooth.'

She kept up a running commentary as they worked together on the pies. Nesta learned that the common folk — smallholders, labourers, tradesmen — would be served in the courtyard, sitting on benches at the trestle-tables. After the meal there would be music and dancing, lasting far into the night.

'And it won't surprise me if there'll be plenty of work for you, mistress, nine months from now,' she cackled. 'Free ale does more than loosen tongues. I'd keep an eye on that granddaughter of yours, if I were you, mistress.'

Nesta said nothing. She was trying to work out how she might get to serve the tables in the great hall, where the gentry would be eating their meal. That was where she could observe the Critchleys and their kin. She had no idea what she hoped to find, or how she might achieve that aim, but it was somewhere to start.

Fortunately, the cook gave her the opening she needed. 'I must tell you about the menu for the grand folks, Mistress Davies. You've never seen the like of what they'll be having. All the courses I've been told to make. Why, I doubt they'll have better at Court!'

'Roast peacock or swan?' Nesta had heard of such fare at Oxford, although naturally she had never sampled it.

'Well, no,' the cook admitted, 'Sir William wouldn't go quite that far. But there'll be salmon, and woodcock, and honey-baked ham, and manchet with real butter to go with it.'

'I've never had manchet,' Nesta said wistfully. This was the fine white bread which ordinary people never saw.

'I'll slip you a bit, once we start cutting the loaves,' the cook promised. 'You'll like the butter. I coloured it myself with marigolds.'

There was a stir at the door, and the pair looked up to see a brightly dressed young gallant swaggering in.

The cook beamed with pleasure. 'Master Will! Here you are, then. All grownup and about to be wed.' He leaned over and kissed her on the cheek, which turned crimson with pleasure. He reached over to snatch one of the honey cakes which was cooling on a nearby table.

'None of that, my lad, or you'll get a taste of my rolling pin!' the cook threatened, with all the pretended insolence of an old family servant who had known the bridegroom all his life. 'Them's for the guests. You'll eat your fill on your wedding day, that's if you can tear your eyes away from your lovely bride!'

He grinned, and sauntered down to the end of the kitchen where, at the sight of him, the girls were beginning to twitter like a flock of birds.

So that was Kate's light o'love, Nesta thought. Handsome enough, she supposed, if you like that sort of blond colouring. To her mind, his chief attraction lay in his confident air, and the colourful doublet and hose he wore. That sort of confidence only came with being born into the upper classes. Young Will had never had to tug his forelock when encountering his betters. The most he had to do was to doff his feathered cap when coming across some beautiful lady. The months he had spent at Court had probably honed his skills.

Nesta felt a brief pang at the thought of shy Blanche being yoked to such a one. He was just the type to take his pleasure without thought for her feelings, and her wedding night was likely to be everything the girl feared, and more. After he had ensured that his bride was safely *enceinte*, he would then return to the excitements of Court, while she would be left alone in a strange household, with only the servants and her new father-in-law for company. Perhaps she might be glad of that.

All this went through Nesta's mind while she was bent over the table, filling the pastry cases with chopped mutton. As a result she didn't see what was happening at the other end of the vast room.

The girls were gathered around the bridegroom, shyly vying for his attention, while one of them, bolder than the rest, dared to flirt. Then he noticed Kate, who was lagging back trying to avoid his eye.

'Why, is it Kate Davies? What are you doing here, sweeting?'

This caused even more whispering and surprise, especially when Kate refused to answer. Will strode forward and grasped her wrist.

'I want a word with you!'

'Don't! Everybody's listening!'

'The whole world can listen, for all I care.'

'I don't want to talk to you, Will Mowbray. In fact, I never want to see you again! Just go away and leave me alone!'

There were gasps of astonishment from the wide-eyed girls. Will narrowed his eyes.

'I'll show you who's master here, my girl! If you won't talk here, then we'll go outside.

Come on, don't keep me waiting.'

Nesta had seen enough. She marched down the room and stood in front of Kate, shielding her from his furious gaze.

'You heard what she said, Master Will. Now leave the child alone. Please!'

'Who do you think you are, woman? I'll have the pair of you dismissed for this, and that's a promise!'

Nesta shrugged. 'I'm not your serf, Master Will, and neither is my granddaughter. We came here to help with the preparations for your wedding, but we can easily take the money owing to us and go home.' Bosom heaving, she faced the arrogant young man with a defiant look which matched his own. He lowered his gaze, and left.

26

The cook came hurrying up, very red in the face. The maids jumped back hastily to make room for her, like the Red Sea parting before Moses.

'How dare you, girl!' Her whispered rebuke was filled with venom. 'Don't you know that's the young master himself? If he wishes for something you fetch it, with no back answers!'

Kate flinched. 'He'll get nothing from me, the faithless boy!'

'You are here to serve, my girl, and if you don't like it you can leave this minute. And don't expect pay, neither!'

'That's all right with me!' Kate snapped. 'I didn't want to come here in the first place!'

Nesta became aware of the various glances sent their way. Some of the younger servants seemed puzzled, or frightened. One or two seemed pleased or triumphant. Taking the cook by the shoulder she turned her about, at the same time grasping Kate by the wrist.

'Not here!' she hissed, as she propelled the woman towards the main work table, dragging Kate with them. 'And you lot can get on with your work, too,' she called. 'This is none of your business!'

Surprisingly they bent to their tasks. With a sigh of relief she turned to Kate. 'You get outside and wait for me there, gal. I'll be along in a minute.'

'But he might be there!'

'So what if he is? Got a tongue in your head, haven't you? You can put a flea in his ear, lord of the manor or no lord of the manor!'

Reluctantly, Kate sauntered outside, uncomfortably aware that everyone was looking at her, but determined not to show any fear.

'Well, I never did! A fine kettle of fish, this is! I just hope and pray that Master Will don't tell Sir William, or we'll all be in trouble. The blame will fall on me, sure as eggs are eggs, for not keeping proper order in my own kitchen!'

'If he does, I shall have a word to say, and Sit William won't like what he hears!' Nesta spoke with more confidence than she felt inside.

'But what's this all about, then?'

'I'll tell you, but this is for your ears only, mind!'

'Ay, go on.'

'I understand that your Master Will has been paying court to my granddaughter this long while.'

'Paying court! But the girl must have known that nothing could come of it, them being from different classes, like. Begging your pardon, Mistress Davies, but you know yourself there could never be a match between Sir William's son and a cobbler's daughter.'

'Cordwainer, if you please,' Nesta corrected. 'My son works with the best leather, and Sir William himself has his boots made by Jack. Still, I know what you mean. That's hardly the point, though, is it? Kate is young and foolish, and first love hits hard. She believed him when he vowed to love her, and who knows what else? On his part I'm sure it was just a dalliance, and I'm only grateful that matters didn't go too far.'

The other woman grimaced. 'Ay, that's the way of the world with young gallants. But what was all that about, back there?'

'I shan't know until I've spoken to Kate, but I suspect he wanted to take up where he left off, and she wanted none of him. Can you blame her?'

'Surely not, on the eve of his wedding! I expect he only wanted to talk, to explain things to her.'

'What is there to explain? She knows where she stands. Best for him to get on with his life, same as she has to.'

'Tut! What a to-do. I s'pose she's not at fault, so we'll let it ride, so long as Sir William don't get involved. I can't have the girl stay on, though. The rest of them'll be full of questions, I'll warrant, and they're here to work, not to gossip. Look at me; all behind, like the old cow's tail. We've got to get this next batch of pies in the oven.'

'You'll have to give me a few minutes while I go out and see what's happened to Kate. That's if you don't want to sack me, along with her?'

'No, no, I can't spare you, not with all this to do. You can take the time you need, but do make it short.'

Kate was pacing up and down outside but as soon as she saw Nesta she ran to her, with the tears pouring down her face.

'I'm sorry, Gramma! I didn't mean to cause a fuss. He wanted me to come outside with him and he wouldn't take no for an answer.'

'I know, sweeting. I should never have made you come. I did it for the best, but I had no idea that he'd turn up in the kitchens, of all places.'

'But what's going to happen to you? Have you got the sack?'

'No, no, I'm all right.'

'But what if Will's father gets to hear about

202

this? He could see to it that you'll never attend another confinement in Hollyhill. Then where will you be?'

'If the man comes anywhere near me, he'll get a piece of my mind. As for taking my trade from me, who is to attend the women of the area if not me? Men may make the rules most of the time, but when it comes to birthing, no woman would agree to go through her travail alone, without aid, and that's a fact! And that's not all. If I'm still here a year from now, I have no doubt that this new bride will be ready to give birth to the new heir to the manor, and this Sir William will be on his knees, begging me to come. So don't you worry about me, gal.'

She saw Kate wince. Inch by inch, the poor girl was being made to realize that the boy she loved was lost to her in a very real way.

'You'd better get off home, then, 'cause I've gotta get on. Will you be all right, walking all that distance?'

'Yes, Gramma. I can stop to rest along the way.'

'That's all right, then. Be sure to have look in on your mother when you get there. I'm a bit worried about how she's faring, with both of us gone.'

Kate walked away, her head down. Nesta watched her go, hoping she'd be all right. She had not given her any words of cheer. Kate would have to find her courage from inside herself. Just in time Nesta had bitten back the suggestion that the girl would now be free to stand with others outside the church, to watch the bride and groom arriving separately, with their attendants, and later to see them emerge as a newly wedded couple. Kate would not be cheering with the rest. In fact, would she be there at all?

'You took your time!' was the cook's greeting, when Nesta reappeared.

'Ay, well! She's my granddaughter. I had to see she was all right, didn't I?'

'I suppose so. Happen I spoke a bit sharpish, like, but this has left me all of a dither. Never mind, when you leave here I'll see that you get a good parcel of leftovers to take home with you. A nice bit of ham, say, and a few other things.'

'I know my family will appreciate that.' Nesta smiled as their truce was sealed.

Now, with Kate gone, it was all up to her to see what she could find out. Perhaps now was the time to ask, while the other woman was still feeling wrong-footed and anxious to placate.

'I suppose we shan't be able to turn up at the church on the big day?'

'Hardly, mistress. We'll be too busy here to

turn around, let alone go off gallivanting.'

'A pity, that. I'd have loved to see the gentry, turning up at the church in their Sunday best. And all the world loves a bride, all decked out in her wedding finery. I wonder what her gown will be like? I daresay I'll hear about it from others, but it won't be the same. Our Jonno is more likely to gloat over the fine food than to remark on the comings and goings of his betters.'

'You'll see them when they arrive back here for the wedding feast, mistress.'

'I doubt me any of them will come to the kitchens. I don't suppose . . . '

'What's that?'

'The servants will be waiting at table. They'll have a good look at all the grand folks sitting there, won't they? Could they use an extra hand, think you? Who would I speak to about it?'

She held her breath, waiting for the cook's reply.

'I'm not sure. We're all at sixes and sevens without the steward. Young Charlie Howard's taken his place, temporary like, but mainly it's every man for himself. I'm sure if you was to nip in and just looked like you belonged there, nobody would be any the wiser. I can manage without you here when the time comes. Most of your work for me will be getting the food ready for the outside tables, not the hot dishes for the gentry.' Nesta managed to hide a smile of satisfaction.

'Mind you,' the cook went on, 'don't you try handing the dishes, like you was trained to do it. Just speak when you're spoken to, and take away the empties when the time comes. Can you manage that?'

'I'm sure I can,' Nesta replied cheerfully.

27

Kate trudged on, still shocked by her unexpected encounter with Will. She had a dim recollection of Father Wagstaffe saying that the ancient ones believed that the soul was located in the pit of the stomach. While she hadn't fully understood what he was talking about she could certainly testify to the fact that the dreadful pain of loss was eating at her, right below her rib cage. Would it be any better after his wedding took place, and he was lost to her for ever? She thought not. She would carry the yearning to her grave.

'What are you doing here, then?'

Kate's heart sank. Why was it that Frances Cropwell always turned up when you least expected it?

'I said, what you doing here, Kate Davies!'

'I heard you, Fan. I thought you could see that for yourself. I'm on the road home.' She kept walking. Fanny loped along beside her, wearing a sly look on her homely face.

'I thought you was toiling up at the manor house. Getting ready for Master Will's big day. Couldn't stand the thought of it, I s'pose, and had to run away.'

'If you must know, I got the sack,' Kate said stiffly. This wasn't strictly true, but she was not going to share her true feelings with this girl.

'Is that so? And a good thing too, if you ask me. Wouldn't catch me doing menial work like that, I can tell you!'

'Just what sort of work do you do, then, Fan?' She was genuinely curious to know. The other girl lived in a hovel on the edge of the wood with an ageing uncle, but he had no job as far as Kate had ever heard. Surely they must live on something? Even if the man had savings from working at some trade in the past, any such money must have been exhausted long ago.

'Bit o' this, bit o' that One good thing about you losing your job, you'll be able to see the wedding tomorrow. Just make sure you get your share of the food at the feast after. I mean to take a sack with me, fill it up with leftovers. If anyone says anything, I'll tell them it's for Uncle Arthur. Nobody could grudge him a bite or two, seeing as he's too wambly to get up to the manor.'

'My mother is the same. Dad says I should bring her a few bits, to tempt her appetite.'

'Ah, yes, I heard she's like to die, poor soul,' Fanny murmured. Rage welled up in Kate and for a moment she longed to punch

208

the girl in her fat mouth, but she managed to hold herself back. After all, she hadn't said anything that wasn't true.

'Where's your mother, then?' she asked, by way of retaliation.

'Dead.'

'And your feyther?'

'Dead, too. Us and my brothers, we all took the sweating sickness. They all died but me. I didn't have nobody else, so I come to live with Uncle Arthur. Well, he's my mother's uncle by rights.'

'That's awful.'

Fanny shrugged. 'Happens all the time. Feyther Wagstaffe, he says they're in a better place, 'cos they was all shriven before they died. I asked why God didn't take me with them, but all he said was, it's a mystery. It makes you think, though, eh?'

'At least you'll see them again some day.' Kate echoed the pious hope in which most people believed.

'Dunno about that. Anyhow, I'm still here, and this wedding makes for a bit of excitement. I wouldn't want my wedding in November, though, would you? No flowers nor nothing, although they've decorated the church with bits o' green stuff. You should hop along and take a look.'

'I think I shall,' Kate said. She could do

with a bit of a rest, and the quiet of the church would help to calm her jangled nerves. When she reached the ancient Norman building she was thankful that Fanny bade her goodbye and she entered into the gloom with something like relief in her heart.

She genuflected towards the altar, then edged onto a bench near the front; not one on which she normally sat, for her family's place was further back. She had been worshipping here ever since she could remember, and the stained-glass windows, with their depictions of saints and apostles, were as familiar to her as her own family.

Her father had explained to her that the church was almost five centuries old, filling her with awe to think of all the people who had come here before her. Some were now in their last sleep, beneath the leaning crosses in the graveyard, but there must be many more who had no such memorial.

She had said as much to Jack Davies, who had patted her on the head with rough kindness, telling her not to fret. 'Like as not they had wooden crosses at one time. Doesn't matter any more. The people who loved them remember them, see. That's all that matters.'

'But if they lived hundreds of years ago, they'll be dead too, so it does matter.' She had been distressed at the thought, but her father knew what to say. 'Then they're all together again, in Heaven, sweeting. No need to grieve.'

Kate remembered that now, smiling as she got up and began to walk about. The scent of incense was strong, and the flickering candles illuminated the placid face of the stone Virgin in the Lady Chapel, who stood there eternally, holding the Holy infant in her arms. Comforted, Kate went outside to resume her journey.

By the time she reached home, her mind was made up. She would not go to the church to watch the wedding guests arrive. Why torture herself with the sight of the newly married pair? It was best to stay away, and try to busy herself with some job around the house. Nesta had been heard to say that work was the best cure for a broken heart, although privately Kate thought that was nonsense.

However, she had no sooner set foot in the house when her younger brother hurled himself at her, his small face aglow with excitement.

'We didn't know you were coming, Kate! Mumma never said.'

'I didn't know either, Jonno, but they didn't need as many up there any more so I thought I might as well come home.' And that's another lie I'll have to tell the priest about, when I go to confession next, she thought. Father Wagstaffe was always insistent that there was no difference between what some people liked to call a white lie, and a thumping good one. Both were sins, and if you weren't careful they would count against you when you landed in purgatory.

'Oh, good! Then you can come with us to the church tomorrow after all.'

'I thought I'd have a lie-in instead. They've kept my nose to the grindstone up at the manor, and I'm tired out.'

'Why do they want to get married so early in the morning, anyhow?' he grumbled.

'You know why, Jonno. Everyone has to go fasting to Mass. That's why they call the feast a wedding breakfast. If the wedding was later in the day the poor bride would faint from hunger, not to mention Feyther Wagstaffe.'

'But we're to go to the feast at dinner-time, aren't we?'

'I know, but everyone will go home and have something to eat in between time.'

'Then why — '

'Oh, do stop asking silly questions, Jonno! How is Mumma? Have you seen her this morning?'

''Course I have. I took up her gruel, but she couldn't eat it. She said it tasted burnt, but not to tell Dad, cos he did his best.'

As if on cue, Joan called out from upstairs.

'Is that you, Kate?'

'Coming, Mumma!'

'What on earth are you doing back so soon, child?' Joan's thin face bore an expression of dismay.

'Why does everyone keep asking me that? This is my home, isn't it?'

'You know what I mean, gal.'

Kate considered repeating the tale of a sacking, but she knew that was no good, for Nesta would put her in the wrong in due course. She hung her head.

'I saw Will, Mumma.'

'You mean Will Mowbray?'

'Who else do I know called Will? He came into the kitchen and showed me up in front of everybody. He wanted me to follow him outside; to talk, he said, but I have nothing to say to him. The cook was annoyed, and I could tell I'd be in trouble if I stayed, so Gramma and me, we thought it best if I came away.' Joan made no reply to this, and Kate broke the silence by saying that wild horses wouldn't drag her to the church when the wedding was taking place.

'Oh, but you must, gal! I was promised that someone would tell me all about the gowns the women wore, and how the bride looked.

I'll be that disappointed!'

'Dad will be there.'

'Pooh! A fat lot he'll notice. Typical man. Say you'll go, for my sake, please?'

Unwillingly, Kate agreed, and was rewarded with her mother's grateful smile.

28

The bell had not yet begun to toll, to summon the congregation to the church, yet already a crowd had assembled near the doors. They must have come from miles around, Kate thought, for many of the faces were strange to her.

Others were neighbours, and as she patiently responded to the inevitable questions about her mother's health, she remained alert to the arrival of Will, who so far had not put in an appearance. Of course, he would not come until the guests were assembled, and the bride would arrive last of all.

Before long, the first guests rode up to the lychgate, dismounting stiffly and handing their mounts to an ostler, hired for the occasion. Whispered comments greeted their arrival.

'Who be they, then? See the fur on her cloak? That cost a pretty penny, I'll be bound! Feed my lot for a year, that would.'

'Looks like coney to me.'

'Naw. 'Tis fox at least; mebbe beaver.'

Kate wondered if many people were coming from Court. Will must have made friends there. Perhaps not members of the aristocracy, but at least young gentlemen. But this pair could not have come far. Their horses were not lathered in the least.

The thought of her mother, all alone at home, gave her a pang. Would she ever rise from her bed again? Miracles did happen, but it did no good to hope too much. Mindful of her promise to recount every detail of the guests and their apparel, Kate did her best to commit things to her memory.

The ladies, now. Obviously well-to-do, and richly dressed, but not in the style of the great ladies of the Court. Not that Kate had ever seen any of them, but she imagined them all decked out in costly gowns, emblazoned with jewels. These women had a lesser style. They were the sort who might own two or three gowns, and some modest baubles. What characterized them most was the air of confidence which went with breeding. You couldn't imagine any of them trudging to the village well with pails of water suspended from a yoke on their shoulders.

Someone plucked at her sleeve, and she spun round to find her younger brother.

'We just got here,' he panted. 'I thought we'd miss everything.'

'What kept you, Jonno? It's not Mumma, is it?'

'Nay, she's well enough. 'Twas a pair from Hardwick, with an order for boots. Said they'd heard as Dad was the best cordwainer in these parts, and seeing as they'd come for the wedding they thought they might as well stop at our place. Dad takes ages to measure up, you know. 'If a thing's worth doing at all, it's worth doing right', is what he always says.'

'I'm surprised he didn't tell you to run on ahead and he'd follow later.'

Jonno grimaced. 'One of them was a woman and you know he doesn't like to measure them in the workshop. I had to show her into the parlour as usual, and keep her company until he was finished with the husband.'

Kate nodded absently. That sounded like Dad, all right.

'Look, Kate! Tis Master Will. Riding in with another chap, see?'

Kate felt her stomach sink. At least, that was what it felt like. She forced herself to look.

Both men, travelling on fine, tall horses, looked as proud as peacocks. Despite the cold, they were not wearing the usual long coats, but had on short jackets over their doublets. Will's green sleeves were slashed, showing glimpses of crimson underneath. His flat hat was also green, with a huge red feather. Later, Kate could not have told you what his companion was wearing, except that he, like Will, had a finely pleated white ruff around his neck, a fashion which had not yet reached Hollyhill.

'Who be that, then?' asked a voice at Kate's elbow.

The woman beside her craned her neck to see. 'That be young Master Will, you fool. Dint you recognize him?'

'O' course I know him, but who's the other lad, all decked out like a popinjay?'

'The groomsman, no doubt one of his fine new friends.'

And so the talk went on. A murmur went through the crowd as they recognized familiar faces. Adam Critchley was there, and his new wife, followed soon after by the Dilleys and the Robinsons. Sally sent a half-smile in Kate's direction as she walked past.

The bell began to toll, but by this time the church must be full to bursting, as Jonno remarked. Only the bride and her attendants were still to come. Within the hour the bells would ring again, this time pealing joyously, and Will and Blanche would appear at the door as man and wife.

'Where she be, then?' an old gaffer groused. 'Time that gal was putting in an appearance, keeping us all waiting like this!'

'What's it to you, old man? Not coming to wed you, is she?' Laughter rippled through the crowd.

'Not me. I've had two wives, and that's enough for any man, king or commoner. Naw, let the priest get on with his job, and then we can sit down to eat. That's what I'm looking forward to!'

'And the drink!' another wag called out.

The rumble of wheels on the road signalled the approach of a coach.

'That's the one that stopped at our house when the wheel came off,' Jonno said. 'That'll be her, won't it.'

First out of the coach was an older man, who was a stranger to those in the waiting crowd. Then a girl, blonde and pretty, obviously a bridesmaid. Last of all, out stepped Blanche, pale as death itself.

'Don't look too steady on her pins, do she?' one onlooker said. 'Not looking forward to wedded life, I s'pose. I wouldn't have, neither, if I'd known it would bring me eleven childer and a one-room cottage.'

'Shouldn't have married a labouring chap, then, should you? Anyway, 'tis different for this gal. She'll want for nothing all her days, lucky wench.'

Kate forced herself to study the bride's attire. As they paused at the church door, the bridesmaid folded back Blanche's cloak, a heavy affair of dark-blue wool, revealing a gown of a slightly lighter shade, all embroidered with golden lovers' knots. In the fashion of the day the gown was split open at the front, showing a kirtle of rose-pink, made from some costly fabric which shimmered in the early-morning sun.

Blanche's hair was spread over her shoulders, left loose to signify virginity. A fine veil was suspended from her close-fitting coif. Kate absently fingered her own long plait as she watched the other girl. Blanche had given no sign of recognition although she had passed close by to Kate. Did she even know that her rival was present?

The trio disappeared inside the church, and the door clanged shut. Now there would be a long wait before they all emerged again.

'I think I'd better go home, see how Mumma is,' Kate whispered. 'Are you coming with me?'

'Oh, you mustn't do that,' Jonno told her. 'What if they throw coins to the crowd and us not here? Sometimes that happens at weddings. Gramma told me. She's seen it happen at Oxford.'

'I doubt they'll do that here. Not when Sir William's had all the expense of feeding all these people. Do come on, Jonno. I'm getting cold hanging about here.'

But at that moment Jack Davies appeared beside them.

'Phew, I thought they'd never go. Have I missed anything?'

'They're all inside the church now, Dad. They won't be leaving for a while.'

'Good, good.'

'What took you so long, Dad? Did you get a good order from those people?'

'Boots for each of them, in the best leather. Trouble was, the woman couldn't make up her mind between two colours. I got the idea she was hinting at getting two pairs made, but her man didn't rise to the bait. Anyhow, they paid a deposit, so if she comes back later and says she's changed her mind and doesn't want the dark brown after all, at least I won't be out of pocket.'

Kate looked up suddenly at the sound of the church door opening. There was a concerted gasp from the crowd as they realized that the bride was framed in the doorway. They stood back automatically as she stumbled down the path, and out onto the road.

'Come back, girl! What are you doing?' All eyes swivelled back to the steps, where Father Wagstaffe was standing, quivering with outrage. The new Mistress Critchley was at his side, her face a picture, as Kate reported to her mother later. Other guests peered over her shoulder, their expressions varying from horror to glee. Of Will Mowbray there was no sign. Probably standing at the altar with his mouth hanging open, Kate reflected, with a surge of joy in her mind, quickly dampened when she considered the possibilities.

The thing was, were they already wed, and their union never to be torn asunder, except by death? Or had poor Blanche made her escape before the fateful words had been spoken? The assembled crowd waited with bated breath to see what would happen next.

29

Tabby the cook returned to the kitchen, white-faced and shaken. Crossly shaking her head at the interruption, she had gone outside when summoned by one of the men who were setting up tables in the courtyard.

'Some fellow wants yer, mistress, says he's come straight from Sir William,' he sniffed, wiping his nose on his sleeve.

'What now!' she fussed, grimacing at Nesta. 'Don't tell me he wants some fancy new dish for the feast, and us pushed to the hilt as it is! Well, better go and see, I s'pose!'

But now Nesta could tell from Tabby's face that whatever Sir William wanted, it was more than a request for cossetard tarts.

'You look like you dropped a groat and found a farthing. What is it, in the name of all that's holy?'

Tabby sank down on the nearest bench. 'There's been no wedding, Nesta! What do you make of that?'

'No wedding! Don't tell me somebody else has died, or been set upon?'

'Almost as bad. It seems the priest barely got started before the bride ran away.'

'She ran away!'

'That's what I was told. It was that Reynard, Sir William's coachman, so it must be true if Sir William sent him back here at this hour.'

'And did they catch up with the girl?'

'Apparently not. Nobody seems to know where she's gone, or why. What a scandal.'

'Of course, the girl wasn't very keen at the outset,' Nesta mused. 'Said she didn't want to wed at all, never mind getting married off to some chap she'd never met.'

Tabby's eyes opened wide. 'How would you know a thing like that? Is that what the old gossips at the pump are saying? You can't believe half you hear, and that's a fact.'

'Oh, it's true enough. Some time back Jane Pettapiece — Critchley, as she is now — was on her way here with the girl, for the betrothal ceremony. A wheel came off their coach right outside our place, and they took shelter with us while it was being seen to. The woman told me all about it. More to the point, young Blanche herself spoke to our Kate and told her the very thing I've said now. She was being forced into it, against her will, as happens to many a girl with a bit of wealth behind her.'

'Even so . . . ' For a moment Tabby was lost for words, and then the significance of the disaster struck home. 'Oh, no! What am I supposed to do with all this food, then? You tell me that! What a wicked waste, and after all our hard work, too.'

'If I'm any judge of people, all the ordinary folk will turn up anyway, hoping they'll still get fed. I know what they're like, when it comes to free food. That's what I'd do, in their shoes. Even if Sir William cancels the feast, we can still give out the pies and bread at the door, can't we? I'm sure there would be a riot if people tramped all this way without receiving as much as a crust.' Nesta was only half-joking.

'I daresay you're right,' Tabby said, gnawing on her thumbnail. 'But it's the gentry I'm worried about. They're the ones expecting a hot meal. Do we go on with that, or do we not? Look, I've got pans on the hob at the moment, with dishes half-finished, and enough sweetmeats prepared to feed a family till doomsday. Drat that Sir William! Trust a man to forget to tell me what to do now!'

'I expect he's too shocked to think straight,' Nesta said, but she could sympathize with the cook. 'I think we should go on as if nothing has happened. That's what we're getting paid for, after all. It's a bit like my trade,' she went on, as Tabby dithered. 'Once labour starts, there's no turning back. The only way out of it is to go forward.'

Not a very helpful comparison, she thought, but at least it had the virtue of spurring Tabby on. They couldn't loll about wringing their hands.

'I s'pose they'll still want feeding,' Tabby muttered. ' 'Specially those who've come from afar. Sir William would never hear the last of it if all those high and mighty folk were turned from his door with empty bellies. Then there's all those musicians and actors coming to do the entertaining. They've started turning up already. One big red-headed fellow had the sauce to come to the door, begging for something to keep him going. You'll get fed when you've done your job, and not before, I told him. He started to give me an argument, but he soon stepped back when I brandished my cleaver at him.'

Nesta tuned out. None of this was her problem. What did concern her was that if the feast was called off, her chance to do a bit of detecting would be gone with it. Meanwhile, she could hardly wait to speak to someone who had witnessed Blanche's headlong flight from the church. Had they caught up with her by now? Would her guardians drag her back into the church and force her to make her vows, as if nothing had happened?

An hour later they learned more, and it was

Sir William himself who brought the latest news. Tabby fainted when she saw him enter the kitchen. He had never been known to do such a thing before, and, as she explained to Nesta later, 'I come over all queer.' Now, though, it was up to Nesta to revive the cook, having the presence of mind to hold a burning feather under the woman's nose.

'And if you don't come round right this minute,' she hissed, having seen Tabby's eyes flicker, 'it'll be a bucket of water over you next.'

She was not impressed by Tabby's 'Where am I?' delivered in a weak voice. Stalling for time, that's all she was doing.

'She'll be all right in a minute, Sir William. I'm Nesta Davies. Is there something I can do for you?'

'Not unless you can catch that fool of a girl, and bring her to her senses,' he growled.

'Oh, dear! So they haven't found her, then?'

'No, they have not! And she can keep running, for all I care! How dare she shame us all like this? Gives people the idea there's something wrong with my son, a fine, upstanding young man whom any girl in her right mind would be happy to marry! If she had no mind to wed, why couldn't she have said so before it came to this?'

She did say it, Nesta thought, but wisely she held her tongue.

'What I've come to say is that food must be provided for my guests. I thought that should be obvious, but the girl's aunt tells me it should be made plain. Under the circumstances, my cook might not know what to do, she says. It's coming to something when a man has to speak to his own cook, but nothing has been the same since my steward died.'

He glared at Tabby, wrinkling his nose in distaste. 'Is she capable of carrying on?' he demanded.

'She'll be better in a minute, sir. 'Twas only the heat from the fires. We've been cooking for days. Everything will be ready on time, you'll see.'

'I hope you're right. If anything else goes wrong, I won't answer for my actions!'

As soon as he had gone, slamming the door with a violence that made the dishes rattle, Tabby sat up. 'Phew! He's cross as a ferret down an empty hole! I thought he was going to fetch me a wallop when he come in, all purple in the face.'

'He's gone now, and you can hardly blame the man. As he says, everyone will be sniggering behind his back. It will be interesting to see if young Will turns up at the feast after all.

Mebbe he'll turn tail and go straight back to Court after this.'

However, it seemed that the young man was made of sterner stuff, for he did indeed come to the table, taking up the place of honour as if nothing had happened. He entered the hall leading the bridesmaid by the hand, and she, simpering and blushing, allowed herself to be installed in the chair which had been reserved for the bride.

She probably has hopes of filling her shoes, Nesta thought, as she peered round the door. She'd best not get any silly ideas, or she may get more than she bargains for. That young man has far too high an opinion of himself for any girl to be safe around him at the moment.

The guests seemed to be making polite conversation now, carefully avoiding Sir William's eye. He in turn was ignoring Mistress Critchley, who sat at his right hand. Her face was sombre as she toyed with her food, moving it about without bringing any of it to her lips.

The words spoken by the guests were hardly distinguishable over the singing of a young lute player who was manfully belting out words of love and loss. Hardly appropriate, after what had happened, Nesta considered, but probably he had practised his repertoire before coming and could not change it now.

She was conscious of a feeling of great disappointment. She had hoped to find some clue here to the crimes which had plagued Hollyhill, but with all the noise that was going on she couldn't hear herself think, let alone eavesdrop to any purpose.

Then the great door was flung open, and the blacksmith burst in. For a minute he stood as if frozen, before striding up to Sir William, whose eyes opened wide with fury.

'Sorry, sir, the priest told me to come and fetch you. 'Tis the young miss that was to wed Master Will. Drowned herself, she has. We found her shoes and cloak on the riverbank, and no sign of the gal herself. She's a dead one, surely.'

30

A loud scream rent the air. Sally Robinson had risen to her feet, rapidly working herself up into full-blown hysteria. Nesta hurried forward, ready to assist, but before she could act, Tom Robinson had delivered a resounding slap to his wife's cheek, and her cries receded to a whimper.

Nobody else moved, or seemed to care. A slap in the face was of course the accepted treatment for a fit of hysterics, never mind that husbands had the right to chastise their wives when necessary. However, in this case it seemed like cruelty. Surely the girl was reliving her own dreadful experience?

Jane Critchley leapt to her feet, her hand over her mouth. Lot's wife could have been no less rigid than the poor woman was at that moment, Nesta decided. Adam Critchley tugged at a handful of his wife's skirts and she sank down again, gasping.

Sir William snatched up his goblet and downed the contents in one gulp. Holding it out to a servant for it to be refilled, he beckoned the blacksmith closer.

'An accident, you say?'

The man swallowed hard. 'I doubt it, sir. I saw her cloak, all folded up neat-like, and her two poor little shoes, side by side like you might put them at your bedside, ready for morn. I'd say she done away with herself, deliberate like.'

'That's all. You may go.'

Inclining his head, the blacksmith marched the length of the room, all eyes following. Nesta sidled up to him. 'Go into the kitchen, will you? I'll see you there.'

She waited until a babble of talk broke out before following him out. She found him standing beside the fire, looking lost.

'Sit down, man!' she ordered. 'You'll take a mug of beer and a bite of something before you go.'

'I don't mind if I do. I'm that mazed I don't know which way is up!'

When she returned with the promised food he looked at her, bewildered.

'Don't I know yer, mistress? You look familiar, like.'

'Of course you do. I'm Jack Davies's mother.'

'What you doin' here, then?'

'I've been hired to help with the wedding feast. What else?'

'But you're a midwife, ain't yer?'

'That don't mean I can't turn my hand to

other work. Now then, can you tell me what all this is about?'

He blinked at her, owlishly. 'Nothing else to tell, but what I already said.'

'Who found her clothes?'

'I dunno, exactly. Folk was coming this way for the feast, and some youngster spotted the things from the bridge. Let out a yelp, and everyone came gathering round. 'Looks like she topped herself' someone said. I dunno who. Then someone else said as we had to let Sir William know, and I got told to come, seeing as I see to Sir William's horses, and he'd know I'm a sensible sort o' chap.'

'Poor child,' Nesta murmured.

'Stupid child, if you ask me. Now if she'd been wed for a bit, and found her husband hard and cruel, she might have had cause, even though 'tis mortal sin. But to drown herself now, when some might say she had everything to live for, that don't make no sense. You take that Sally Robinson, now. She was another one. Oh, she's sorry now, o' course, and tries to make out she were pushed, but who believes a word o' that? She has to say that, after they fished her out. She'd be in big trouble, else.'

Nesta said something noncommittal. With the way this conversation was going she didn't want to get involved, in case she said something which could be repeated later and misconstrued, but she was thinking furiously. Unfortunately for her train of thought, they were interrupted at that moment.

A man whom Nesta didn't know strode into the kitchen as though he owned the place. 'They need a new barrel of beer out there, and we're running out of pies,' he announced.

Nesta looked around, but there was no sign of Tabby. 'I'll send the maids out with more food, but you'll have to find Charlie Howard to see about the drink. He should be about somewhere. A chap with long black hair and a squint.'

'I'll do that. The dancing is about to start, and 'tis thirsty work, is dancing.'

'I wouldn't know about that. My dancing days are over.'

'Naw, you look like you could still shake a leg, missus, specially with a drop of ale inside you. You come looking for me later and we'll see what we can do.'

'Get along with you, man!' Nesta cried, not sure whether she should feel complimented or insulted. When she turned back to the table it was to find that the blacksmith had disappeared. On his way back to the scene of the crime, she supposed, for suicide — if that was indeed what it was — was against the law.

Poor little Blanche, Nesta sighed. She was too young to die. Younger than Kate, if she remembered rightly.

When Nesta's work was done she returned to the great hall, where the tables had been cleared and the musicians were tuning up their instruments, readying themselves for the dancing to follow. Nesta was keen to watch the company taking part in this sport, for, as she knew from her time in Oxford, the gentry performed the popular moves with grace, always as part of a group. The country folk outside would be bouncing about energetically, but for all that enjoying themselves just as much as their betters, who were following patterns laid down by some courtly person.

In the corridor near the other entrance to the hall, Adam Critchley and his wife seemed to be engaged in a heated argument. Nesta drew back into the shadows, straining to hear what was being said.

'Brought disgrace on my house.' That was Adam.

'Hardly my fault,' his wife pleaded.

'She's your niece, woman.'

'So what? I did not have the raising of her. And don't call me woman! 'Tisn't seemly.'

'I'm your husband now, and you won't tell me how to speak, unless you want to feel the weight of my hand.'

Oh, dear! Nesta thought. So that's the way the land lies, is it? Married for barely two minutes, and a rift in the lute already. However, it seemed that Jane Pettapiece was not to be quieted so easily.

'I was as shocked as you when the girl broke away and ran from the church, husband. Embarrassing as it was, it wasn't the end of the world, though. I'm sure that Blanche wasn't the first bride to change her mind, nor will she be the last. And don't shout, Adam! Do you want the whole gathering to hear you?'

This as he raised his voice in anger, but to Nesta's annoyance he did lower his tone, so that she missed what came next.

'I don't believe you care at all that the poor child is dead,' Jane countered.

'Such a girl is better off dead if she cannot obey her elders and do what is expected of her. That was a fine marriage we'd arranged for her. How could she throw our goodwill back in our faces in such a manner?'

'Better off! Taking her own life, and going to meet her maker unshriven!'

'I'm only saying what everyone else must be thinking, wife. And you might spare a thought for me. I'm the one who has to live here for the rest of my life. I doubt if Sir William will speak to me again after this.'

Nesta tiptoed away, having eavesdropped on what she realized was nothing more than a family argument. Minutes later she returned, humming loudly to warn them of her approach, but they had already gone. She shrank back against the wall as young Will appeared, held up by the erstwhile grooms-man. Both young men were swaying and giggling, obviously very drunk. They took no notice of her.

She glanced into the hall to see that a dance was already in progress. Anne Dilley was dancing with great vigour, partnered by her husband, Peter. Sally was hunched over on a bench, ignored by the throng, as well as by her husband, who was partnering a buxom wench with whom he exchanged lascivious looks.

Nesta made her way over to Sally, and sat down beside her.

'Are you feeling all right, dearie?'

Sally raised her tear-stained face to meet Nesta's gaze. 'I wish we'd stayed at home, that I do. I told Tom I didn't want to come, but he insisted, and now look at him. He's all over that slut, with never a thought for me.'

'I daresay you're upset about that poor girl, aren't you?'

'Of course I am. And not just for her own sake, Mistress Davies. People are looking at me and whispering. A lot of people don't believe me when I say I was pushed into that river, you know. But I was, and I'll swear that on my poor mother's grave.'

'I believe you, and I mean to find out who did push you, and why.'

'That's kind, but I don't know how you can. Sam Fowler's been trying hard enough, and we're still no further ahead.'

'I don't know about that,' Nesta said slowly.

'What do you mean?' Sally asked, and was surprised when she received no reply.

31

Lying in bed, Nesta found that sleep eluded her. Having dragged her aching bones up to the room she shared with a servant named Bessie, she'd thought she'd fall asleep at once, being exhausted after the day's work, but that wasn't the case. Part of the problem was the pallet they'd given her to sleep on. A piece of straw was sticking out through the worn fabric, scratching her painfully on the hip. She was used to sleeping on a good feather bed and this was a bit of a come-down.

Surely Sir William could have done better by his servants than this? In a household where good food was the norm, there must be plenty of feathers left over from plucking birds. Making a feather mattress was more difficult than stuffing straw into a sack, but the result was far more satisfactory.

She turned over onto her right side, and minutes later rolled back again. Bessie snored on, oblivious to her companion's struggles. With a sigh, Nesta got up and tiptoed over to the window. Bessie had protested mightily when Nesta had insisted on having it open a crack and had promptly shut it again. Everybody knew that night air was bad for you. Now Nesta opened it and leaned out. All was quiet below, save for the far-off hoot of an owl, and the bark of a hunting fox.

Once again her mind turned to the mysterious doings of the day. She realized suddenly that one thing had been puzzling her. The blacksmith had mentioned that poor Blanche had left her cloak on the river bank, neatly folded, with her shoes nearby. Why would the girl have done such a thing?

Suicide wasn't the only reason for a person to enter the river. You might have to wade across if there was no convenient bridge. Perhaps dive in to rescue a person in trouble, as the men had when Sally Robinson was in danger. In such cases one would naturally leave one's good clothing on the bank, for fear of spoiling it. As for shoes or boots, they would drag a person down. It was only sensible to slip them off.

But why would Blanche leave her things behind? If she hoped for a quick death, she wouldn't want to float, would she? Or was she so distressed in her mind that she hardly knew what she was doing?

Nesta's hand flew to her mouth. What if — think carefully, now — what if the girl hadn't drowned at all? Nobody would know for sure until her corpse was discovered, as might well be the case. However, what if she had purposely left her garments there as a means of calling off the hunt while she made her getaway?

Nesta clicked her tongue in annoyance, causing Bessie to mumble in her sleep. This was November, and the nights were cold. The girl would hardly go flitting through the woods in her bare feet, with nothing to keep her warm.

She dismissed this train of thought and turned her mind to her encounter with Sally Robinson. She believed Sally's story, although it seemed that others were sceptical. Yet there was still the question of who had attempted to harm the young woman, and why? At one point she had wondered if the husband had been responsible, but that was before the women at the well had explained Adam Critchley's plan to leave his land to a legitimate male heir.

As long as Tom Robinson was married to Sally, he still had a chance to inherit. If she died, that was the end of that, so obviously he would not kill the girl, no matter how many pretty wenches he chose to dally with in front of his wife.

So far, Nesta had been inclined to believe in some link between all the attacks, probably stemming from the Critchley connection. But how did poor Blanche's disappearance fit into this pattern? She did not belong.

Oh, yes, she does, a little voice seemed to say. She's niece to Jane Pettapiece as was, and that lady is now wed to Adam Critchley! But that idea only produced a dead end.

Nesta sighed again. The likely answer seemed to be that some madman was at work, and the strange occurrences had no rhyme or reason to them. If that were the case, they would never get to the bottom of it all.

The next day Nesta set off for home, with several coins in a bag hidden in her apron pocket, and a large bundle of good leftovers for the family.

'It's been good having you here,' Tabby said, as she pressed the food on her erstwhile assistant. 'I hope you'll come again, to visit me, if not to help out.'

'That I will,' Nesta told her, 'and if you learn anything more about this wedding business, I trust you'll let me know. You're more likely to hear something, seeing as you live here at the manor.'

'Well, one thing I do know! Young Will isn't stopping here to help in the search for his missing bride. He and his friend set off back to Court at first light. When our girl came down to light the fires she heard them go.'

'I don't think much of that, then, do you?'

'Well, I don't know as I blame the boy.' Tabby came to his defence at once. 'A real let-down, is that. Him left standing at the church door, with all eyes on him, while she runs off to goodness knows where, rather than wed him.'

'The poor child has drowned herself,' Nesta reminded her.

'So they say! They haven't found the body yet. And that makes it worse, eh? How's he supposed to feel, thinking she'd rather die first?'

'He seemed cheerful enough last night. He and his friend were certainly making merry when I saw them last.'

'Ah, drowning their sorrows, I'll warrant.'

There was no more to be said, so Nesta made her farewells and took to the road.

It was a fine crisp morning and she made good speed on her way. The sound of hooves on the hard-baked road caused her to swing around, hoping it was someone she might flag down for a ride. She was glad when her old friend the carter drew his horse to a stop beside her.

'Hop up, mistress, if you want a ride. Drop you at the crossroads, shall I?'

'That would be a big help, though I trust

I'll fare better than the last time I rode with you!'

'What do you mean by that?' He looked so indignant that she had to laugh.

'Oh, I thought you might have heard. After I left you I came across Sam Fowler. He'd been set upon and left in the ditch. A good job I didn't pass the spot a bit sooner, or mebbe I'd have got the wallop over the head.'

'Oh, that was you, was it? I heard as somebody found the constable lying there pollaxed.'

'And I should have left him there,' Nesta went on, 'for now he's accused me of being the one who attacked him.'

The carter clucked his tongue at this, which caused the mare to break into a trot.

'Whoa there, Brownie! Wasn't talking to you! I s'pose you've heard the latest, mistress, about that young miss who run off from the church door!' He slapped his knee in glee. 'I wonder what become of her? Halfway back to her old home by now, mebbe.'

'That's not the latest,' Nesta informed him. 'They think she drowned herself. Some of her clothes were left lying on the riverbank yesterday.'

'Never! What's she want to go and do a thing like that for, eh? Any girl of mine tried a thing like that, and I'd give her what for!'

'You'd have to find her alive first, I think.' They exchanged sober glances.

When she reached home at last, there was nobody about. Jack and Jonno were probably in their workshop at this time of day, and she knew better than to interrupt them. Regrettably, her grandson was still at the stage when he welcomed any distraction from the work on hand. She peered in at Joan, who appeared to be dozing. No point in disturbing her, either. The poor soul was tormented by sleepless nights.

The sound of the latch being lifted on the house door brought her downstairs in a hurry, but it was only Kate, struggling inside with a bucket of water in each hand. Nesta noticed that the girl hadn't made much of a fist at the task because the buckets were only half-full, but she managed to bite back an acid comment. At least the child had shown willing, which was more than could have been said about her a month ago.

'Good morrow, Gramma!'

'You were at the well, I see. Did you hear anything of interest while you were there?'

Kate blushed. 'I wanted to hear what folk were saying about Blanche, but there was nothing new.'

'Were you at the church yesterday?'

'We all were. Dad, Jonno and me. I meant

to leave, but then Blanche came running out and that put the cat among the pigeons, I can tell you. I wonder what Will thought about that!'

'Not much, apparently. He went back to Court early this morning.'

'Oh!' Kate looked stricken for a moment, and then she lifted her chin. 'He's probably pleased she ran away. He no more wanted her than she wanted him.'

'You can't know that, child.' Nesta was being cruel to be kind. If Kate had any silly ideas about Will being free to return to her now, the sooner she was dispossessed of that notion, the better.

32

Nesta flinched and almost dropped the pot of broth she was holding as there came an almighty pounding on the door.

'All right, all right, I'm coming! Just keep your hair on!'

She flung the door open, half-expecting it to be the constable come to give her another earful, but the man who stood there was a wiry little fellow, holding his hat in his hands. She could tell from the ancient smock he wore that he was a shepherd by trade.

'Yes, what is it?'

'Is Jack Davies at home, mistress?'

'Who's asking?'

'Job Hervey, mistress. I've been sent to collect all the men I can find, and take them up to the pasture. I thought Master Davies should be here.'

'Who sent you? And why?'

'Constable, mistress. Seems they found a corpse under a hedge, up by long meadow, and they need men to bring 'un home on a gate. I got to get back to my beasts, so if you'll tell me where I can find Master Davies I'll be on my way.'

'He's in his workshop, out the back.'

Job tugged his forelock, and disappeared round the side of the house. Nesta carefully moved her pan to the side of the hob, and made for the door. So poor young Blanche had been found, then. No reason why she shouldn't be there to see what was going on. That Fowler wouldn't like it, but he could whistle. So far he hadn't done much to solve Hollyhill's crime wave so it was up to others to do what they might. And besides, she was sorry for the girl, who deserved a friendly face at the scene, even though she was long past knowing anything about it.

'Just going out for a bit,' she bawled up the stairs to Joan.

'Where to?' came the faint answer.

'Tell you later!' Nesta grabbed her shawl from its hook and stepped outside. Jack was already striding off, with the little shepherd close on his heels. Jonno hovered nearby, hopping from one foot to the other.

'What's the matter with you, boy?' Nesta demanded.

'I wanted to go and look at the corpse,' he muttered, 'but Dad says I have to stop here, in case a customer comes. Said to tell them he's had to go somewhere but he'll be back any minute.'

'So get on with it, then!'

'Aw, there won't be nobody. They'll all be going to see the corpse.'

'Never you mind that. You'll see plenty of dead folk before you get to my age. Now don't just stand there; do as you're bidden, child. Or do you want a clip round the ear to help you along?'

He glared at her, but obeyed with a show of annoyance. She began to trudge after the two men.

'No need for you to come, Mumma!' Jack called over his shoulder, when he realized she was following.

'Let me be the judge of that!' she puffed. Reluctantly he halted, to give her time to catch up.

'We'll be bringing the corpse home on a gate, Mumma. Takes strong men to do that. It'd be too much for the likes of you.'

'If it's young Blanche, I certainly should be there,' she countered. 'There are some things a man can't do.' She meant to straighten the girl's skirts, make sure the poor young thing's garments were arranged in a seemly fashion.

But when they reached their destination she saw that it wasn't Blanche at all, but a man who, on closer inspection, proved to be Tom Robinson.

'Let me take a look,' she insisted, elbowing her way in among the group of men. They made way for her, knowing that her store of medical knowledge, scanty though it might be, was more than any of those present possessed.

'No sign of a wound,' she murmured.

'Hit over the head,' the constable grunted.

'Mebbe, but then why's he lying on his back? You'd think he would've fallen forward. Could have been stabbed, though. Help me turn him over, somebody.'

Jack went down on his knees to help her. There was still no sign of any injury, and she said so.

'Could have died natural-like?' the shepherd ventured. 'Struck down with an apoplexy, mebbe. My old dad went that way, he did. Hale and hearty one minute, and dead as a doornail the next.'

'He's still breathing,' Nesta said suddenly. 'Best bring that gate and take him to our house. We can look after him properly there. All right with you, Jack?'

'What do you reckon is wrong with him, Mumma?'

'Drunk as a lord to start with,' she muttered, having come close to the fellow when she knelt down to examine him. 'Probably fell down last night and couldn't get up again, and then the cold got to him.'

'Ay, 'twas a hoar frost last night, right

enough,' the shepherd said.

The constable turned away in disgust. 'A common drunkard! And they fetched me all this way for nothing!'

'Don't make it sound as if you come all the way from Banbury,' the blacksmith grunted. 'We all know as you've been at my place, seeing as I give you a bed for the night. And they done the right thing. It could have been another murder, so far as we knew. It's your place to look into crimes. That's what you're paid to do, Sam Fowler!'

'I got better things to do than seeing to drunkards!' Red in the face, the constable turned his back on them and strode off.

'Well, come on, then, you lot!' Nesta urged. 'What are we waiting for? This chap could catch his death yet if we don't get him in the warm. And for goodness' sake don't let his arm dangle like that. It could catch on something going through the wood and he'd be hurt worse. Put it across his chest, do! Has none of you the sense you were born with?'

Grumbling almost inaudibly, but unwilling to make a sharp retort while her son was present, they did as they were told, and in due course they arrived back at the house.

'And let him down gently! Gently, I said! Down there, close to the fire, where he can thaw out.'

With a great deal of stretching and rubbing of backs they did as they were told, only leaving when she flapped a hand at them.

'I can manage now. Where's Kate? I want blankets. And you stay here with me, Jack Davies. What if he comes to and acts violent, not knowing where he is or what's going on? You just nip out and let Jonno know you're back, and then go up and tell Joan all's well. She'll have heard the noise and may be wondering.'

It was a while before Robinson came to his senses. 'Wha's the matter?' he groaned, struggling to sit up.

'You're all right, Master Robinson. Just lie there for now.'

'Aw, my head!'

'Nothing that time won't cure,' she told him.

He sank back on the rolled-up sack she'd used for a pillow.

'We found you lying under a hedge, Master Robinson. You must have been there all night. Have you any idea what happened to you?'

He gazed up at her, bleary-eyed. He shook his head, wincing.

'Had you been in the Bird in Hand? Looks to me like you had a few too many and when you were on your way home you stumbled and fell.'

He scratched his forehead. 'Dunno.'

'Find out anything?' Jack had come back into the room and was staring down at their visitor with some distaste.

'No big mystery, Jack. My guess is he'd been in the tavern and was on his way home when he tripped over and was too mazed to get up again. He's lucky someone came across him when they did, or that might have been the end of him.'

'See any bogles while you were going through the wood?' Jack laughed. 'Running away from them, were you?'

'Not bogles, ghosts.' His voice was still slurred but he seemed certain enough.

'Ghosts! Old Goody Clapton, was it, come back to haunt her poisoner?'

'Not the old gal. The young one.'

Nesta sat up at once. 'What young one was that, then?'

'The bride, o'course. Her as run off from the church.'

Nesta spoke urgently. 'Where did you see her? Where did she go? Think, man! This is important.'

'How do I know where they went?'

'What do you mean, they?'

'There was two of them, wasn't there?'

'Oh, the drunken fool was seeing double!' Jack said in disgust.

33

Nesta continued to replenish the fire, hoping that Robinson would soon recover and go on his way. She'd had little sympathy for the man once it had become apparent that he was drunk, not injured or ill.

When at last he stirred again she bent over him, pretending to be concerned.

'Is there anything I can get you, Master Robinson?'

'Eh? Whassat?'

'Would you like water to wash before you set out for home? You won't want your wife to worry if she sees you so unkempt.'

'Fat lot she'll care!' he grunted.

'Up you come, then!' She took him by the elbow to help him into a sitting position but he shook her off angrily.

'I don't want no help from you, mistress!'

'Mebbe we should have left you lying there, then, drunken sot that you are!'

'Here, don't you speak to me like that, woman, 'less you want to feel the back of my hand!'

'I speak as I find. And don't you dare threaten me, Tom Robinson, or you'll have my son to reckon with.'

'Huh!' He struggled to his feet. 'And don't think you'll get no more custom from me,' he muttered, as he lurched towards the door.

There's gratitude for you, Nesta said to herself, not that she cared. She'd heard far worse in her time, and she had no doubt that, if Sally Robinson was unfortunate enough to find herself *enceinte* to that boor again, her services would be required just the same. There was no other midwife for miles around, and when it came down to it the fellow wouldn't take chances, not if the long-awaited son was to be born alive.

As she worked, she mulled over in her mind what Robinson had said about seeing two girls the previous evening. Could one of them have been the missing bride? If so, who was the second girl? Or was it as Jack had suggested, and the fellow had been seeing double? Or his wits had been addled by the drink?

It was time to attend to Joan. The poor soul sweated a great deal, and it would do her no good to be left in damp sheets. Probably she would enjoy hearing Nesta's theories as a means of forgetting about her own troubles.

'Ay, he always was a surly beggar, that Tom Robinson.' Joan agreed.

'Makes you wonder why they ever married in the first place,' Nesta remarked. 'They don't seem suited at all.'

255

'Ah, well, she has expectations, doesn't she? That would have been all the attraction Tom needed. As for poor Sally, well, I suppose he was a good-looking devil in his young days, sort of black and dangerous, if you know what I mean. Oh,' she went on, blushing, 'not a patch on my Jack, of course, but there's no harm in looking, eh?'

'No harm at all. But what interests me is that he mentioned seeing two girls in the wood, just before he fell down.'

'Two girls! Who would they be, then?'

Nesta laughed. 'According to our Jack, it was probably the drink talking. But let's say it was true. One could be Blanche, of course, but who was the other?'

'Never! If she knows what's good for her, she'll be over the hills and far away.'

'Making for home, you think?'

Joan frowned. 'Every rabbit knows its own burrow, I s'pose, but she'd be a fool to go there. She must know she'd be dragged back and forced to do as she's told.'

'So you think she's still in the district, then?'

'I didn't say that. Truly, I don't know what to think. As for the girls Tom saw, they could be anybody. Most families hereabouts have a few daughters.'

'Where was Kate last night?' Nesta said suddenly.

'Kate? Why, snug in her bed, I s'pose, same as the rest of us. Why do you ask?'

'Don't take this amiss, dearie, but think about this for a moment. What if young Blanche is hiding somewhere nearby, and Kate is helping her?'

'Why on earth should she do any such thing?'

'Don't get up on your high horse, Joan. It's just that she must have a certain sympathy for the girl, that's all. She might help her, without considering the consequences.'

The hectic colour in Joan's face faded for a moment, leaving her complexion the colour of buttermilk. 'Ay, if she were found out, it'd be gaol for her, I daresay.'

'I didn't mean that. Blanche Bellefleur is no runaway servant. It could affect Jack's trade, though. I shouldn't like to cross Sir William at a time like this. But we have no reason to believe that Kate is helping Blanche. We don't even know if she was one of the girls whom Robinson saw. Just forget I said anything!'

But the more Nesta thought about it, the more her theory seemed to make sense. Young Will had broken Kate's heart. This could be her way of getting revenge. No doubt the lad would be made a laughing-stock once the word got out. His wealthy young bride had bolted from the church and gone to ground like a hunted fox, rather than bring herself to wed him. Furthermore, at the back of Kate's mind there could well be the faint hope that he would now turn back to her, which he could never do once he was lawfully married.

Nesta reminded herself that this was mere supposition. She must be most careful not to alert Kate to the way the wind was blowing. Instead, she would have to watch carefully to see where the girl went by day or by night. Was any food missing? Hard to know, with young Jonno always ready to eat like a starving horse. He'd had his knuckles rapped more than once when she'd caught him helping himself in the larder.

The rumble of wheels and the shrill neighing of a horse drew her attention. She went to the window to see who the visitor was. It was a lady, heavily muffled in a fine cloak. Nesta's hand went to her mouth. She flew around the room, tidying up the mess left by Tom Robinson. There was nothing she could do about the pallet but she hastily folded the blankets and bundled them out of sight. A knock came at the door.

'Why, Mistress Pettapiece, what brings you here?'

'Mistress Critchley now,' the woman

reminded her, as she brushed past Nesta on her way inside.

'Of course! Of course! I do beg your pardon.'

Jane flung off her cloak and handed it to Nesta. Exactly as if I was her servant! Nesta reported to Joan in some indignation, but that was later. For now, she accepted it meekly and hung it on a spare hook. The weight of it pulled the hook from the wall and the cloak fell to the floor. Red-faced, Nesta put it on the table, first feeling the wood with her hand to make sure there were no spills or crumbs remaining.

Jane Critchley, meanwhile, had pulled a chair closer to the fire and sat down, without so much as a by-your-leave. Trust the gentry! They thought they were entitled to behave as they liked! Nesta felt her temper rising, but curiosity triumphed and she, too, sat down beside the fire.

'What news of young Blanche?' she asked, boldly.

'I wonder you dared ask,' Joan was to say later.

'But them as don't ask don't get told,' Nesta countered.

Mistress Critchley's eyes flashed in temper. 'Blanche? No news at all, the foolish wench.'

'I expect she's gone back to her home, then.'

'Oh, no, it's the first place we looked.'

'Very worrying for you, I'm sure.'

'I doubt she's come to grief, or she'd have been found by now. Adam — my husband — believes that somebody has taken her in.'

'Well, mistress, I hope you don't think we're hiding her here!' Nesta said, trying to instil more indignation into her voice than she felt.

'What? No, of course not! This is nothing to do with the silly girl! My husband has sent men out to search for her, and there's nothing more I can do. No, I've come to speak to you about something quite different.'

Nesta waited. The woman looked slightly embarrassed.

'I believe . . . that is, I'm hoping . . . ' Her voice broke off. Nesta knew at once what this was about.

'That you may be *enceinte*?'

Mistress Critchley nodded.

'But surely it's too soon to tell, mistress. You'd need to have missed your courses at least two months to be certain.'

'I understand that, but still, it is possible, isn't it?'

'Of course, but what do you want of me?' Surely to goodness the woman wasn't foolish enough to ask for some sort of spell to make her hopes come true? It wouldn't be the first time that Nesta had been approached for such a thing, but spells and incantations smacked of witchcraft.

'I'd like to have you come to stay in the house for a time,' Jane Critchley said. 'Maybe you thought I was barren, but I did become *enceinte* by my former husbands, only to miscarry in the early weeks. I want to avoid that now. Please say you'll come, Mistress Davies. Time is running out for me, at my age.'

Nesta hesitated. At this stage she could do nothing more for the poor woman than any attentive maid or stepdaughter could do, but she relished the chance to see at first hand what was going on in the Critchley household.

'Very well, I'll come!' she announced.

34

Jonno was the only member of the family who expressed no interest in Nesta's plans. He was dimly aware that his grandmother went into other people's houses 'to help women' and although he had only a vague idea of what this meant, he readily accepted the fact that this was more of the same.

His father pulled a face, asking why she needed to attend Mistress Critchley at this juncture, when she quite obviously wasn't near her time, but when Nesta told him it was 'women's problems' he dissociated himself at once, not caring to hear more.

'What are you up to, Mumma?' Joan asked, giggling. 'I've lost babes before their time myself, and there's nought to be done about that! What does Mistress Critchley think you can do for her, if indeed she is *enceinte*?'

'It's not what she wants, but what I may be able to do for her, Joan, and that's keep her alive!'

Joan's expression sobered. 'You mean try to keep her from bleeding to death if the worst happens?'

'That, and other things.' Nesta turned to

her granddaughter. 'And I trust I can leave you in charge this time, gal? No running off around the countryside instead of attending to your duties at home?'

'It's the middle of winter, Gramma!'

'Ay, so it is, and that makes me wonder what that poor gal is doing, out there all alone, with never a roof over her head.'

'What gal? Do you mean Blanche?'

'Who else? She's never returned home, and she's not been found dead. Where else would she be, eh? What would you do if you'd had to run off, Kate? You tell me that.'

'I'd go to some big place, like Oxford, say, and get me a job in some household where nobody knows me.'

Nesta's eyes narrowed. 'Is that what's become of Blanche? Do you know something the rest of us don't?'

'Of course not, Gramma.'

'Then why say what you did?'

'Because you asked me what I'd do, and I told you.'

Nesta frowned at Kate, but when the girl gazed back innocently she was forced to accept that the girl genuinely had no idea of Blanche's whereabouts. She spent the next half hour explaining what needed to be done while she was absent. Under her guidance Kate had learned to cook a number of simple dishes, as well as food to tempt her mother's appetite, and she should be able to cope.

'And don't let that brother of yours eat too many sweet things,' she finished. 'We'll need what honey we have as the winter wears on, especially if any of you fall ill.'

Nesta was soon settled in at the Critchley house. Having expected to receive the rough side of his tongue, and told there was no necessity for her presence, she was pleasantly surprised when Adam greeted her kindly.

'Anything you can do for my lady's comfort will earn my gratitude,' he told her, smiling. 'And if at the end of her travail she presents me with a fine son, you will be well rewarded, Mistress Davies.'

Nesta smiled and nodded in return, but inwardly she was alarmed. His wife must have already told him that she was with child, although that was by no means certain. Many a slip twixt cup and lip, she reminded herself. He would not be pleased if no son resulted from all this care and attention. And who would get the blame then? His poor wife, certainly, but Nesta would not escape his wrath. Could it be that Jane Critchley had invited her here to use as a scapegoat, if she failed to produce the longed-for heir? What else did she expect Nesta to do, unless she was extremely naive?

There was little anyone could do if a woman miscarried. Sometimes staying in bed could help, but that didn't always provide the desired result. Once the womb had lost its hold on the child nothing on earth could prevent what the body had set in motion. Jane Critchley must know that, since she had already lost babes in the early stages.

Sometimes Nesta wondered what God was up to. The priests were fond of saying that he was a mystery, and never was a truer word spoken. She had seen it all before. Women who were worn out with childbearing continued to bring babes to term, children they could hardly afford to feed and clothe, while others, who would have given almost anything for a living child, were defeated time and again.

Adam Critchley was strutting about like a turkey-cock. Nesta intercepted a few sly glances, directed at his son-in-law, Peter Dilley. Dilley himself grew glummer by the day, as Adam couldn't fail to notice.

One morning, when Adam could contain himself no longer, matters came to a head. 'Cheer up, lad!' he bellowed, delivering a hard slap to Dilley's dejected back. 'Go and pay attention to your wife, and see if you cannot get yourself an heir. Look at me, a grandfather. Yet I'm able to beget more children, while what do you have to show for years of marriage? Your nose will soon be out of joint, my lad, when my wife presents me with the son she's carrying.'

'He ain't born yet,' Dilley growled, 'and mebbe never will be. I'll see my day with you, Adam Critchley, make no mistake about that!'

'A cockerel may crow on a dunghill,' Adam countered, somewhat obscurely, Nesta felt. For the first time she experienced a thrill of fear. The situation was beginning to fester, like a wound gone bad, and it was only a matter of time before it became dangerous. She knew nothing of the law of inheritance, but surely Adam could change his will if he so chose? After all, the land was his to do as he liked with.

What if Dilley's anger boiled over and he contrived to murder his father-in-law? She chided herself for wild thinking. That would get the man nowhere. Even if he could manage it without getting caught, there was still Jane's babe, which could be a boy. Failing that, Sally Robinson had proved her worth as a breeder; she was likely to have another child before her sister produced her first.

Nesta was so lost in her thoughts that she failed to hear Jane coming up behind her until the woman spoke.

'You near made me jump out of my skin!' she blurted, holding a hand to her heaving bosom. Thoughts of murder had set her nerves on edge.

'Perhaps you'd like me to walk about with a bell in my hand, like a leper!' Jane retorted. 'Heavens, you're jumpy as a cat!'

Nesta said nothing. How could she explain what was on her mind without getting the woman all upset?

'I want to know when I shall be certain about the babe,' Jane went on. 'Am I *enceinte*, or am I not?'

'You have some of the signs,' Nesta answered cautiously, 'but it's early days as yet. In any case, haven't you told Master Critchley that you do expect his child? Why else would he have hired me to come here?'

'I only said I might be. He was the one who jumped to a conclusion.'

'Oh, yes? And what if you are wrong, mistress?'

'How so? My courses have not returned.'

Nesta sniffed. 'Let me tell you something, mistress. There are times when great worry can stop a woman's courses. I've known it to happen. But then, when the problem is resolved, or the grief overcome, everything returns to normal. Have you thought that might be the case with you?'

Jane's blank look said it all. Nesta wanted to shake her.

'Your niece has gone missing, woman, and may be dead for all we know! That's enough to upset anyone, is it not?'

'Oh, that!'

'I can see that doesn't worry you overmuch, mistress.' Nesta was too disgusted by the woman's lack of concern to bridle her tongue.

Jane shrugged. 'Of course I care, Mistress Davies, but what do you expect me to do about it? My husband has sent some of his labourers to search for the silly wench, and I know that Sir William has done the same. A watch is being kept on her old home, in case she tries to go back there. We have done all we can. Now I have our own child to think of. Should I not care for him?'

'Of course you should,' Nesta sighed. 'I spoke out of turn. All I can advise you to do is to possess your soul in patience. When the time is ripe we shall see the signs, and know the truth, one way or the other.'

For her part she couldn't wait until the woman was safely carrying a child and she could leave them all to their own devices. She was sorry that she'd come here in the first place. Despite all her nosing around she'd learned nothing of interest.

The next day she was surveying the linen press, more from the need of something to do than anything else, when she heard a blood-curdling scream coming from the hall, followed by a series of shouts. Moving as fast as her legs would carry her she arrived to find Jane Critchley sprawled on the stone flag floor, surrounded by a several gaping onlookers.

'Out of my way and let me see what's going on,' she insisted, feeling her heart in her mouth. Apparently the Hollyhill murderer had struck again.

35

Kate arrived at the market with a mental list of items she needed to buy. Because her father was a cordwainer rather than a farmer they could not produce all the food they needed, although they did have a large vegetable garden. In past years Joan had put away many dried or salted items for winter, but this year, because of her illness, she'd been able to do very little.

Kate felt guilty enough, for Gramma had made it plain that she had failed in her duty to the family. 'A great girl of fifteen summers ought be able to do better than this, when her poor mother is so badly in need of help,' Nesta was fond of saying. Too fond, in Kate's estimation! She loved the outdoors, and not only toiled in the garden, and cared for the hens, but she also scoured the countryside, gathering fruits in season. Surely all that was of greater importance than scrubbing floors and washing linen?

Going to market was a treat, because she was in the open air. She did wish that the family possessed a horse, though. Going to market and back was a bit too far to walk.

She had said as much to her father, who laughed.

'And where would we keep a horse, child? Or feed it, for that matter?'

'Farmer Benson would let us keep it in his field, Dad, and that would take care of the feeding problem as well.'

'Is that so? Then you double the size of your garden so you have vegetables to sell, and you learn to bake as well as your Gramma does, and then I'll think about it.' He went off, chuckling as if someone had told him a good joke. So here was Kate, travelling by Shanks's pony, as always.

'Not often we see you here, Kate Davies!'

Kate's heart sank. Everywhere she went these days her footsteps seemed to be dogged by Fanny Cropwell.

'Not much time for gadding about. My mother is ailing.'

'So I've heard. That's why your Gramma come, in't it? To look after the family, like.'

'Ay, but she's not able to come to market today, so I've got the job.'

'That's right! She's at old Adam Critchley's, eh, looking after the new bride!' She laughed unpleasantly.

'How do you know that?'

'Not much happens round here without me knowing about it.'

For some reason this rubbed Kate up the wrong way and she felt the need to retaliate. 'If you're so clever, tell me what's become of that Blanche Bellefleur, then.'

'Ah, there's a lot of folks would like to know that, most of all that lover of yours.'

'I don't know what you mean!'

'Ah, but I'm sure you do. Sweet on him, aren't you? And to think he threw you over for that whey-faced miss, all because she's got a great dowry, and you ain't.'

'He did nothing of the sort!' Kate suppressed a desire to smack the smug look off the other girl's face.

'Mebbe there's a chance for you again, now she's dead and gone,' Fanny went on. 'Leastways, I 'spect you think so.'

'Nobody knows if she's dead. They haven't found the body, have they?'

'Haven't you heard? They found her mantle, all folded up neat-like, and her fancy little shoes perched on top. On the riverbank, they were, right where she must have gone in.'

'And mebbe she left them there on purpose, to put people off the scent.'

'Oh, yes? And what's she doing in the middle of winter, then, in a flimsy wedding dress and barefoot? She'll be lying somewhere dead by now, you mark my words.'

Kate fingered a knot of blue ribbon, wishing she had the money to buy it for herself. It would look well on her red hair, although her mother always said that green was a better match. The stallholder looked on idly. She had been in business long enough to be able to distinguish prospective buyers from mere dawdlers. The trick now was to make sure the customer didn't transfer it to a pocket or basket, when her attention was distracted. That Fanny Cropwell, now, she was a sly one, and merited watching.

'That's Peter Dilley over there,' Fanny went on, pointing. 'Him that's married to one of the Critchley girls. That's his brother-in-law with him.'

'I know Tom Robinson,' Kate said loftily. 'I was there when his last little girl was born.'

'Oh, him! You don't want to have nothing to do with him, Kate Davies!'

'Of course not. He's a married man.'

'Huh, that won't stop him! Famous for it, he is. Dallying with some poor girl and then leaving her in the lurch when it suits him. Just like you and that Will Mowbray.'

'You don't know what you're talking about.'

'Don't I? Let me give you a piece of advice for nothing, then. In this world a girl has to watch out for herself. There's always someone waiting to drag her down. Well, it's time

273

somebody took a stand, see? Get them before they get you, and if that ain't likely, then make sure you get your revenge after.'

Kate shuddered. The girl sounded positively mad. Best not to get on the wrong side of her. 'I'll remember what you've said,' she responded. Mumma was fond of saying that 'a soft answer turneth away wrath', a maxim which seemed to fit the case here. Fanny nodded, apparently satisfied.

'I'm going to speak to Tom Robinson,' Kate said. 'Mebbe he'll give me a ride home; save me a walk, carrying all this heavy stuff.'

Tom agreed readily enough, saying it would be a pleasure to ride with such a pretty maiden, and Kate realized too late that he had not brought his cart, as she had assumed, but had travelled on horseback. She tried to retract her suggestion, but he would have none of it.

Later, riding pillion, she found that she had nothing to fear. From what Fanny had said, she half-expected the man to make some lewd suggestion and she was prepared to slide down from her perch and run off, but nothing untoward happened. He said very little as his horse plodded along, and when they came to the crossroads and he assisted her to get down from the great beast, he behaved in a gentlemanly manner. She thanked him prettily and marched away in the direction of home, not looking back to see if he was staring after her.

Still feeling a little unsettled she mentioned this encounter to her mother.

'Oh, he's all right, really,' Joan said. 'I've known him since we were children. He's inclined to be glum at times, but there's no harm in him. Your grandmother doesn't have much time for the man, seeing as he's so gruff with his wife, but you can't blame him for hoping for a son.'

'Why do people make such a fuss about getting boys?' Kate asked crossly. 'Aren't daughters just as good?'

'Of course they are, sweeting; better, if the truth be known, although you mustn't tell your brother that! I only meant that so much hangs on the matter in Tom Robinson's case, with his father-in-law having made such a silly decision regarding his estate. Still, it may not matter now, when Adam has married again. His new bride may give him all the sons his heart desires, and then Tom's nose will be out of joint.'

Kate thought this highly unlikely, given the advanced age, as she saw it, of both Adam Critchley and his new wife.

'What do you know of Frances Cropwell, Mumma?'

'Fanny? Oh, a strange girl, I must admit. I'm not sure where she hailed from in the beginning; she wasn't born in Hollyhill. When her parents died she came to live with her mother's uncle on the edge of the wood, and a miserable life she must have had of it. He was a farm labourer in his working days, but that was long ago. Nobody has seen him about for years, not since he broke a leg falling on the ice one winter. I should imagine he's still there, for I doubt he could get about much.'

'So Fanny has to look after him?'

'If he's still in the flesh, yes.'

'No wonder she's so odd, then. She's always making sly remarks, as if she knows something nobody else does.'

Joan leaned forward, patting her daughter on the hand. 'Poor gal. It's probably to make herself feel better. She can't have much else to boast about.'

'She seems sure that Blanche is drowned, Mumma.'

'Does she? I'm afraid she may be right. It's been too long since she ran from the church, and there's been never a sight of her, unless you count what Tom Robinson said, about seeing two of her.' Joan laughed gently. 'Your grandmother believes that was all nonsense, though. That was the demons of drink talking. No doubt she's right.'

There was a crash downstairs as someone burst through the door. Kate jumped, thoroughly worked up from her experiences of the day.

'That'll be Jonno,' Joan remarked. 'One of these days we'll teach him to come in quietly, not like a bull at a gate, letting the door swing to behind him.' Moments later she was proved right, as Jonno's plaintive voice wafted up the stairs.

'Mumma? Is there anything to eat? I'm hungry!'

36

'Out of my way!' Nesta snapped, not caring if she sounded rude. The servants here seemed to resent her and ever since her arrival they had been slow to respond to any request she might make. One of them, a ruddy-faced maid, had dared to mutter something to the effect that Nesta was 'only a servant like us' which had greatly annoyed her. Now, however, they deferred to her as being the only person with some medical knowledge, however scant.

She sank to her knees beside Jane, trying to suppress a groan as her muscles protested strongly. Getting down was one thing; getting up again was quite another! But she would worry about that when the time came.

'Mistress Critchley! Can you hear me?' There was no reply. Not dead yet, heaven be praised, she thought, noting the rhythmic rising and falling of the woman's bosom.

'Mistress Critchley! Try to answer me, please!' Nesta was aware of the group of onlookers pressing ever closer, as they tried to see what was happening. 'Step back, all of you! Give the poor soul room to breathe, do!'

'She must be gone,' she heard someone mutter. 'Stands to reason, falling down all that way. Like as not her neck is broke!'

Jane's eyelids fluttered. 'Come on, mistress! Wake up, so I can see what's wrong with you!'

'Fell down,' she whispered.

'Yes, yes, I can see that! Can you move your legs?' Nesta had a vague idea that this had something to do with whether the back was broken or not. She felt it important to sound confident, in order to convince the onlookers that she possessed more knowledge than she actually did. She was relieved when Jane managed to move her toes.

'Back hurts' Jane moaned now.

'I daresay it does. We'll get you to your chamber and you'll soon be more comfortable. Now, then, you lot! Fetch a good strong pallet of some sort. Not a worn one, half-stuffed, mind! We're going to carry Mistress Critchley on it, and we don't want it giving way at the wrong moment.'

There was a shuffling of feet. 'Well, don't just stand there! Go!'

When the pallet came Nesta directed six of them to lift Jane onto it. 'Take care, now! And I'll take her head.'

They were not out of the woods yet. 'That old pallet's not much use,' a manservant complained. 'A gate is what we want,

279

mistress! Always bring bodies home on a gate, we do, a good strong 'un as won't bend.'

'Do you see a gate here?' Nesta barked. 'Just do as I say, or we'll be here all day. Steady, now. One, two, three!'

Moaning in fear, Jane was deposited on her bed. When they were alone Nesta managed to remove her gown. 'Did you tumble all the way from the top, mistress?'

'I'm not sure. I can't remember.'

'Never mind that now. Where do you hurt? Is there any cramping in your belly? No? Then you should be all right in time. You'll have a few bruises, but nothing that won't mend.'

Later, when Nesta went to the kitchen to ask for hot water to bathe her patient, she found the servants gathered together, nudging each other and whispering.

'Your mistress will be all right,' she announced. 'No harm done that I can see, at least, not to the body.'

'What do you mean?' the cook demanded. 'Has she lost her wits, then?'

'No, no, just her memory. She has no idea what caused her to fall. The first thing she remembers is opening her eyes to see me looking at her.' This was an exaggeration, of course, but if somebody had pushed Jane it would be just as well if that someone felt safe from discovery.

'But she will remember, in time?'

'I doubt it. People seldom do.' Again, this was an overstatement of the facts. Nesta picked up the bucket and returned to her patient. When she reached the bedchamber she was surprised to find Sally Robinson seated beside the bed.

'Is she unconscious?' the girl asked, her eyes wide and troubled. 'I spoke to her, but she doesn't reply.'

'Just sleeping,' Nesta told her, looking at Jane with a practised eye. 'I gave her something to soothe the pain. Sleep is the best thing for her now. What are you doing here, Mistress Robinson?'

'It's such a fine day I thought we'd come over to make a visit. The baby is teething and fretful, and every time she cries it sets young Catherine off as well. The sway of the wagon seems to calm both of them, so here we are.'

'Where are they now, then? I don't hear them about.'

'Polly has them outside. We heard the commotion when my stepmother fell, and we didn't want the children to be frightened. What do you think happened to her?'

'Tripped over the hem of her gown, I shouldn't wonder. Would you mind sitting with her for a while longer? I shan't be far away, but there is something I have to do.'

Sally nodded, and Nesta hastened away. The stairs leading to the gallery were steep enough, yet a woman of Jane's age should not have fallen so easily. Had she perhaps fainted? If she was indeed with child that was not impossible. Many women did feel sick or dizzy in the early stages.

Nesta studied the staircase carefully. If Jane had not been pushed, could she have tripped over a string, cunningly placed by someone wishing to do her harm? But no, there was no such thing there, nor was there any nail or hook in an appropriate place, where a string could have been placed.

Climbing the stairs at a crouch, almost on her hands and knees, she ran her hand carefully along the treads, until she came to one which felt greasy. Raising her hand to her nose, she gave a great sniff, before gingerly tasting the substance with her tongue. Mutton fat? But how could it have come there? Candles were made of tallow, of course, but this was of a much softer consistency, almost as if it had been rendered down. Frowning, she straightened up and returned to her patient.

'How is she, Mistress Robinson?'

'She hasn't moved since you left, Mistress Davies.'

'Thank you for staying. I mustn't keep you

any longer. I expect you want to get back to your children now. Or is your husband helping the girl to keep an eye on the babes?'

'Tom?' Sally laughed at the thought. 'That's women's work, that is, or so he would say! No, he's gone to market with Peter Dilley.'

When Sally had left, Nesta picked up the soft shoes which Jane liked to wear in the house. There was a faint smear on the sole of one, and a faint scent which might or might not have been the odour of mutton fat.

Why would someone have been carrying mutton fat up to the gallery? It seemed an unlikely thing to do. It was more likely that someone had smeared the step with it deliberately, so that Jane would lose her footing. People seldom went up to the gallery, which was only used when musicians were present to entertain the family and guests. Christmas was coming, a time when wandering minstrels arrived at country houses, hoping for a meal and a bed and perhaps a few coins, in exchange for their skills.

But in the meantime, what was to say that Jane would go up the gallery at all? And if the stair had been greased to trap somebody, what guarantee was there that Jane was the intended victim? It might equally be that it was meant for one of the maids. Had one of the girls been told to go to clean the gallery, in preparation for Christmas? And did somebody in the household carry a grudge against her, vowing to pay her back for some slight or misdeed? Such things did happen among servants, all cooped up together in a house and jealous of their relative positions.

She would have to ask about that. But when she spoke to Anne Dilley, that lady shook her head. 'I can't think why you want to know about a thing like that, when you're here to nurse my stepmother. But since you ask, no, I've sent nobody up to the gallery at all. When the time comes a quick flick with a duster will be all that's needed.'

'Then I wonder why Mistress Critchley went up there at all?'

Anne shrugged. 'Nothing better to do, I suppose. Wanted to see what the hall looked like from up above.'

Having settled that, Nesta returned to her earlier theory that someone had greased the stair in the hope of Mistress Critchley coming to grief. But who? According to Sally, both Tom Robinson and Peter Dilley had been away all day. They could not have been responsible, unless, of course, the grease had been there for more than a day.

Surely none of the servants would have reason to harm their new mistress? As for

Adam Critchley, he had every reason for wanting Jane to remain in good health. He had even brought Nesta here for that reason. *And so far I haven't done a very good job of protecting her*, she thought soberly.

What about Anne Dilley, then? That was a possibility. Until now she had been mistress in her father's house, but now she had been ousted by Jane Pettapiece. And Anne stood to lose far more, if Jane should give birth to a living son.

37

Nesta was torn two ways. On the one hand she was determined to get home for Christmas, 'home' meaning Jack's house; on the other she was afraid to leave Jane Critchley without any protection.

Christmas was a time for being together with family, attending church, enjoying special delicacies at table, and lazing around a roaring fire, with no work to go to. Perhaps Joan might be well enough to come downstairs for an hour or two. If she wasn't strong enough to sit in a chair she could at least lie on a pallet in the warmth. Nesta thought sadly that her daughter-in-law would not see another Christmas, so memories of this one would have to suffice for the rest of their lives.

Jane Critchley, though! Heaven forbid that anything should happen to her. In the normal run of things she should have many Christmases to come. And what of Nesta herself? If she left the house and something happened to her patient, she would get the blame. She would never hear the last of it from the bereaved husband. Come to that, she would find it hard to forgive herself.

Weighing everything up, however, she decided that her own family must come first. How to tell the Critchleys, though; there was the rub. As it happened, she need not have worried.

'We're having a houseful of company over the season,' Jane told her, eyes sparkling. 'Margery, my husband's sister, among others, and her boy, Philip. I'll be waited on hand and foot, so I shan't need you. Doubtless you'll want to spend Christmas with your own folk?'

Perversely, Nesta was annoyed. All that fretting, and now to be told she was unwanted! Some people! she fumed.

'I was expecting to spend the twelve days here,' she lied, wanting to rub it in.

'Oh, dear, were you? Well, I expect we can find a corner for you somewhere, if you really want to stay.'

'Never mind. I should be with the family, I suppose, especially when my poor Joan is so low.'

'Yes, yes, of course. And I'll tell the cook to make you up a nice parcel of bits and pieces. How will that be?'

It was on the tip of Nesta's tongue to say that they didn't need charity, her son being well set up in his own trade, but she managed to swallow her pride. She hadn't had time to prepare any special food before being summoned here, and since all the catering was left to Kate, there would be slim pickings.

'A nice roast chicken?' Jane coaxed.

'That would be very nice, I'm sure.' As indeed it would. Such luxury! It was many a long year since Nesta had tasted chicken.

'I'll stay until Mistress Dawes arrives,' she decided. 'When I've given her my instructions, then I'll be off.'

'I'm much better now, you know, thanks to your ministrations.'

'Someone has to apply the ointment to your poor back. You can't reach round there by yourself. Besides, I want her to keep a close eye on you. We can't have any more accidents, can we? Think of the babe.'

'I suppose you're right, but I did so want to make this a wonderful Christmas for everyone. I'm so newly come to this house, I wanted to show my husband what a good housewife I am.'

'I'm sure Mistress Dilley will be able to cope very well, and as for Master Critchley, wouldn't a fine son be the best gift of all?'

And so it was that on the day before Christmas Eve Nesta was bowled along in the equipage owned by her friend, the carter. He never had much to say for himself, but he was a comfortable sort of person to be with, and they sat in companionable silence for most of the way.

'God rest you merry!' she called, as she alighted at the crossroads.

'Wassail!' He raised his battered hat in salute as his mare ambled forward.

She had almost reached the spot where the constable had been struck down, when she felt the hairs prickle up on the back of her neck. She stopped uncertainly.

'Who's there? Oh, it's you, Fanny Cropwell. You did give me a fright.'

'Good morrow, Mistress Davies.' For once the girl spoke quietly, with none of her usual smug looks and foolish remarks. 'Will you come with me, Mistress Davies? It's my uncle. He's dead, I think. Someone must lay him out, but I'm afraid to touch him.'

'The dead can't hurt you, child. What did he die of, then?'

'I don't know. He just dozed off in his chair, and when I went to wake him with his bowl of broth, I saw that he was gone.'

'Ah, well, it comes to us all, and he must have been quite old, surely? Not such a bad way to leave this world, after all.'

'But can you come, and do what has to be done?'

'I suppose I might, but first I must go

home and let them know. You come along with me, gal. We'll make better speed if I have help carrying these bundles.'

Nesta had a strange feeling about this. Of course she wasn't afraid to see a dead man; she had laid out plenty in her day. No, it was the idea of going off through the wood to some unknown place, with nobody knowing where she had gone, or why. She decided that it was probably Jane Critchley's 'accident' which had made her jittery.

'Mumma!' Jack Davies threw the door open wide, pleasure showing in his handsome face. 'Come in, come in! Sit by the fire, and Kate shall fetch you a tankard of ale.'

'I haven't come to stay, at the moment.' Nesta indicated Fanny, who was hovering near the garden gate. 'It seems that Master Cropwell has passed away, and I'm needed to lay him out.'

'Jackson, his name is,' Fanny corrected, coming forward. 'He was my mother's uncle, not mine.'

'You've time for a bite and sup,' Jack said gently. 'Master Jackson won't mind waiting. For the love of heaven come inside so I can shut this door. We're letting all the cold air in.'

Kate and Fanny stared at each other warily. Fanny was the first to lower her eyes, and

Kate relaxed visibly. Nesta noted the interchange, but said nothing. Time enough to question her granddaughter when she returned from her duties. Having gulped down her drink, and chewed the slice of stale bread that went with it, she bustled about gathering the old rags she would need in her task.

'I suppose you've got an old sheet we can use as a shroud?' she asked Fanny. The poor old man could not go to his grave without a shroud, yet she balked at the idea of sacrificing a good sheet from their own meagre supply. Poor Joan needed frequent changes of linen, and at this time of year it was hard to get things properly dry. Put them on the line and they immediately grew stiff and hard.

'Have you notified the priest?' she asked, as they were partway through the wood, Fanny sure-footed from her knowledge of the path, and Nesta stumbling along in her wake.

'No, I never thought. I mean, he was gone when I found him, so what could the priest do for him?'

'That's not for you to say, gal. Your uncle isn't the first to die sudden, nor is he likely to be the last. The priests must have something they can do in such cases, even if the poor soul died unshriven. Now, as soon as we get to the house, and you've shown me where things are, you must come back and find Father Wagstaffe. Do you hear me?'

Nesta had been expecting a modest dwelling, perhaps a tumbledown cottage, but the hovel to which Fanny led her to was a shock. It must once have been a woodsman's shelter, or some such thing, but now it was more like something an outlaw might take refuge in, for want of anything better. In the dying light it was just possible to make out the roof, where weeds of all descriptions were growing out of the thatch. Nesta felt a sudden pity for this girl, who was forced to live here. No wonder she wandered the countryside so much, if this was all she had to come home to.

'Let's get inside, then,' she said briskly, 'and you can show me what's what. Then I can get started.'

The water in the chipped basin was cold, but poor old Jackson wouldn't care. The candle flickered once or twice and went out, leaving Nesta in the dark. She swore softly.

'Stay where you are, mistress, and I'll bring a light,' a soft voice said.

Nesta, who had believed herself to be alone with the dead, spun around, puzzled, peering into the shadows. 'Who is it? Who's there?'

The speaker bent over the smouldering

fire, lighting a taper which she brought to the candle. As the room came into focus again Nesta was able to make out the features of a slender young girl.

'Blanche Bellefleur, by all that's holy! Can that be you, or are you a ghost, sent to plague me?'

'Yes, 'tis I,' the girl said with a sigh, coming into the light.

38

Darkness came early at the time of the winter solstice. Knowing the track out of the wood like the back of her hand, Fanny reached the priest's house without difficulty. After hammering on the door she waited to be admitted but it was some time before anyone came. Just as she raised her fist to try again, a man's voice came from behind the heavy wood.

'Who is it? What do you want?'

'I thought priests were supposed to help people,' she muttered, under her breath. Then, more loudly, 'There's been a death. Will you come?'

The door opened slowly. Father Wagstaffe frowned down at her. 'Who are you? I don't recall seeing you at Mass.'

'No, well . . . ' She had no answer to that. 'It's my uncle that's died. Master Jackson.'

'Are you sure he's gone, girl?' No point setting out to hear the man's confession, if he was already departed. 'How did he come to die?'

Fanny shrugged. 'I dunno. I went to feed him his broth and he didn't answer me. Sometimes he used to doze off. I took him by the shoulder and he sort of fell sideways. That's when I knew he was a gone 'un.'

'Had he been ailing?'

'Not so's you'd notice. Old as the hills, he was. I reckon 'twas his time to go.'

'And you've left the corpse alone, with nobody to watch by him?'

'Mistress Davies is there to put him to rights. She told me to come to you.'

A large snowflake settled on the sleeve of the priest's black soutane. More fell damply on Fanny's hair.

'It looks as if this is settling in for the night,' the priest said, gazing up at the sky. 'Where did your uncle dwell, child?'

'At Joby's well, Feyther.'

'Ah.' He had only a vague idea of where the place was. Somewhere in the depths of the wood. Long before he had come to Hollyhill there had been a murder there. The old people still talked of the place, saying it was haunted. The present inhabitant — now dead, it appeared — had never come to Mass. Had the man even been baptized? That would need looking into. He came to a decision.

'Seems to me the poor man can wait till morning. If I send the sexton out with a cart to bring the corpse in he may be stranded overnight.' He glanced at Fanny, who by now was shivering in the evening air. 'Nor should you return this night. Do you know where Mistress Glover lives? Go there. Say I sent you. She'll take you in.'

He shut the door in Fanny's face. 'Well!' she grumbled. 'Fat lot of good that was, coming to you!' She debated whether to make her way home, but the thought of sharing the crowded little room with the dead man was daunting. The priest wasn't the only one who had heard tales of hauntings. For all she knew, the murdered person might have come for her uncle, or at least to warn him of approaching death.

The sexton's wife gave her a better welcome, removing the girl's thin cloak and leading her to the blazing fire. 'Of course you must stay with us, if you've no objection to a pallet in front of the fire, gal? And your uncle is gone, you say, poor wight? Don't tell me the priest wants to send my man out in this, to bring him in? By the looks of that sky we're in for a good dose of snow.'

Rob Glover grunted when his wife repeated her remarks to him. 'Just as well Feyther had enough sense to say leave it till tomorrer. I ain't taking the hoss out in this. Not fit for man or beast, and going to get wuss afore it gets better. And if it sets hard, how am I going to dig the grave? You tell me that! Hard as iron, that ground will be.'

Fanny let the talk flow over her. It was enough that she had shelter for the night, and a hot meal to come. Tomorrow could take care of itself. Much later, when she was out of earshot, the Glovers, being snug in their beds, held a whispered conversation.

'Mebbe the poor man won't be buried in the churchyard at all,' Mary Glover suggested. 'Not shriven, poor man, so dying in his sins. And never set foot in the church, so far as I can remember.'

'That'll be up to Feyther Wagstaffe to say.'

'But what I meant was, mebbe you won't have to dig his grave after all?'

'Gotta be buried somewhere, gal, even it in't in holy ground. Who's to dig it, if not me? It's not as if the man has sons of his own to look after it. Can't leave him lying in his cottage till doomsday, specially not when that little gal that brought the news has nowhere else to go.'

'Say he's buried in potter's field. Will you get paid, same as usual?'

'How do I know, gal? Just roll over and go to sleep, will you? Morning comes early and there's lot to do tomorrer, it being Christmas Eve.'

They slept.

★　★　★

Back at the hovel Nesta finished her task, although her thoughts were in a whirl. 'That's that!' she said, wiping her hands on her already grubby apron. 'I'd best be off home. Seems there's some nasty weather settling in.'

Blanche gave a little whimper. 'Don't leave me, Mistress Davies!'

This decided Nesta, once and for all. 'I'm not staying here, Blanche. If you don't want to wait for Fanny, I'll have to take you with me. Come on, get your things.'

Blanche drew back, obviously frightened. 'No! I can't let them find me. I don't know what they'll do to me, after what I did.'

'Make up your mind, gal!' Nesta snapped. 'It's one thing or the other. Either stay here with the dead, or come along with me and face up to whatever may come. I hope you know that you've caused a lot of grief and woe to your kinfolk, what with them thinking you must be dead, or abducted.'

As if they care about you, she thought, but didn't say the words aloud. Young Will had gone back to Court, quite jauntily, and even the girl's aunt seemed more concerned with the family's reputation than whether Blanche was alive or dead.

'I suppose you'll tell them,' Blanche snivelled.

'I haven't made up my mind yet what I'll

do. We can't send word tonight, in any case. Meanwhile, let's leave this god-forsaken hole and get home to my Jack. He'll be worried, wondering what's happened to me.'

Nesta headed for the door, not looking to see whether the girl would follow, or no.

'Wait for me!' The girl appeared at Nesta's side.

'You can't come like that? Where are your things?' Blanche was shivering in a linsey woolsey gown, wearing felt booties on her feet. It occurred to Nesta then that her proper shoes and her warm mantle had been left on the riverbank. That would need explaining, eventually, but in the meantime they must get home. She took off her apron and arranged it around the girl's shoulders. Not that it would provide much warmth, but it would at least keep the snow off for a short while.

They stumbled through the wood, Nesta hoping desperately that they were going in the right direction. A whippy branch gave her a painful slash on the cheek, causing her to cry out. She was greatly relieved when she saw a bobbing light coming towards them.

'Mumma! Is that you!'

'Jack! Thank goodness! Can you give this child your coat? She'll be cold as charity by now.' Jack obliged at once.

Cries of amazement greeted Nesta when

she walked into the house, holding the door open for Blanche. 'Make way there. Let us get to the fire, you two. Jonno, fetch a blanket. Kate, a hot drink.'

'We thought you were dead,' was Jonno's helpful remark to Blanche. 'You look like a skinned rabbit.'

'That's enough of that, Jonno Davies! Fetch that blanket, before I give you something you won't like!'

'But I want to know what's happened,' he insisted, dodging out of Nesta's reach.

'All in good time,' she told him. 'We've more important things to think about now, such as getting out of these damp clothes, for one.' Disappointed, he opened the wall press and removed a blanket.

★ ★ ★

The hovel at Joby's well was dark, except for a tiny glow from the fire. The room was cold, for in her hurry to leave Blanche had not fastened the door securely. The wind blew it open, and the draft caused the fire to flare up momentarily. A spark flew from the hearth and landed on a bundle of rags which had been left on the floor. Another gust of wind caused the pile to ignite, and in moments the whole room was ablaze. The ancient walls, made of wattle and daub, went up immediately, and the mouldering thatch was the next to go up. In no time at all the hovel was a bonfire.

Perhaps fortunately for the inhabitants of Hollyhill, the little cottage had been built in a clearing. At a different time of year the fire might have spread to the trees, and from there to the hamlet, but that wasn't possible now. It eventually burned itself out, aided by the thick covering of snow which accumulated before morning. Old Jackson had a funeral pyre fit for a Viking jarl.

39

'I want you to see if Joan is well enough to come downstairs for an hour,' Nesta told Jack, who looked alarmed.

'Downstairs!' he repeated. 'Do you think she's well enough, Mumma?'

'She'll be the best judge of that, son.'

'But we planned for her to come down on Christmas Day. Why now?'

'Because I want her to hear what this young woman has to say, Jack. Being in at the kill, so to speak, will buck her up no end. She feels cut off from life, being stuck upstairs all the time; that I do know.'

'We could go up to her,' he suggested.

'It's cold up there, and I for one need this fire. I'm chilled to the marrow. If I get the lung rot, where will we all be?'

Jack winced at the reminder. Moments later he edged down the stairs, carrying his beaming wife. Introductions were made.

'Right, then!' Nesta announced. 'Let us hear from you, young Blanche.'

The girl lived up to her name, turning pale as a lily. 'What do you want to know?'

Jonno jiggled up and down with impatience.

'Why did you run away? Where have you been all this time, and why aren't you dead?'

'That about covers it,' his father agreed, with a wry smile, but the girl wasn't so easily persuaded.

'First I want to know what you mean to do with me. Shall you send for Aunt Jane, or Sir William? Because if you do, I won't stay here. I will not!'

'Whoa!' Jack said. 'That snow is coming down thick and fast. It won't be possible to get a message to either of those good people for some time to come. Nor should you think about fleein' into the storm. You'd be dead before morning, my gal!'

'He speaks truly,' Nesta murmured. 'You might as well tell us the whole story, gal. Come time you get it off your chest, you'll feel better, I trow.'

Blanche looked at Kate. 'You remember what we said, the first time I came here?'

Kate nodded. 'I think so.'

'I told you I don't want to marry anyone, least of all a man I'd never set eyes on. Aunt Jane kept saying it would turn out well enough in the end; other girls have arranged marriages and love follows in time. There is no life for a woman without marriage, she kept telling me. You'll spend your life in other people's houses, and end up dependent and neglected in old age. Better by far to marry and have children.'

'So you agreed to go through with the marriage?' Joan put in.

'I could not see any way out of it, Mistress Davies. It was only when we were standing in front of the priest and I realized the awful solemnity of what I was about to promise, yoked to a stranger until death, that I could not do it. I ran away, and the rest you know.'

'Not quite all,' Nesta remarked. 'How did you come to take refuge in the old man's cottage, with Fanny Cropwell?'

Joan gasped on hearing this. She had not been privy to Nesta's earlier explanations.

'Oh, yes,' Nesta said. 'I was alone in that hovel, seeing to the old man, when Blanche here came out of hiding.'

'I ran into the wood, and Fanny was there, watching everything that was going on. She often does that, I think. She doesn't miss much, by what she tells me. She didn't ask why I was running, or what I meant to do. All she said was: 'You come along with me. I'll hide you, never fear.' So I went with her, and that's where I've been ever since.'

'And I suppose it was that young woman's idea for you to leave your things on the river bank, so everyone would think you were drowned! And what was to happen after that, pray?'

'I hoped to make my way to the nuns near Oxford.'

'You want to be a nun!' Jonno sounded incredulous. Blanche smiled sweetly at the boy.

'I meant to seek sanctuary with them. It doesn't mean that I have to take vows, for many a widow or young girl choose to enter a convent as what they call a parlour guest. I have money, you know. I could afford to do that.'

'But have you thought?' Joan cried. 'I daresay your dowry has already been paid over to Sir William or his son. A wife's money becomes the property of her husband.'

'But I'm no wife yet, nor ever shall be. They'll have to hand the money over to the nuns, if not to me.'

'Easier said than done,' Jack told her. 'The lawyers will have to get involved, and at your age you could be made a ward of the king. You'll have no say over your money, or your person. I'm surprised you knew nothing of this.'

'That remains to be seen,' Nesta said, shaking her head slightly at Jack. Poor Blanche was shocked by the day's events, and there was little point in frightening her with things which might never happen.

'I wonder why Fanny helped you?' Kate

was bewildered. 'It's not like her to put herself out. I've always found her to be quite the opposite, full of bitterness and spite.'

'She told me quite a lot about herself. How she's been let down by men, or one man, at least.'

Nesta cocked her ears. 'I wonder who that could be?'

'She had a lover once, and expected to wed him. Then, when the time came, he abandoned her and married a girl who was more to his advantage. Perhaps I shouldn't say this, but I wondered at the time if she'd been *enceinte*. If it wasn't for the old uncle, letting her stay with him, she'd have been destitute, she said.'

But if that was the case, then where was the babe now? Nesta wondered. She did not continue this train of thought aloud, while Jonno was listening, all agog. Little jugs have big handles! And if there had been a child, Goody Clapton would have known about it, unless the girl had miscarried. Unless . . .

It was common knowledge that the old woman had possessed a knowledge of herbs and simples. This was good, so far as it went. Nesta herself had picked up one or two ideas along the way; marigold ointment, for example, such as she had given Adam Critchley for his gout.

306

But there were other uses for plants, which could be administered with evil intent. The old midwife herself had fallen victim to the poisoner's art. Nesta was well aware, having heard talk when she was learning her craft, that some herbs could be employed to end unwanted pregnancy, although she herself did not know with any certainty what they were.

Horse-parsley was useful to help expel the afterbirth, when the seed was boiled in wine; garden basil likewise. There were others she could think of, all good when properly used. But could they also be made to abort a child, either given in a larger dosage, or perhaps mixed with something else?

To do such a thing would be mortal sin. It was also against man's law. Any midwife procuring an abortion could be tried and hanged, as the mother would be also, if suspicion fell on her.

Nesta gave herself a mental shake. She had no cause to think that either Goody Clapton or Fanny Cropwell had been involved in such a thing. But someone had murdered the old dame. What if . . . ?

This would bear looking into. It might also be useful to discover who the girl's sweetheart had been. Fanny wasn't likely to tell her anything, of course, but apparently she had confided in Blanche to some extent. Could

Blanche be persuaded to question the other girl further?

But no. Fanny had helped her in her hour of need. The girl must feel a measure of gratitude for this and would not be inclined to betray her friend. Kate, then. They knew each other, even if there was little love lost between them.

Nesta made up her mind. When the snow had melted, they would return to the cottage, bearing a basket of Christmas fare for Fanny. It was quite usual to take food to a household where there had been a bereavement, and normal enough for Nesta to see how the survivors were getting on, since she had performed the last offices for the old man. Somehow she would have to get the conversation turned towards Fanny's betrayal.

How would that be possible, though? Perhaps it would be better to let Kate take charge. Somehow, it appeared that Fanny already knew about Will's dalliance with Kate. Then he had thrown her over and allowed himself to be betrothed to Blanche Bellefleur. Never mind that Kate was the cordwainer's daughter, with hardly a groat to her name, while Blanche was an heiress of sorts. The stories were the same.

Kate could bleat about the way she'd been set aside, and this would lead into Fanny's parallel story. If she was indeed as bitter as Blanche suggested, no doubt she would be glad to spill it all out. That would be Kate's cue to say 'who was he, then, your sweetheart?' and with any luck Fanny would name him.

Joan was beginning to look weary, and Nesta stood up then. 'Time for bed, dearie. This has been your first time up and we mustn't tire you. Come along, Jack, do your stuff!' Jack rose, stifling a yawn. The evening's excitement was over.

40

'Whatever be going on out there? Come and take a look, Robbie.' Mary Glover huffed on the window, trying to clear the frost away, the better to see out.

'Can't I even break my fast in peace, woman?' he grumbled.

'But there's a knot of people on the greensward, Rob, just standing there like they're waiting for the Second Coming!' The greensward, that strip of unoccupied land beside the road opposite the church, was white with snow this morning. Her husband got up from the table and lumbered to the window.

'What the devil?'

'I told you, Rob, I told you. What's happened?'

'I dunno, but whatever it is, it'll mean work for me! Where's my boots, woman? I'd best get out there and find out.'

Just as he joined the group the priest appeared, seemingly intent on dispersing the crowd.

'What do you people want? There's no Mass this morning, as well you know. Come back tonight, prepared to welcome the Christ Child in.'

'But, Feyther, we've had a sign!' one woman cried, her voice tremulous.

'A sign? What sort of sign?'

'A great red light in the sky, over yonder!'

By the expression on their faces his parishioners were very much afraid, and they had come to him for reassurance.

'Ay, we all saw it!' the blacksmith chipped in. 'I thought mebbe 'twas a beacon, like.'

'We're not at war, man! And even if we were, we shouldn't see the warning bonfires this far inland.' The priest frowned. He had the power to control his people, even to quell a threatened riot, by sheer force of personality, if not the threat of divine retribution, but this was something different. He had to know what they had seen before he could act.

'Where exactly was this light?'

'In the sky, Feyther, over the wood.'

'A warning of more snow to come, I expect. Red sky in the morning, shepherd's warning.'

The blacksmith shook his head. 'Not like that. All in one place, and leaping up, like flames.'

Flames! Father Wagstaffe grasped at this. 'It sounds to me like a house on fire. Doubtless somebody piled the wood too high, against last night's cold, and the thatch caught. Yes, that's what it will be.'

'But there's no dwelling in that direction, Feyther, not unless you count the hut at Joby's well.'

The priest let out a long-drawn sigh. 'There was nobody there to set a fire last night. Old Jackson died in the afternoon. I was waiting until the snow stopped before sending Master Glover here to bring in the corpse.'

'But that girl was there! Young Fanny Cropwell! Burned to a cinder she'll be, poor wight!'

There were murmurs of regret. Fanny wasn't well thought of — no better than she should be, according to some of the housewives — but nobody would wish a fiery death on another human being. The sexton cleared his throat.

'Fanny's with us, see. Spent the night 'cos it were too mucky out to let her go home in the dark. Come to tell Feyther about her uncle's death, and he sent her down to us.'

There were murmurs of satisfaction at this. Nobody had died — at least, not in the fire — and this left them free to enjoy the drama without feeling guilty.

'Now the weather has cleared, some of you men had best get over to the wood and see that the fire is mainly out, and not likely to spark up again and spread to the hamlet,' Father Wagstaffe directed. 'For all we know some wayfarer may have taken shelter there for the night and fired the place, either by accident or design. Be so good as to report back to me with your findings.'

'Shouldn't us send for the constable, Feyther?' a woman piped up. 'Sounds fishy to me. First the old man dies, then his house burns down. Wouldn't be the first bit of trouble we've had here lately!'

'As far as I know, the poor man died a natural death. As for his house burning down, we shan't know if that has happened until you men go and look. But yes, I suppose we should summon Fowler, just to be on the safe side, though we'll get no thanks for dragging him from home on Christmas Eve. One of you with a horse had better carry the message. Tell him it's from me so he knows there's no mistake.' He turned and went to his house, black skirts trailing through the snow.

'There's mebbe been a fire the other side of the wood,' Glover told Fanny. 'Could be your house has burned down. The men have gone to look.'

'I've got to go and see,' Fanny cried, pulling on her shoes. 'Tell them to wait and

I'll go with them!'

'No, no, you stay here, gal,' Mary said, taking the girl by the shoulders and forcing her down on a chair. 'They'll come back soon enough and let us all know.'

'But where will I go if the cottage has gone? And what about my belongings?' Tears sprang to Fanny's eyes. She owned very little other than a change of clothing, a blanket and a few pots and pans, but even those were irreplaceable without money.

'There, there,' Mary said, patting her on the back.

'I must go and see for myself!' Fanny shouted, struggling to free herself from the older woman's grip. But Mary Glover had raised a family of sturdy boys, now gone out into the world to fend for themselves, and she brooked no nonsense.

'You'll sit right there, my girl, and wait until my Rob comes back to let us know what's happened. It may not have anything to do with your home at all. And don't think you can go sneaking off when my back is turned. I'll have my eye on you, make no mistake about that!'

Fanny subsided, biting her lip. Her greatest fear was for Blanche Bellefleur, but she couldn't tell Mary about that. There was no doubt in her mind that Blanche had done something to cause the fire, and was now dead. Either that, or she had escaped and stumbled out into the storm, where she would surely have become lost and died of exposure.

Fanny could well imagine what had happened. All the while she had been there the stupid girl had moaned about how cold she was, blaming Fanny for leaving her heavy mantle on the riverbank. It was true that the cottage was cold; the wind whistled in through every cranny and the roof leaked in places. Blanche had constantly begged Fanny to pile more wood on the fire, and Fanny had refused, explaining that their meagre stock of firewood had to last the winter.

'We can go out and bring in more,' the foolish girl had insisted. Useless to explain that everything was damp from the rains.

'Break branches from the trees, then.'

'Green wood won't burn. It will only smoulder and fill the house with smoke.'

Blanche had looked blank. 'Oh, if only I could be back at home! They'll have fetched in the yule log by now, and the house will be so snug and warm!'

'Better go back there, then!' Fanny was tired of the whining. The girl showed no gratitude at all for what had been done for her. She was nought but a weak, pampered thing who wouldn't last a month if she had to live in the real world that most people inhabited.

Fanny could guess what had happened. As soon as her back was turned Blanche would have piled the fire high. The chimney, which hadn't been swept since Adam was a boy, probably caught fire, and that was the end of that. She longed desperately to be with the men when Blanche's corpse was found. Either her charred body, unrecognizable, pray all the saints, or frozen stiff and covered with a blanket of snow.

Not that she cared much. Whatever might have happened, the stupid wench had brought it on herself. At this very moment she might have been celebrating Christmas in the manor house, dressed in fine clothing and eating more good meat than the average person saw in a year. So what if she did hate the idea of married life? All she had to do was endure it for a time, and then her husband would scurry back to Court, leaving his bride to please herself. But no! The little fool must run off, like a vixen with the hounds behind her, and cast herself on Fanny Cropwell's charity!

What Fanny did care about was what might happen to her when it was learned that she had assisted Blanche Bellefleur in her bid for freedom. That alone would surely be a punishable offence and she could imagine herself spending time in the stocks, or the pillory. Mebbe both! But if Blanche was dead, even if that was accidentally caused by her own doing, how much more would Fanny be blamed, and punished? If found guilty she might even be hanged. She caressed her neck, without realizing it.

Mary Glover watched her through narrowed eyes. Something was wrong; she could tell. She'd always known when one of her boys had been up to something he didn't want known. The girl was far too agitated to be mourning the loss of a few bits and pieces, easily replaced. She would get to the bottom of this, she promised herself.

41

Nesta opened the door to the blacksmith, who smiled at her genially.

'I've come to pick up them new shoes for my daughter's Christmas fairing, but there's nobody in the workshop.'

'Christmas Eve, isn't it!' she told him, as she stood aside to let him pass. 'My Jack's giving himself the day off. Sit down, do. I'll give him a shout.'

She went to the foot of the stairs and bawled up to him. 'Blacksmith's here, Jack!'

'Down in a minute. Give 'un a drink while he's waiting.'

The smith moved closer to the fire, smiling at Kate as he did so. His eyes widened when he noticed Blanche, up to her elbows in flour. The womenfolk were busy preparing the Christmas fare, and Nesta had accepted the girl's offer of help, saying that she might as well get a lesson in pastry-making while she was at it.

'Here! You look like that little bride that ran off the other day. Everybody thought you was drowned, and we wasted a lot of good working hours trying to find your corpse! You been here all the time, have you, then?'

'No, she has not!' Nesta retorted. 'Who do you think we are? This is a God-fearing house, is this. I found her last night and brought her in. There's been no time to notify her people, but as soon as the snow goes, my Jack means to do something about it.'

'Well, I never did!'

'Where was you all this time then, gal?' The smith peered at her fearfully, as if wondering if she was a ghost.

'Best not to say,' Nesta warned. 'Her people should be the first to know. After that, it's up to them to decide who should be told what.'

'Aw, you might give us a hint, missus! Besides, I've got a tale to tell you, if you haven't already heard. You know what they say; exchange is no robbery.'

'What's that, then?'

'You know that hut over to Joby's well?'

'What about it?'

'Burned down, it has, right to the ground. Nothing left but ashes.' Nobody noticed the great gasp Blanche gave, nor that her hands ceased to work over the pastry.

'Well, that can't be right, for a start,' Nesta insisted, 'for I was there myself afore supper time yesterday. Young Fanny called me in to lay the old chap out, for he died yesterday.'

'It's right enough, mistress. It must have started after you came away.'

Nesta thought for a moment. 'Did they get the corpse out in time, do you know?'

'Naw. Burned to a crisp. Saves digging a grave, though, with the ground hard as iron, and makes no difference to the old man.'

'Fanny! What about her, I wonder?'

'Oh, no need to worry about her. She's safe enough in the sexton's house. When she come to notify the priest, he sent her there. Told her there was no point trying to get back while the storm was so unket.'

'How did it start, then, this fire?' Nesta wondered.

He shrugged. 'Who knows? A spark from the fire, I suppose. It wouldn't have been old Jackson who got up and stoked it. More like the devil came to take him away, for the old man was never known to darken the door of the church!' He guffawed, and Nesta shot him an old-fashioned look. Any more of that and she'd land him a good one round the chops, she thought. Whatever the dead man had done or not done during his life, no call to drag his memory in the mire now. It was bad luck to speak ill of the dead.

Luckily Jack came thumping down the stairs at that moment, and the smith stood up to greet him.

'I hope as you've finished them shoes, Jack Davies! My gal's set her heart on them.'

'Finished a week ago. I'd have brought them round, only we've been extra busy. Everyone wants something special for Christmas, and I'm not wanting to turn work away.'

'So Fanny is staying just up the street,' Nesta remarked, when the smith had completed his errand and gone on his way. 'That means you can pay a call on her, Kate, and see what you can find out.'

'Aw, Gramma!'

'Don't you 'aw Gramma' me, gal. I've got a plan, I have, and you're just the one to carry it out.'

Kate was not the only person who wanted nothing to do with Fanny Cropwell just then. The sexton's wife was thoroughly out of countenance. Rob Glover had come home to break the news that the cottage was in ashes.

'You didn't find anybody there?' Fanny asked, her white face betraying her anxiety.

'S'pose you mean what happened to your uncle? Not a trace. Gone beyond finding. Of course, it's not like he was alive when it must've started. He didn't suffer. There's many as would be glad to say the same, when a dwelling goes up in flames.'

Obviously distressed, Fanny snatched up her cloak and went outside. With a black look

321

on her face Mary Glover watched her go.

'She'll be back when she comes to grips with it,' her husband said, thinking he was being a comfort to his wife.

'That ain't what I'm worried about. I hope you ain't thinking of letting her stay on here, Rob Glover. Too soft, that's your trouble.'

'It's Christmas, woman. We can't turn her out, just like that. 'Taint Christian, and I've a position to keep up, being sexton at the church.'

'She can stay till St Stephen's Day,' Mary said firmly, 'but after that, out she goes.'

'Twelfth Night,' he bargained.

'I'll have to see. She's a lazy little toad. We've taken her in and she hasn't even offered to help me with the chores. I don't mind being a servant to my own family, but I wasn't put on this earth to be a slave to a chit such as Fanny Cropwell.'

'But where is she supposed to go after this? That hovel is the only home she's known ever since she come to Hollyhill.'

'She's able-bodied, Rob Glover. She can hire herself out as a scullery maid or suchlike. And don't tell me this is not the season for hiring fairs. That's not the only way to get a job. Let her go up to Critchleys and ask there. Mebbe Mistress Critchley will be soft-hearted, her being a newly wed woman.'

Her husband knew it was useless to argue. He muttered something about needing to go up to the church, to make sure that all was in readiness for the night to come.

Fanny, meanwhile, was wondering what had become of Blanche, and how she herself was affected by this. Perhaps she should get out of Hollyhill while the going was good. She had no wish to spend the cold months in the gaol while the constable, or perhaps the sheriff, tried to decide what her fate was to be.

As she turned to go back to the sexton's house, she made up her mind. It was plain from Mistress Glover's attitude that she was only here on sufferance; she would wait until after Christmas and then leave. She might as well enjoy the good food on the Glover's table in the meantime; even the poorest folk managed to provide themselves with a few treats at this time of year, before the hard days of January when many came close to starvation. Besides, if she took to the roads now, there would be nobody abroad to beg from. Every man to his own fireside during the winter festival.

'This floor needs sweeping,' Mary Glover remarked, when Fanny entered the house.

'Oh, yes?'

'Oh, yes!' Mary mimicked. 'I suppose you

know one end of this broom from the other? Or perhaps not. I doubt if you had much use for a broom in that pigsty where you lived.'

Fanny controlled her rage with difficulty. It would be so easy to snatch the broom away from the woman and beat her with it. Uncle had done that more than once during his spells of vile humour. But at least he was master in his own house, and entitled to beat his womenfolk if they displeased him. This woman had no such hold over her. She wasn't a servant. Nor, if she had her way, would she ever become one. She took the broom and began to sweep.

I should think so, too, Mary thought, with grim satisfaction. We take her in, out of the goodness of our hearts, and see what we get in return! Idle good-for-nothing. Glaring at me like that, just because I asked her to give me a hand. Even my boys would clear the table or clean out the fireplace, if they did need a prod now and then. Rob is right, it wouldn't be Christian to turn her out at Christmas. What would the neighbours think? But as soon as the festivities were over, out she should go, neck and crop!

It did not endear the girl to Mary when she realized that she would have to confess her sin of failing in charity, when she next went to the priest. Still, he would surely see eye to eye with her, and impose a very small penance. Which reminded her! The hussy had stated quite firmly that she never went to Mass at all, never mind confession! Well, she would go to church on Christmas Eve, like it or not! This was a Christian household, and all under its roof would behave accordingly.

42

Christmas Eve wrought its usual magic. For Jonno Davies, part of the joy lay in the days off he was given from the boredom of work. The idea of eating his fill at every meal also held a great appeal, for he was a growing lad and needed to fill every inch of his growing frame, or so he told himself.

Then there was Midnight Mass. It was thrilling to get up in the middle of the night and go out in the frosty air, carrying a lighted torch, which flickered as he walked. Like everyone else the Davies family went to bed early in winter, for what was the point of wasting good candlelight, just to loll about?

It was wonderful to come into the brightly lighted church, filled with men, women, children and babies, all waiting to hear the age-old message, that Christ was born!

Now, in the year of Our Lord 1533, Nesta, Jack Davies, Kate and Jonno were among that crowd. Blanche had been left behind to keep Joan company. The traditional lighted candle had been placed in the window to welcome the Christ Child in, and Nesta had given the girl strict instructions to watch it carefully.

Blanche shuddered. She didn't need telling twice. Nobody knew how the fire had started in the hovel at Joby's well, but it had been a disaster, and she was lucky to be alive. If she hadn't fled the scene with Nesta, fearing to be alone with the dead man, what could have happened? Would she have managed to put the fire out, or might it have taken hold too quickly, so that she perished before she had time to escape?

It was customary after Mass for people to stand outside the church for a short while, exchanging greetings and news. Nesta found to her dismay that the blacksmith had blabbed to all and sundry, so she was obliged to face a barrage of questions.

'I hear you found that gal! Where is she now?'

'They'll bring young Will back from Court, won't they, and make the naughty wench wed him now?'

'What did Mistress Critchley say when she heard the news? That girl was given a good drubbing, I'll warrant.'

Fanny Cropwell, standing nearby, listened to all this with amazement. So Blanche was alive, and here in the hamlet. That put a different complexion on matters. A pang of fear went through her as she remembered some of the things she had told the other girl in the long, dark nights while they were cooped up together. Having been deprived of any confidante for so long, she had said too much. Far too much. She wasn't sure whether Blanche could be trusted to keep her mouth shut. She sidled up to Kate, who was leaning against the wall of the church, waiting for her family to leave.

'Is it true, then? Blanche has been found? Where has she been all this time?'

'You know that very well,' Kate snapped. 'Gramma found her at your house. You took her in, and you hid her, heaven knows why!'

'I felt sorry for her,' Fanny whined, changing her tune in a hurry. 'Being forced to wed a man she doesn't love. You of all people should feel for her, after the way Will treated you! What I meant was, where has she been since she left our cottage?'

'If you kept your ears open, you'd know that, too. She's at home with Mumma, keeping her company till we get back.'

'She should have come to church.'

'Mumma? She's far too ill to come out in the cold night air.'

'I mean Blanche, of course.'

'Don't be stupid! This lot would fall on her like a swarm of bees, especially Sir William.'

'I must speak to her, Kate. Will you take me to her now?'

Kate was about to give a curt refusal, when she remembered Nesta's instructions to her about trying to pump Fanny for information.

'All right, but quiet as a mouse, if you please! My mother isn't well, and I don't want her disturbed. When she wakes in the night she can never get back to sleep, and that isn't good for her.'

Blanche's mouth dropped open when the two girls came through the door. Was Fanny about to blame her for the fire at Joby's well? She stood up, her knees shaking. Fanny glanced at Kate.

'This is private, Kate. Can you go somewhere else and let us talk?'

'This is my home, Fanny Cropwell, and you can say what you have to say in front of me, or not at all!'

Fanny hesitated. 'Well, get on with it, then!' Kate insisted. 'Dad and Gramma will be here in a minute, and if you're here to make trouble they'll have you out, neck and crop!'

'You may think you're safe here,' Fanny pointed out, turning to Blanche, 'but when they find out where you are, they'll come and take you away to face your punishment. And the Davieses won't be spared, either. You've got to leave now, while there's still time, and I'm coming with you.'

'But where can we go?'

'To the nuns, as you planned.'

'You, a nun?' Kate scoffed. 'That's rich!'

'Did I say I want to take the veil? All I'm seeking is sanctuary, to give me time to think. Besides, what I do is my look out, and no business of yours.'

'But there's snow on the ground,' Blanche bleated, 'and I don't even have my mantle. 'Tis a long way to walk, and we dare not beg along the way, for fear that word would get back to my people. You go on, Fanny. I'll stay here.'

'You'd let yourself be taken, all for the want of a cloak? Take mine if you must. I'll get another, if I must beg, borrow or steal. Nay, Blanche Bellefleur, I helped you in your hour of need, and you won't fail me now.'

'Blanche will stay where she is. As for you, Fanny, you'd best hie back to the sexton's house, before he bars the door for the night and you find yourself truly without shelter.' Nesta, entering the house quietly, had overheard Fanny's last words. Blanche looked at her with relief.

'My aunt and her husband; were they at Mass this night?'

'They were not. Feyther Wagstaffe goes to say Mass in the manor chapel in the morning, and the Critchleys will be there, or so I heard from a woman whose niece is a servant in

330

Master Critchley's employ. I wonder that Fanny here did not think to tell you that your aunt was not present tonight.'

'How do I know what her aunt looks like?' Fanny's expression was sullen.

'You know the rest of the family, though,' Blanche muttered. 'Her stepdaughters and their husbands. Tom Robinson was your lover once upon a time, was he not?'

All eyes swivelled to Fanny. Even Jonno, who had come into the room looking for food as usual, gazed at her with interest.

'That can't be true!' he piped up. 'Master Robinson is a married man, so he couldn't be Fanny's lover!'

'Oh, do be quiet, Jonno!' Kate snapped. 'You don't know what you're talking about!'

'But I only said — '

'Jonno! Help yourself to a honey cake and take yourself off to your bed,' Nesta told him, not unkindly. 'This is women's business.'

'Why does nobody ever tell me anything?' he grumbled, but when his grandmother raised her hand in a warning gesture he obeyed in a hurry. He did not want the Christmas festivities spoiled by a sore jaw.

'I don't want to hear any more of this!' Fanny announced. 'I'm leaving now, and if you want to stay here and take what's coming to you, Blanche, that's not my problem.' She wrenched the door open and fled into the night.

'At least close the door behind you!' Kate bawled, but there was no reply.

'When I return to Master Critchley's you shall come with me,' Nesta told Blanche. 'They are to send a wagon for me on St Stephen's Day. And don't look at me like that. It will be pleasant there, with the celebrations going on until Twelfth Night. You'll enjoy yourself well enough, I expect.'

'That's if they don't lock you in your room, on a diet of bread and water!' Kate said, grinning.

'Now, Kate, that's enough of that! Don't bully the gal!'

'But she's right, Mistress Davies. I will be punished. I'd be better off if I had jumped into the river and drowned.'

'Now, now, we'll have none of that talk here. 'Tis mortal sin to do away with yourself. Life is precious, gal. Better to be alive and wed than in your grave at your age, and a suicide's grave at that!'

Blanche's mouth set in stubborn lines. 'What if I say I won't go back?'

'We certainly can't keep you here,' Jack said, joining the conversation for the first time. 'I've a position to keep up in this place. Let it be known I hide runaways and bang goes my trade! Seems to me you'd be best to go quietly, before they come and drag you away. You've no chance to avoid it, child. Go back, show proper repentance, and do as you're told next time. Wed young Will as has been arranged; that's if he'll still take you after the shame you've brought on his family. Or, if your heart is set on entering the cloister, tell them that, and mebbe they'll see reason.'

Blanche made no reply to this, choosing instead to hang her head.

'All right, Jack, that will do,' Nesta murmured. 'She'll come with me, just as I said. Now, hadn't we all better go to bed and get some sleep?'

43

'So you've come out of hiding at last, have you? Take that, you wicked hussy!' Jane Critchley delivered a painful buffet across her niece's cheek. Blanche stepped back with a cry of alarm.

'Take care, Mistress Critchley!' Nesta cried, equally alarmed, although for different reasons. 'Hold your temper in check, lest you mark the babe, or worse!'

'I'll thank you not to address your betters in such a manner!' Jane snapped, but Nesta stood her ground.

'If I'm not welcome here, mistress, I'll be glad to return to my family, but I'll have you know that the girl is returned to you through my good graces alone. I mean to see her fairly treated before I leave her here.'

'Then come to the solar, where we may talk in comfort. And you, girl, come with us, but keep a still tongue in your head unless you want to be locked in the cellar. Well, do you hear me? Say something!'

'Yes, Aunt.' Blanche hung her head so that Nesta was unable to read her expression. Fear? Rebellion? Meekness? Who could tell?

Several other women were already seated around the fire, patiently stitching at various forms of embroidery, when the newcomers entered. Nesta recognized Sally Robinson and Anne Dilley.

The older woman must be Margery Dawes, Adam Critchley's sister. She looked at Nesta with a question in her eyes before turning to frown at Blanche, but it was obvious that all three were expecting Jane Critchley to make the first move, and she said nothing.

'Sit there!' Jane ordered, pointing to a stool at some distance from the fire. Blanche obeyed, huddling into the mantle she had been forced to borrow from Kate.

Nesta divested herself of her cloak and took up a place closer to the flames. She had come all this way on a bitter morning and hadn't even been offered a hot drink! Not good enough, she grumbled to herself. When this woman stopped at my door, didn't I treat her like a queen? Well, she'd better not try her airs and graces on me, not if she wants me to care for her in her delicate condition.

'Why did you dare to behave as you did, you wicked child?' Jane demanded, almost spluttering in her rage. 'Oh the shame of it. Such a disgrace to befall our family! And in front of everyone!'

'I told you I did not wish to wed!' Blanche

335

said. 'Nobody listened to me. You made me stand still while you dressed me like a doll, and then I was forced into the church and expected to vow to love and obey a man I didn't know. I would rather die!'

'Stuff and nonsense! You had the chance to marry a fine young man, the son of a baronet, and perhaps even go to Court some day and mingle with the highest in the land. Any one of us here would give much to be in your shoes.'

'Yes, indeed,' said Mistress Dawes. 'And what will happen to you now, do you suppose?'

'I mean to go to the good nuns at Oxford, if Sir William will give back part of my dowry.'

'No need to pretend you've been called by God,' Jane snapped, 'for we all know better. That dowry has been already paid to Sir William. No, my girl, you'll go to him on your bended knees to beg his pardon, and you'll make sure you show the proper contrition. Do not forget that he is your father now, according to law, and he may deal with you as he wills.'

'But William and I are not married,' Blanche insisted. 'How can he do anything of the sort?'

'Little fool! You were betrothed before

witnesses, and set your hand to the document. Do you not know that a betrothal is as binding as a marriage? Whether he wishes it or not, young Will must wed you, and you will behave accordingly next time, if you go there in chains! You cannot escape this marriage, Blanche. All you have succeeding in doing is to turn him against you, and you have only yourself to blame, if he beats you at every opportunity.'

Sold into slavery, Nesta thought. She at least had been able to marry for love, although the marriage had ended aforetimes, when her husband had died. At times they'd had trouble making ends meet, and she had envied brides who could bring wealth to the marriage. Her own dowry had been a woollen blanket and some second-hand pots and pans, purchased by her mother from a neighbour whose parents had died, leaving her with extra chattels.

Now, though, she considered herself more fortunate than any of the women in this room, apart from Margery Dawes, whose story she knew nothing of. Sally and Anne Critchley had husbands who had wed them in the hope of inheriting their father's land, and because of the cock-eyed will he had made, that was all up in the air. As for Jane Critchley, she had been married three times, and always to older men. Had she gained any satisfaction from that, apart from the knowledge that a single woman was disparagingly called an old maid, and had no social standing?

Nesta had believed Blanche Bellefleur to be a meek little thing who couldn't say boo to a goose, but now it seemed that she was unwilling to go down without a fight.

'Better to serve God than a man who only thinks of his own advantage, Aunt! Queen Catherine has learned that the hard way, cast aside for Nan Bullen! Faithful all these years she has been, yet that means nothing to the king. He's no better than the lowliest peasant when it comes to keeping his marriage vows.'

'Hush, child! You speak treason!'

'I speak truth, Aunt.'

'We all feel for the Queen,' Sally said softly, 'or the Princess Dowager, as we are told to call her now. But marriage for many of us can be a good thing. Why, I take joy in my two little girls, and it pleases me to do what I can to make a happy home for my husband.'

'Your husband!' Blanche scoffed. 'I could tell you a thing or two about that man of yours!'

Sally paled. 'I don't know what you're talking about, Blanche Bellefleurt! Oh, I know that people blamed him for my accident, but that was a mistake. Whoever pushed me into the river, it certainly was not Tom. Without me, he would have no chance of inheriting this land when Dad dies.'

There was an uncomfortable silence. Nesta noticed that Jane was red in the face, while Anne Dilley's expression was grim. She could guess what was coming next, but felt powerless to stop it.

'So you see, Blanche dear,' Sally went on, 'you should not fear marriage. It might bring you great happiness, as my union with Tom has brought me.'

'Fiddlesticks! Your blessed Tom has a lover, who has borne him a child.'

'Fiddlesticks yourself! Who is she, then, this lover?'

'Fanny Cropwell, that's who.'

Jane sprang to her feet and slapped the girl on one cheek after the other. 'Take that, you miserable little vixen! How dare you spout such lies at poor Sally's expense, just to divert our attention from your own bad behaviour!'

'I dare because it's true, Aunt!'

Jane leaned over and snatched up a small hand bell from the table. She rang it furiously until a young maid appeared, bobbing a curtsy.

'Yes, mistress?'

'Blanche is to have the green room, Betsy.

Show her upstairs and lock her in.'

'Lock her in, mistress?'

'Isn't that what I just said? Lock her in, and bring the key down to me. And as for you, Blanche, you'd better not try any more of your tricks, or you'll be sorry you were ever born.'

By now, Sally was crying softly. 'It can't be true, can it?'

'It probably is,' Mistress Dawes responded, sniffing loudly. 'When you've lived as long as I have you'll know that men are easily drawn to temptation, whether they be king or peasant. The thing to do is pretend you know nothing about their little lapses, and then your marriage will be secure.' At this, Sally sobbed even harder.

'Mistress Davies,' Jane began. 'What do you know of this? Is there any truth in what Blanche tells us?'

'I know nothing of a certainty,' Nesta replied, wondering how much to tell them. 'I have a shrewd idea that Fanny thinks herself in love with Master Robinson, but that does not mean that he returns her feelings.'

'But has she a child?'

'Not as far as I know. Of course, she may well have had a child before I came to Hollyhill, but if she did, it must have died. There was certainly no baby in the house when I went to Joby's well to lay out her old uncle.'

'Goody Clapton would know,' Anne Dilley mused, 'but she is dead, and the dead can't talk!'

'Just so,' Nesta said. 'All I can suggest is that we forget what Blanche has said. As Mistress Critchley says, the girl wants to take your attention from her own plight.'

44

Early on the morning of St Stephen's Day, Fanny Cropwell looked out of the attic window to see the small painted coach passing by. This, she knew, was the property of Jane Critchley, or had been the last time she'd seen it. Since the woman's marriage to Adam Critchley everything that had been hers now belonged to him.

There was a second man sitting on the box beside the driver. Some sort of house servant or groom, Fanny surmised. Probably sent along to prevent Blanche from running away during the journey to her aunt's house. Father Wagstaffe would have passed on the news that the girl had been found alive, and the Critchleys would be taking no chances.

Sure enough, the conveyance passed the sexton's house again, on the return journey, but this time there was no sign of the second man.

'Probably sitting inside, to keep the silly girl in order,' Mary Glover remarked.

'I feel sorry for the little wench,' the sexton remarked.

'You'd feel sorry for a dying duck, Rob

Glover! Too soft, you are, by half! No we all has to do our duty in this world, and hers is to marry the squire's son and spend the rest of her life in comfort. Some people have all the luck!'

'I haven't done so bad by you, gal, have I?'

'Oh, I s'pose not, according to your lights. Let's face it, though, we don't have what she's going to, do we? No tapestries hanging on these walls, and no velvet couches!'

It was not very long before there came a knock at the door, which Rob flung open to reveal a very disgruntled constable.

'Are you going to let me come in, or do you mean to keep me standing on the doorstep on a bitter day such as this? Bad enough I'm dragged away from home on a high holiday, without perishing of cold!'

'If you're looking to speak to the Bellefleur gal, she's gone.'

'What! You mean she's alive?'

'Of course she is. She was hiding out at Joby's well. Isn't that why you've come?'

'I've been ordered by the sheriff to investigate the death at Joby's well. Why else do you think I'd be out and about on St Stephen's Day?'

'How'd he hear about it so soon?' Glover asked, standing aside to let the constable enter.

'Blessed if I know. Anyhow, I went to the priest first, seeing as he has to deal with any death round about, and he said as Fanny Cropwell is biding here with you. Where is she, then? Not run off, has she?'

'Upstairs, helping Mary. I'll give her a shout.'

Fanny came downstairs with all haste, propelled by Mary's large hand in her back.

'What now?' Mary demanded. 'A fine Christmas this is turning out to be. I told you, Rob Glover, we'd rue the day we took this one in!'

'Now, Mary!'

'Don't you 'now Mary' me, Rob Glover! I suppose you know, Sam Fowler, that this one here has kept Blanche Bellefleur hidden all this while, and the girl's people half-demented with worry, thinking her dead!'

'Well, now!' Fowler rubbed his hands together. 'Seems like we may be able to kill two birds with one stone, eh?' He sat down heavily on the nearest bench. Fanny watched him like a hen who has sighted a weasel.

'Now then, Fanny Cropwell, I have questions to ask of you, and don't even think about lying to me. First of all, what killed old Jackson? Left him lying there helpless, did you, while you set fire to the cottage and let him burn with it?'

'Nay!' Glover interrupted. ''Twasn't like that at all. The gal was here with us when the fire started.'

'That's what she'd like you to think, Master Glover! She could have arranged it so she was well away before the fire took hold.'

'Mistress Davies was the last one to leave the house,' Fanny told him.

'That midwife? Not her again! Every time I turn round she's there.'

'She came to lay my uncle out. She was still there when I came for the priest.'

'Then I'll talk to her next.'

'You'll have to go to the Critchley place then,' Glover put in. 'She left this morning, taking the Bellefleur gal with her.'

'What did Jackson die of, then, if he wasn't killed in the fire?'

'My uncle was very old,' Fanny replied. 'Well past eighty, as far as I know. He'd been going downhill for some time. If it wasn't for me looking out for him he'd have gone home long since.'

'How is it you had an uncle of that age, then?'

'He was my mother's uncle, not mine, and much older than her own mother, being the first of his family. When my parents died of the sweating sickness I came to live with him, having nowhere else to go.'

'Probably with an eye to his bit of money,' Mary mumbled.

'What's that, Mistress Glover?'

'Everyone knows he had a bag of gold buried under his floor. It's been the talk of the hamlet for years.'

Fanny took a step towards the woman, her fist clenched. 'That is a lie!'

'Then what did the pair of you live on? You tell me that! You needed more than the few vegetables you grew, and mebbe a coney you snared now and again. And come to that, what was you doing in that cottage? Jackson had no right to it, far as I can tell.'

'You'd better explain that,' Fowler grunted.

'My uncle was a drover. He served Sir William well, and years ago he managed to save his herd of cattle, when thieves tried to make off with them. Sir William was grateful, and when uncle got too lame to work, he let him have the cottage, seeing as Joby had just died. Sir William sometimes sent us a few coins, or a joint of pork when there had been a pig killing. You ask Sir William about it. He'll tell you I speak true.'

'Rest assured, I shall. Meantime, it may be that you are innocent of the old man's death, and the fire as well, but there's another charge, just as serious. Hiding a fugitive! What do you say to that?'

346

'All I did was let Blanche stay with me. Where's the harm in that? I did not kidnap her, if that's what you're thinking!'

'Ah, but whose idea was it to leave her belongings on the riverbank, eh? Making everyone think she'd gone to her death?'

Fanny said nothing. The constable smiled unpleasantly. 'All right, my gal! It's the gaol for you! Fetch your cloak, if you have one, and look sharp about it! If I'm to get up to Critchley's before the snow starts again, I mustn't dally.'

'You can't leave the poor gal in that gaol, not in this weather! It's cold as the tomb. She'll freeze to death!'

Rob Glover spoke urgently. The gaol was a solidly built stone building with a floor of beaten earth. The small barred window was devoid of glass, and the heavy door was barred from the outside with a heavy plank which slotted into sturdy iron stanchions. There was no furniture inside, and nothing to keep out the cold. Even in summer the place was dank and chill.

Mary Glover plucked at her husband's sleeve. 'Constable knows his business, Rob. She's done wrong and must take her punishment.'

He stood by mutely as the girl marched out, without a backward glance.

'See! Didn't I tell you? That girl's no good. Not a word of thanks for all we've done for her!' Mary reeled back under the weight of her husband's fist. 'That's right! Take it out on me. It's true what they say, work like a slave and do your best, and nobody gives a tinker's damn. Have a pretty face and a lying tongue and you can do no wrong, at least where men are concerned!'

Glover banged his way out of the house, disgusted that his wife exhibited not an ounce of charity. And why judge the gal so harshly? She would not get off so lightly. The constable was determined to convict her of something, all the more so because he needed a scapegoat, in order to prove to the sheriff that he was capable of solving the crimes that had recently beset the hamlet.

Jack Davies opened the door when the sexton knocked.

'Come in out of the cold, man. Tis enough to freeze the nose off your face!'

'Not working today, then?'

'Nay, time to take a few days to enjoy the season. We've worked hard all month, seeing to all the Christmas orders. 'Twill be quiet for a while, I know.'

'Then you'll be able see to this glove of mine. You'd think I could deal with it myself, with a name like mine, but each to his own trade.' He held out a sturdy leather glove. 'My Mary is a dab hand with a needle, of course, but hard stuff like this is a bit beyond her. Weather like this, I daresay I'll have graves to dig ere long, and I'll need my gloves.'

'It's just the stitching come loose,' Jack noted. 'I'll set young Jonno at it tomorrow.'

Glover hesitated. 'That gal of yours. Is she at home, or did she go up to Critchley's?'

'Kate? She's somewhere about. Why do you ask?'

'It's young Fanny. She's been clapped in gaol. She's likely to perish in there, and I wouldn't wish that on man or beast. I was thinking, mebbe Kate could take her a blanket, and a bite to eat.'

'Surely.' Jack didn't ask why Mary could not have done the same. He knew the sexton's wife of old.

45

'Are you sure the man was dead when you got there?'

Nesta bridled. 'What on earth are you talking about, man? I'm not in the habit of laying out living people!'

'Did you notice anything unexpected?'

Nesta clicked her tongue impatiently. 'You mean was he covered in blood? Had his head been severed from his body? Had he been frothing at the mouth? No, constable, as far as I could tell he had died a natural death. Had I had any cause to suspect otherwise, would I have washed him and sewn him in his grave cloth? Rest assured I would have sent for you if I had found aught wrong.'

'And what of the girl?'

'Fanny? She left before I did. I sent her to notify Feyther Wagstaffe, not that there was anything he could do at that stage, but I had to follow the rules. She did not return. At least, not as far as I know. The Glovers will be able to tell you more about that.'

'I have already spoken to them, but I meant the Bellefleur girl. You knew she's been staying there ever since she ran from the church?'

'I knew no such thing, Sam Fowler, so you can stop trying to trip me up. Nobody could have been more surprised than me, when I turned round and found her standing there in the gloom. Gave me quite a turn, in fact. For a minute there I thought her a spectre.'

'I'm sure!' He turned to Adam Critchley, who had been listening carefully. 'Now I'll speak to the girl Bellefleur, if you please.'

'Send for the girl!'

Jane Critchley obediently turned to her little bell, which she rang with more force than strictly necessary. In due course Blanche appeared, visibly trembling but with her head held high. But no matter how cunning the constable's questions, he was unable to trick her into any variation of her story. Fanny had kindly offered her shelter, while she tried to decide what to do. Yes, the old man had been alive when she came there; if you could call it alive. He spent the hours mumbling on his cot, opening his mouth like a little bird when Fanny fed him his gruel.

'She told me she owed him everything, which is why she cared for him so tenderly.'

This revealed a new side to Fanny's character, Nesta reflected, but there, wasn't there some good in everyone?

The constable seized on that remark. 'What do you mean, she owed him everything?'

'Why, I understood her to mean that he had taken her in when her parents died, and given her a home, such as it was.'

'What is to happen to the girls now?' Jane asked.

'I leave this one in your care, mistress. The family will decide what becomes of her now.'

Jane nodded. 'And the other? This Fanny?'

'I have her locked in the gaol at present. The sheriff will say whether she comes to trial. There seems no proof of her involvement in her uncle's death, or indeed the destruction of his cottage by fire. However, harbouring a fugitive is serious business and she must answer to that.'

'She is young yet,' Nesta pleaded. 'Surely she meant no harm? She found a fellow creature in need, and acted out of charity.'

'Stuff and nonsense!' Margery Dawes cried. 'She's broken the law, and must pay for it. Why, if a child of mine had acted so, I should say just the same.'

Nesta intercepted a black look from Jane Critchley. Obviously there was no love lost between the sisters-in-law. She recollected that Mistress Dawes's son, Philip, was one of the heirs to the Critchley lands, a prize which could be snatched from his hands in the event that Jane bore a son.

Out of the corner of her eye she noticed

that the lad in question had come into the room and appeared to be listening intently. Perhaps he was in love with Blanche, and cared about what happened to her now? But no. As soon as the constable had finished speaking, the boy was gone.

Soon afterwards the constable also left, pleading that he must be on the road before nightfall. He directed a hard look at Nesta, who ignored him. She had better things to do than worry about Sam Fowler, who in her opinion would have trouble finding the nose on his own face, let alone any criminal who might be lurking at Hollyhill.

'This has been a difficult day for you, Mistress Critchley,' she murmured, taking Jane by the arm. 'You must come to lie down. Think of the babe.'

'Indeed, yes, my dear,' Adam insisted. 'We must think of the babe.'

'But what to do about her?' Jane wailed. 'I'm responsible for the silly wench. Sir William must be told, and only then shall we know what comes next.'

'Leave all to me. A messenger shall go to the manor house first thing in the morning. Meanwhile, this niece of yours may go back to her chamber and contemplate her sins a while.'

Blanche rose with dignity, and walked out of the room.

'Well, go with her, one of you!' Critchley bawled. 'Make sure she doesn't run off again!'

Anne Dilley rose and followed. Sally Robinson's expression was hard and cold. The Robinsons were due to stay in the house until Twelfth Night, but Nesta felt sure that the storm would break long before that, to judge by the way the girl refused to look at her husband. In that she was correct.

Some time later, when she had Mistress Critchley tucked up in her bed, and had made sure that there was nothing else the woman required, Nesta returned to the solar. Adam Critchley had evidently left, and there was no sign of Anne Dilley, who doubtless had gone about her duties in the house.

Only Margery Dawes and Sally Robinson were present; Mistress Dawes was stitching away crossly as if her life depended on it, and Sally was staring into space. Of her children there was no sign. They must be off somewhere with the maid, Polly, playing, perhaps, or having a nap.

Nesta was about to enter the room, braving the annoyance of Mistress Dawes, who persisted in treating her like a servant, when Tom Robinson came in by another door. Nesta shrank back, waiting to see what would happen.

'Come, wife! Gather up the babes and let us go home. There is an uncomfortable feeling about this house since that girl was found.'

'And can you doubt it, after what you've done?' Sally spoke without meeting his gaze. Mistress Dawes looked up sharply, but remained where she was, her needle poised for another attack on her piece of tapestry.

'I'll thank you to remember your marriage vows!' he said sharply. 'You promised to obey, and I say that we return to our own home forthwith. I might get a bit of peace and quiet there.'

'And what about your vows to me, Tom Robinson? Or have you forgotten about your little dalliance with that Cropwell wench? And if what Blanche Bellefleur tells us is true, that girl has borne you a child. Was it a son, Tom? That son you are so anxious to get from me? Of course, born out of wedlock, such a boy is of no use to you, not when it comes to getting your hands on my father's land!'

Tom took a step towards her, his fists clenched. Behind him, Mistress Dawes cleared her throat. He swung about, as if realizing for the first time that she was there. With a muttered oath he rushed from the room, almost knocking Nesta down as he pushed past her. Clutching at the door frame for support, she waited to hear what would happen next.

Why had Mistress Dawes remained on the spot when what was happening was so obviously a private dispute between husband and wife? Had she perhaps stayed in order to protect Sally, in case the pair came to blows, or was it just that she was curious and wanted to be in at the kill, so to speak?

' "Tis Christmas, the season of forgiveness and new beginnings,' the woman said suddenly. 'You should go home and try to forget what the foolish man has done.'

'Forget!' Sally snapped. 'And what then? Do you suppose I can remain silent if he insists on bringing his bastard into my home and expecting me to care for it? And what's to say he'll give up this Fanny, once he knows he can twist me round his little finger? I'll die first.'

'You courted death once before, as I recall. Methinks you knew of this love child long since, which was why you meant to drown yourself?'

'I tell you, I was pushed!' Sally shouted. 'Why does nobody believe me? I've finished with Tom Robinson, and there's no more to say!'

'Then what next? Do you intend to remain in your father's house for the rest of your days? That's if he allows you to do so. Don't be a fool, girl. He's more likely to make you go back to your husband, especially if his new wife puts a word in his ear. What God has joined together, let no man put asunder!'

Nesta decided it was time to intervene. She walked into the solar, smiling as though all was right with the world. Mistress Dawes took one look at her and left the room.

46

'For the love of heaven, let me out of here!' Fanny grasped the iron bars as she peered out through the gaol window. There was a look of anguish on her pinched face.

'You know I cannot do that,' Kate told her, although she pitied Fanny greatly. 'And do take care. If you hold the bars like that, your fingers will freeze to the iron.'

'Come to mock me, have you?' Fanny's teeth chattered madly.

'I've brought food, and a blanket. I'll try to push them in through the bars.'

After a tussle, they succeeded in getting the blanket through. Fanny immediately wrapped it around her shaking form and reached out again for the food. Cramming bread into her mouth and gulping it down, she grabbed for another piece as Kate watched, appalled.

'Where is the constable, Kate? Is he coming back?'

'I cannot say. Surely he won't leave you here overnight, though? This weather is enough to freeze the birds in the trees. Already there is a layer of ice on the river.'

'They'll drag me out to hang me, I

suppose. Perhaps freezing will be a kinder death.'

'They'll have no cause to hang you, Fanny. When it comes to the matter of your uncle's death my Gramma will speak for you, and we all know that you were here when the fire started. I'm afraid they will punish you for aiding Blanche, but not by death. Be of good courage, and all will come right in the end.'

Kate spoke with more bravado than she felt. She wasn't the one who was in this mess, although she might well have been, had circumstances been different. If she had come across Blanche she, too, might have hidden her, although more to spite Will Mowbray than for any other reason.

'It cannot come right, for there is much you do not know,' Fanny wailed.

'Shall I fetch Feyther Wagstaffe? If you make your confession it will give you ease.'

Fanny shuddered. 'I could not bear to confess to him. He would only threaten me with the fires of hell, and I know well enough where I'm bound, without him to rub it in. Oh, why did I ever believe in that faithless Tom Robinson?'

'Then why not tell me?'

'Tell you! So you can run to the constable to seal my fate?'

'I won't. I swear by my mother's blood!'

Kate quailed inwardly as she said this, knowing that her mother might not have long to live, in any case.

There was silence for a while as Fanny considered this. Kate, hopping from one foot to the other to ease her numbed feet, was thankful for the sheepskin jerkin she wore underneath her mantle.

'Very well, then, I'll tell you, but remember, you swore an oath! Well, then, Tom Robinson and I were lovers, long since. It was in the spring, when all the world was green, and sweet with flowers and birdsong. He promised to marry me so I lay with him, and it did not seem wrong to me then.'

She paused. Kate was not shocked, for, young as she was, she knew that many a bride reached the altar only a short while before her child was brought there for baptism. Country people were inclined to turn a blind eye to such shortcomings, for it was important for a man to know that his wife would not be barren. Large families were a boon, if enough children survived infancy, for even the youngest could earn a pittance by scaring crows in the fields, and older ones could earn their own way as labourers and contribute to the family purse. In old age, parents could not survive without grown children to support them.

'Then I knew I was expecting his child. I hoped he would wed me then, but when I told him he only laughed, saying that what had been between us was only a bit of fun. I begged him not to abandon me, but he left me just the same.

'In the end I had to tell my uncle. It was he who told me that Tom was betrothed to Sally Critchley. 'You can't bear the child,' he told me. 'We have little enough to live on now, and with a bastard child at your skirts you'll be shunned by all the old crones in the hamlet.' I knew that to be true so when he told me to take my trouble to Goody Clapton, I did as he said.'

'And she helped you get rid of the child!' Kate whispered.

'And almost did for me, as well, after taking her potion! But I recovered, and for a while I thought that was to be the end of it. Then one day I met her in the wood, and she told me she wanted money, or she would tell the world what I'd done.'

'She could hardly have done that without disclosing her own part in it,' Kate said.

'Perhaps so, but I couldn't risk it. I didn't want to hang! I told uncle, and he pulled out his little purse and gave me a groat. That was the beginning. At last he had no more to give, and he said we must put a stop to it, once and for all, for she had bled us dry. He had me make a mess of pottage to take to her. I was to say that it was in place of money, for we had no more. I would promise to bring her food from time to time, and that would have to do.'

'So it was you who poisoned the old woman!' Kate breathed.

'Not really. Uncle had a knowledge of herbs and 'twas he who put the poison in the dish. He told me it would give her the collywobbles for a few days, and that would serve her right for the way she'd leeched off us for so long. I believed him, and she took the food greedily enough. But when I went back later, to see if it had worked, I found her dead. I could hardly bear to stay in the same room with her, but I managed to find the money, which I took from under her mattress. It was ours, after all. Why should I leave it there for someone else to steal? Then I went home. On the way I was as sick as if I'd taken the poison myself.'

The words continued to come tumbling out while Kate listened, saying nothing. The sound of horse's hoofs, ringing on the hard ground, made her look up.

Philip Dawes reined in the animal beside her, his breath white on the frosty air.

'Fanny's in there, is she?'

'I've brought her a blanket and some food.'

'Ay, trust Sam Fowler to leave her there with nothing! And what of you? Could you not have let her out?'

'Me! Would you have them hang me, too?'

'Nobody's being hanged, if I have aught to do with it.'

'What's it to you?' Fanny snivelled, watching though the bars.

'You forget I was kept in there myself, and likely to be hanged on account of that fool, Sam Fowler! I heard of your story from Blanche. She's set the cat among the pigeons with her wild tales. Nobody knows how much to believe.'

'Do you mean to help me?' Fanny's tone was devoid of hope.

'That I will.'

'You'll be outlawed, then. And what of your inheritance?'

'Not much hope of anything there, with the three Critchley women likely to produce babes to put my nose out of joint. As for being outlawed, who's to say that I had aught to do with your escape, if Kate here holds her tongue?'

'If you let her out, I'll get the blame!' Kate roared.

'Then you get off home, and you'll see nothing.'

'I'm not leaving my blanket here, then.'

'We'll leave it behind, never fear. You come back later, with food or something, and you can raise the hue and cry then. Not too soon, mind!'

Kate went home in a daze. Had she done the right thing? Yet there was no denying that she felt sorry for Fanny. Would she have left her there to certain death? She knew of course that she could not. She had proved that to herself by walking away.

But she was involved up to a point, having gone to the gaol with food and a blanket. She would most certainly be questioned, and she hoped she could stand up to that. She must, of course, deny all knowledge of seeing Philip Dawes, and she had sworn not to betray Fanny.

As she hobbled along, keeping her frostbitten hands in her armpits for warmth, she rehearsed her story. She had gone there with charitable intent, handing over the bread and the borrowed blanket. She had not stopped long. That part, at least, was true. She would tell this to her father as soon as she got in. He could see for himself how cold she was; obviously she would not have loitered outside the gaol. When the constable came to question her, as he surely would, Jack could attest to her tale.

When supper was ready she would take a portion to Fanny, saying that the girl must need something hot. Kate would walk to the gaol, find it empty, and rush home at once, crying that Fanny had somehow escaped.

By this time, late in December as it was, it would be getting dark. As an honest citizen, Dad might well decide to let somebody know what had happened, but nobody would set out to find the constable before dawn. Therefore Kate had hours to spare before being interrogated, hours which would help Fanny and Philip on their way.

When the constable eventually appeared, once again Dad would come to her defence. It could not have been my daughter who let the girl out, he would say firmly. She wasn't gone long enough. And even if she was responsible, where could Fanny have been hidden? She could not return to her home, which was in ashes.

'Godspeed, wherever you are,' Kate whispered softly.

47

Jane Critchley gave a great wail of distress. Nesta was at her side in an instant, folding back the sheet to see what had caused her patient to howl like a wolf at bay.

'Ah!'

'I'm losing the babe, aren't I?'

'I believe this is merely your natural courses, mistress. A miscarriage would manifest itself in a more frightening way.'

'But I know I was *enceinte*. I have not bled for some weeks now.'

Nesta sought for words to comfort the distressed woman. 'Alas, I have seen such a thing many times before. A wife who longs for a child manages to convince herself that she is in a delicate condition, when she is not. Nobody can explain why the body acts in such a way.'

Jane wiped away a tear. 'But what am I to tell my husband? He is so pleased to think of the coming child, and now this!'

'And he will be pleased again, I am sure. Do you suppose you are the only woman who has ever suffered a disappointment? Or, come to that, miscarried? Why it has happened to me, in the past, so I know whereof I speak.'

'I cannot bring myself to tell him,' Jane mourned. 'Perhaps you could give him the sad news?'

Nesta was about to agree when she remembered why she was here. Adam Critchley had hired her to watch over his wife, in particular to prevent any threatened miscarriage. As if any human hand could ensure that, once nature had taken its course! She didn't care to face the man when he had worked himself up into a rage. Even if she said that Jane had been mistaken, that, too, could be laid at Nesta's door. Midwives were supposed to know the workings of the female body.

'You must tell him you were mistaken, Mistress Critchley,' she said firmly.

'I cannot! He'll accuse me of lying, to make him look foolish. Better I had miscarried than that.'

Nesta thought carefully. 'I suppose we could say that it's a delayed response to your fall down the stairs the other day.'

'Then he'll want to know why it didn't happen at once.'

Nesta sighed. 'I daresay the stress of the past days has made matters worse.'

'Yes! That's it. Nobody knows the shock I felt when Blanche came through that door, just when I'd become used to the idea that the girl was dead.'

Nesta closed her eyes momentarily. Shock? But a happy one, surely? She would never understand the gentry. They always seemed to have their priorities twisted.

'I think I'll make you a posset,' she said. ' 'Twill calm your nerves.'

When she reached the kitchen she found the place in a turmoil. The cook was shouting at the maids, one of whom was weeping.

'Perhaps I've come at the wrong time,' Nesta murmured. 'It's just that your mistress needs something to calm her down.'

'Calm her down, is it!' the cook muttered. 'And she's not the only one. I swear, if them Robinsons don't leave and go back to their own place, I'll go off my head!'

'Oh? How's that, then?'

'It's that woolly-headed maid of theirs, that's what. Coming down here and getting my gals all of a tizzy. 'Tain't right and 'tain't natural.'

'What has the girl been saying, then?'

'What hasn't she said! Acting all mysterious, saying she knows things the rest of us don't, and then refusing to spill the beans. Hinting about murder, and what that Fanny Cropwell's been and done.'

'Oh, that! She's heard what Blanche

Bellefleur has said, mebbe, same as the rest of us. There's naught new there.'

'Ah, but there's more. She says she knows who tried to drown Mistress Robinson, that's what! All lies, of course, but it's getting my girls in a dither, and I don't like it.'

'Is that so! Well, perhaps I'd better have a word with young Polly.'

'Oh, I don't know about that, Mistress Davies! I'm sorry I said anything now. P'raps tis best to leave well alone after all.'

But Nesta's curiosity was aroused. After all, she had been involved in this story, albeit on the fringes, from the beginning. She'd puzzled over it for so long, she'd love to know the rights of it now.

She found Polly attending the little Robinson girls. 'A word with you, please.'

'I can't go far, Mistress Davies. These two can't be left alone.'

'They'll be safe enough for a few minutes,' Nesta said. She looked around the small nursery and saw that the fire was well guarded. Besides which, both children were sound asleep in high cradles. 'We'll be just outside the door. We'll hear them if they try to stir.'

Unwillingly, the girl followed Nesta from the room. Nesta went on the attack at once.

'I hear it was you who pushed Mistress

Robinson in the river, where she might have drowned.'

The girl looked as if she was about to faint. 'I never! As God's my witness, I never did!'

'But you do know who did do it, don't you, gal!'

Polly pressed her lips together and gave Nesta a defiant look, which greatly annoyed her. If they were going to get anywhere, it was time to put the pressure on.

'Very well, if you won't talk to me, we'll fetch the constable, to take you to the sheriff. When they put the thumbscrews to you, or pull your bones apart on the rack, you'll be only too glad to talk, to make the pain stop.' The sheriff's office was hardly the Tower of London, and Nesta was quite sure that Oxfordshire boasted no instruments of torture, but, as she had hoped, the silly girl didn't know that.

'It was Fanny!' she gasped.

'Fanny, you say? Convenient that, putting the blame on someone already accused of misdeeds.'

'I swear! We were friends, her and me, so when she asked me to pretend we'd had a message, I didn't see no harm in it.'

'But what did she have against poor Sally?'

'It was Tom Robinson she wanted to get back at, after what he done to her. She thought if she could get Mistress Robinson out of the house she could tell her everything, and that would put paid to Tom's hopes of getting Master Critchley's land left to him. It would've worked, too, for you see how things are between them now.'

'But why push the poor woman in the river?'

'I don't think she meant to do that. They had a tussle and the mistress came off worst. That's what Fanny told me, anyhow.'

Yet Sally says she doesn't know who pushed her, Nesta thought. 'One thing has always bothered me,' she mused. 'Who was the boy who brought the message to Sally, asking her to go to her injured husband?'

'Oh, there was no boy. We made that up.'

Nesta nodded in satisfaction. So that was one little piece of the puzzle solved. Soon she would be able to see everything clearly.

'I suppose you know you could have been the death of your mistress by doing this?'

'Oh, no,' Polly snivelled. 'I love her! I'd never hurt her!'

'Yet had she died you might have been hanged for your part in the business. I suppose you didn't think of that!'

'How was I supposed to know she'd end up drowned? I thought I was helping!'

A sudden thought came to Nesta, clear as

day. 'And when you greased the stair beneath the gallery, that was meant to help her too, was it?'

'It wasn't for her. It was meant for . . . ' she broke off in confusion, aghast at what she had said.

'It was meant for Mistress Critchley, wasn't it? Just a little slip, and down she might go, and with any luck she'd lose her babe. That would give Mistress Robinson another chance to get in first with a boy, and so inherit her father's land. Not very clever, my gal. Anybody else might have gone up to the gallery and fallen, even your own mistress. But then, you haven't been very clever all along, have you? Putting your faith in a knowing gal such as Fanny Cropwell.'

It happened so suddenly that Nesta didn't see it coming. The girl darted at her, pushing her with all her might. It was only by the grace of God that Nesta was able to clutch at the doorframe, or she might have tumbled down the long, winding staircase to land on the stone floor below. She screamed in pain and fright.

Doors opened and questioning faces looked out. 'Stop! Murder!' she shouted.

Margery Dawes came forward and hauled Nesta to her feet.

'I'll be all right in a minute,' Nesta panted, 'but they'd better catch that girl. She knows far too much about the misfortunes which have beset this family of late. The constable will want a word or two with her.'

48

The sound of soft footsteps on the hardwood floor alerted Nesta to the arrival of Philip Dawes. He winked at her as he bent to kiss his mother on the cheek.

'Where have you been all this while, son?' Margery asked. He tapped the side of his nose.

'Something to do with a young lady, Mother,' he replied. 'Other than that, ask me no questions and I'll tell you no lies!'

'Somebody special, is she?'

'Not really. Just someone to pass the time with.'

'Naughty boy!' Margery frowned. 'I do wish you could find a nice girl and settle down, Philip. Time is passing you by, and before you know it the best years of your life will be gone. I can tell you about it, for I know!'

'I'm happy as I am. And with three Critchley women in the running, the chance of my inheriting this place, and all that goes with it, is as slim as you marrying Old Harry and sharing the throne of England.'

'Impertinent boy! Jane Critchley's plans

have come to naught, and your uncle isn't getting any younger. Cousin Sally is fertile enough, but she gets nothing but girls. As for Anne, married for years, and no sign of a babe yet!'

Philip picked up his lute and began to strum idly. Nesta hid a smile. What Margery had said was true, up to a point, but she herself could have sworn that Anne Dilley had a secret. The girl had that particular radiance that comes to some women when they know they are carrying a longed-for child. Then there were the little glances she exchanged with her husband, serene yet joyful. Oh, yes, there was something going on in that quarter, and no doubt Nesta would be summoned to return here in the spring.

Soon afterwards she was on her way home, riding with the carter, who by now was an old friend. His old felt hat was pulled down low over his brow against the cold, giving him a slightly crazed look. Probably she, too, looked odd, with her shawl over her head, all but covering her nose.

'I suppose you haven't heard, you being away from home?' he remarked.

'Heard what?'

'Why, they arrested that young Fanny for doing all them murders.'

'Oh, that. Ay, I did know she'd been

arrested, but I don't believe she killed anyone. Why, I was at her uncle's cottage after he died. I laid him out myself and there was no sign of violence on the body.'

'She must've done something,' he said, stubborn to the last, 'or Sam Fowler would never have taken her in. Anyway, that's not what I wanted to tell you. She's gorn, has Fanny. Got out of gaol and vanished.'

'But there's no way out of that place unless someone removes the plank from the outside. Are you saying that somebody came by and did that?'

'Well, it weren't the Angel of the Lord, missus! No, she's got an accomplice, see. It's as plain as day they were in it together. Did summat to the poor old chap, then lit a fire to cover up their tracks. Shouldn't be surprised if they did for poor old Goody Clapton, as well, and then tried to do for Sally Robinson!'

'Well, well!' Nesta felt it best to keep quiet about the Sally Robinson business. There were enough rumours flying around as it was. Let the Critchleys deal with Polly, as no doubt they would. She had set the ball rolling, and it was no longer her business.

The carter let her down at the crossroads as usual, and she hobbled along the road leading to home. Her chilblains were giving her gyp and she longed to get in and soak her feet. After that she would take a nice long nap. The events of the past few days had taken more out of her than she'd realized. It was at times like this that she began to feel her age.

However, when she came in through the door she was dismayed to find Sam Fowler there, standing in front of the fire and keeping the warmth from everyone else. Jack was there, looking grim, and Kate wore an expression of injured innocence. Something was going on there!

'You again!' Fowler grunted, glaring at Nesta.

'I was about to say the same to you, my good man! As for me being here, this is my home, at least for the present. You're the stranger here. *Again!*'

'Just doing my job, mistress. I arrested Frances Cropwell two days ago, on suspicion of murder, attempted murder and arson. She was locked in the gaol, which as everyone knows is as secure as the Tower of London. And what do I find when I come to take her to stand trial? Gone, like a thief in the night!'

'How could that have happened?'

'Somebody let her out, that's what. And it seems to me as that someone was your granddaughter here.'

'As she's already told you, Kate had

nothing to do with it, man!' Jack's eyes bulged with temper.

'But she can't deny she went to the gaol and saw the girl.'

'I took her some bread, Gramma, and then I left.' Kate appealed to Nesta. 'It was so cold I was afraid she'd freeze to death, so I went back later to see if she was all right. That's when I found the door gaping open, and I raised the alarm.'

'How do I know you haven't got the girl hidden somewhere?'

'You've already looked into my workshop, frightening the life out of my boy,' Jack reminded him. 'You've done all you can here. Time to be on your way, methinks.'

'What's up there?' Fowler began to climb the stairs.

'Here, get out of that! Nobody's up there but my ailing wife, and if you disturb her you'll get a thick ear, constable or no constable!'

Joan gave a squeak of fright when the man burst into her bedchamber, with Jack hot on his heels. She grasped the bedclothes to her throat, watching as Fowler flung open the doors of the great press.

'Perhaps you'd like to look under the bed, too!' Jack suggested.

When at last Fowler had departed,

threatening to return in due course, Jack remained with his wife, thinking to comfort her. He knew she wouldn't rest until she knew what was going on.

'So, what do you know about Fanny's escape?' Nesta asked, moving the kettle to the hob, were it began to sing.

'Nothing, Gramma. You heard what I said.'

'Oh, yes, I heard what you said, gal, but that's not the same as knowing what really happened, is it.'

When Kate failed to answer, Nesta went on: 'Sam Fowler may be a fool, Kate, but there's some things there's no getting away from. Fanny didn't kill the old chap, nor did she start the fire, that we know, but there's other things she did do. For one thing, it was Fanny who pushed Sally into the river.'

'How do you know that?'

'Because I managed to wring it out of Polly, the Robinson's maid. It was that girl who took the message that lured Sally to the river. There never was a boy at all. The girl swears that Fanny wanted to confront Sally, to tell her what Tom had been up to. They argued, there was a bit of pushing and shoving, and Sally went in the water by accident.'

'And you believe that's true?'

'It sounds like a cock-and-bull story to me. I wonder if she truly meant to kill Sally, thereby preventing Tom Robinson from ever inheriting the Critchley land. It would be a just punishment for him, I suppose, although poor Sally would be the one who paid with her life. Personally, if I ever chose to commit murder over a man who wronged me, he'd be the one I'd do away with.'

'Gramma!'

'Don't worry, child. Talk's cheap. It was Fanny who killed Goody Clapton, of course, wasn't it.'

'No, no, it was her uncle really. He was the one who . . . ' Kate stopped, dismayed. 'Gramma, you tricked me! I didn't mean to say anything. I swore to keep it secret!'

'Now you've begun you might as well finish, gal. What's it to Fanny, anyhow? She'll be outside the county by now. Over the hills and far away, never to be seen again.'

Haltingly, Kate completed her tale. 'Remember when someone hit the constable over the head?'

'I'm hardly likely to forget!'

'That was Fanny, too. He'd been back to Joby's well, asking questions, and she thought he was getting too close to the truth about Goody Clapton. She slipped out while he was still nagging at her uncle, and took a short cut through the wood. She was waiting for him when he came along the lane, and that's when she tricked him into getting down from his horse. She whacked him with a branch, and you know the rest.'

'Too bad for her he survived, then.'

'And that's not all, Gramma. It was Fanny who cut down our clothes'-line and let our washing fall in the mire.'

This sounded so ridiculous after all the serious events that had just been revealed, that Nesta had to laugh.

'Why on earth would she want to do that?'

Kate hung her head. 'It was just a bit of spite. She was jealous of me, she said, because I had everything she lacks. Parents, a good home, and the love of Will Mowbray. She saw us hanging out the sheets and something came over her, she said. She wanted to make me suffer, so I'd know how it felt. Later, when Will was meant to wed Blanche, she felt sorry for what she'd done, because she realized that both of us had been abandoned by faithless lovers. Or so she said.'

'That's that, then,' Nesta said, 'and to think that all this evil came about because Adam Critchley was foolish enough to make such an unket plan for his property. Never mind, whatever happens to that family now, 'tis naught to do with us.'

'What happens to Blanche Bellefleur now?' Kate wondered.

'Poor child. There'll be no convent for her, I fear, not that I'd wish that on anyone. I expect she'll be forced to wed young Will, in the end. And don't you have any thoughts of ridding the world of her, just to pay that young gallant out!' Nesta laughed, and patted her granddaughter affectionately on the shoulder.

We do hope that you have enjoyed reading this large print book.

Did you know that all of our titles are available for purchase?

We publish a wide range of high quality large print books including:
Romances, Mysteries, Classics
General Fiction
Non Fiction and Westerns

Special interest titles available in large print are:
The Little Oxford Dictionary
Music Book
Song Book
Hymn Book
Service Book

Also available from us courtesy of Oxford University Press:
Young Readers' Dictionary
(large print edition)
Young Readers' Thesaurus
(large print edition)

For further information or a free brochure, please contact us at:
Ulverscroft Large Print Books Ltd.,
The Green, Bradgate Road, Anstey,
Leicester, LE7 7FU, England.
Tel: (00 44) 0116 236 4325
Fax: (00 44) 0116 234 0205

DEADLY DECEPTION

Peter Conway

Consultant psychiatrist James Cochrane is found early one morning by his neighbour. He has suffered a head injury and drowned in his goldfish pond. The preliminary report from the forensic pathologist is that the victim was certainly murdered, and the police appear to have several suspects. Cochrane is well known to be in serious dispute with one of his colleagues, Dr Audrey Clements, over the nature of ME, the so-called 'yuppie flu', but would she take their dispute this far? How trustworthy is Mrs Cochrane? And are her children as innocent as they first appear?